HE'S GONE

A totally addictive psychological thriller
with a shocking twist

REBECCA COLLOMOSSE

Joffe Books, London
www.joffebooks.com

First published in Great Britain in 2024

Cover art by Nick Castle

ISBN: 978-1-83526-600-7

In memory of my mum, and to my husband Tom,
for all their encouragement and support.

PROLOGUE

Now

The man wears a red tracksuit top, just like the one John was wearing when I last saw him. His dark hair is longer than I remember but is in the same foppish style. Faded grey, slightly scuffed trainers on his feet. Even the walk and the posture are the same — a quick, purposeful gait, hands in pockets, head down. Then when he turns his head, I think it is him. I recognise his profile, the slightly beaky nose, cleft in the chin and patchy stubble. All those times when I thought it was him and it wasn't; this time is surely different. My breath catches in my throat as I sprint forward. "John!" The man stops and turns to face me, an eyebrow raised quizzically.

It isn't him.

CHAPTER 1

Then

The train screamed to a halt and I ran towards its open doors. My foot bounced into the carriage just as a beeping indicated they were about to close. Triumphantly I hauled my other leg inside. Made it.

I thought you were right behind me. But you weren't. Someone else was crammed behind me in the carriage, his armpit close to my nose. Turning to check if you were behind me, I clocked your dark hair behind the door as the train geared up and sped off. A glimpse of your blue eyes. Still on the platform. Oh well. I would catch you at the next Tube stop.

It had been a race for the underground, possessively clutching the bag holding our precious wedding rings, ducking to avoid irritated people as they filed off the train into Oxford Circus, one of London's busiest stations.

Sweat trickled down my forehead and crowds of shoppers invaded my space, their breath on my neck, elbows poking into me. I clutched the bag containing the rings closer to me.

I started dreaming about trying on the wedding band that we had just bought. I imagined it sitting neatly next to the sapphire ring that flashed on my left hand as I got off the train at Green Park.

I positioned myself in the middle of the platform to wait for you and glanced at the screen: only one minute until the next train. Good.

I swung my shopping bags and idly rocked from foot to foot as the next train screeched to a standstill. Except you weren't on it.

I stared at all the faces surging towards me, seeking out your dark hair, your rueful smile at not being quick enough. *You must be here. I must have missed you.*

Fractious children, guided by weary parents. A group of teenagers fooling about. An elderly couple making their way slowly down the platform towards the exit sign. A man tenderly stroking his girlfriend's hair — you weren't among them. The train disappeared into the tunnel, and I was the only person left on the platform.

"The next train will be in one minute's time," came the announcement over the tannoy system.

I shrugged and tried to push away the irritation that was creeping in. It would be a shame to ruin the day that we went to buy our wedding rings with me being in a bad mood. But I was tired after trudging around London. I wanted to get home, put my feet up, and have a cup of tea.

The familiar murmur of a train in the tunnel grew to a roar as it drew closer. *You'll be on this one.* The doors opened. People spilled onto the platform, red hair, blond, an Asian family, a bald man with large spectacles.

Then I saw a flash of red top and dark hair. "John." I started towards you, but the man walked past me, his gaze passing straight through me. It wasn't you.

"Oh, for God's sake," I muttered. I was getting annoyed now. Well, I wasn't going to hang around the stuffy Tube platform. I jumped onto the next train to head home to Tooting Broadway, where our flat was. You had probably decided to head straight there rather than get off at Green Park.

I left the Tube and turned on to Tooting High Street, enjoying as I always did the mix of shops crammed together, brightly coloured fruit and vegetables fighting for space with quirky coffee shops. I turned on to the street that led to our flat.

"John!" My voice rebounded off the walls and the echoey stillness told me all I needed to know. Rocking back on my heels, I prodded my phone to call you. It went straight to voicemail.

"Hi, you've reached my answerphone. I'm sorry I'm not around to take your call but . . ."

Great. You must be on the Tube on your way back.

Not bothering to leave a message, I put the kettle on and snuggled back on the sofa, reaching into my bag to take out the white gold wedding bands that we had just bought. Finally. We were getting married. I held my wedding ring between finger and thumb, moving it down to my finger to slip on with my engagement ring, then stopped, and slipped it back in the box. I'd try it on when you got home. I left the box holding yours unopened.

I glanced at my watch. Two thirty. Ninety minutes since you had failed to get the train. I rang you again. Voicemail. Again.

I shook my head in frustration. You should have been home by now. This was not the way that I wanted to spend the afternoon. There was a bottle of champagne chilling in the fridge. The sun was out, lighting up the autumn leaves. I wanted to be tramping among them on Tooting Common, the warmth on my face.

I switched on the television, scrolling crossly through channels, before choosing a mindless rom-com. I settled back on the couch, debating whether to make another cup of tea.

Six o'clock. Five hours since you missed the train. We were going Jess's to dinner that night, as a belated celebration of both ours and Jess and Jack's engagement. Another couple of friends were going. I needed to start getting ready soon.

I snapped off the TV. The sound of an ambulance filled the room, as it raced to St George's Hospital.

Wandering into our bedroom, I decided to get my outfit for tonight ready, and have a shower.

As I rummaged in a drawer, a glint of silver caught my eye behind the bedside table lamp. I moved closer. The watch that I had bought you for your thirtieth birthday.

"We will never be parted," you had told me jokingly, after I'd slipped it lovingly on to your wrist.

That had been true. You never, ever took it off. Until now.

* * *

"Jess, I know this sounds odd, but John missed the train. He was right behind me and then he was gone, and he hasn't come home, and I don't know what to do." My faltering voice cut through her cheery "Hello" like a knife.

* * *

I didn't always hate her. When we first met, I liked her very much. But that soon changed when I saw how easily things happened for her. The very thing I wanted so desperately, and which had eluded me, came to her with ease. I have information that she needs. I should really tell her. But no, I like the feeling of knowing something she doesn't. I'm going to enjoy this.

CHAPTER 2

"Thanks for coming over." I slammed the door shut behind Jess as she bustled in. I followed her to the sitting room and shuffled around as she walked towards the sofa.

The tightness in my chest dissolved. Jess. My best friend since we started at university. She always made everything okay. Her warm hazel eyes, her gentle manner. She sat on the sofa, her dark curls flung against the cushions.

We had so much in common. We were both journalists, although of very different sorts. She was an editor for a business-to-business pensions magazine, and I was features editor on a weekly women's magazine.

"Sorry if I was a bit dramatic," I said awkwardly, switching from embarrassment to anger to anxiety and back again. "It's just all a bit odd. People miss trains, but he should have been back long ago. Plus, his phone being off makes it worse."

"Honestly, Eve, please try not to worry, I really think there'll be an innocent explanation." Jess's mere presence had helped to take the edge off my worry. "I agree, it is strange, but grown men don't tend to go missing in central London."

I sighed. "Yes, that's what I keep telling myself."

"Maybe he got caught up in an incident?" Jess suggested.

"Yeah . . ." My mind whirled. Someone had fainted on the platform, and you had stopped to help. You had dropped your Oyster card and went to look for it. You had . . . I hit a blank.

"Even if he had done, he would be home by now. It's been ages." I sighed. "Also, why would he leave his watch? You don't think he left it on purpose? Some kind of sign about his feelings for me?"

"Don't be silly, Eve. Why on earth would he do that? People take watches off for all sorts of reasons, even if they generally wear them. It won't have a thing to do with what's happened today." She paused slightly. "Although you guys didn't have a fight, did you? He wouldn't have gone for a long walk to let off steam or because he was annoyed?" she asked, rubbing my arm as she spoke.

"No, no. It's been such a lovely day. We chose our wedding bands today. I'd been so looking forward to it."

You had brought me tea and scrambled eggs in bed, and we had snuggled together talking about buying our rings, and then about our wedding later next year.

Then we had chosen the rings. You had held my hand and gazed thoughtfully at the ring I liked best, a smile spreading slowly over your face. Then champagne at Selfridges to celebrate. We talked about the beautiful lilac flowers I had chosen for the wedding, the number of bottles of wine we had bought for the day and if we needed more. I felt flushed, excited and content.

You had been a little quiet maybe, quieter than usual as you listened to me talk and talk about the wedding, nodding at the appropriate places. I felt a pang of anxiety as I pondered this.

"John was quiet, but I just put it down to the fact that I'm always more excited about the wedding details, and I know he's a bit stressed at work. But I don't know, perhaps he was a bit subdued. Could that mean anything?"

My mind sped forward, in time with the sudden banging in my chest. "Perhaps he has decided that he doesn't want to marry me anymore and has been having doubts? Maybe that's why he just went off. He couldn't face telling me."

"Don't be silly," Jess said instantly. "Him being a bit quiet is a minor thing. I bleat on about my wedding and Jack shuts up. He even admits that the details bore him a bit."

Jess was getting married three months after me.

"And anyway, if he wanted to split up with you, leave you, whatever, you don't go about it like that. He'd have said, 'We need to talk.' Honestly, honestly, Eve, I don't think you should go down that road."

I nodded.

"And he is always so laid-back. That kind of thing wouldn't send him over the edge. He isn't like that," Jess continued, warming to her subject.

"I know. Sorry Jess, you should be getting ready for your dinner party tonight."

"It's cancelled," she said firmly. "I'm not leaving here until we sort this out. It'll be okay, though, there'll be an explanation.

"Now!" She clasped her hands together decisively. "There are things we can do. I suggest that we call some of his friends and his sister, because he could have gone to see them."

"Okay, that's a good plan," I said slowly. "But do you think they'll think I'm being over the top? I feel a bit embarrassed making a big drama. Plus, why would he go to see them without letting me know?"

"People do odd things, sometimes." Jess had her bright it-will-all-be-fine voice on. "And I would say of all the explanations, that is the most likely."

I started scrolling through my phone.

"Do you have his friends' numbers?" she asked.

I nodded. "Most of them."

I hesitated when I got to Sophie's number. "Oh God, I'm not sure about ringing Sophie. She'll fly off the handle when she hears what's happened. I don't want her telling their mum, panicking her, particularly when she's recovering from cancer."

"I know she can be difficult but, Eve, she lives in London, they are close, she may well know what happened.

You have to call. No need to involve their mum yet. Let's just call her and his friends first."

Seeing the concern etched on my face she added, "Tell you what though, try calling her last."

I started with your friend Clive. Not only had you been friends since the age of five, but Clive lived in London, too, just down the road, in Balham. Clive was one of your closest friends and as the phone rang, I prayed he held the key to your disappearance.

"All right, Eve?" Clive spoke loudly down the phone. I could hear a background of noise, laughter, carefree voices. Clive was obviously at the pub. No doubt watching the rugby with several beers inside him.

"Hi Clive, look, is, er . . . Is John with you?" My voice ended in a whisper.

"*What*? You'll have to speak up. I'm down the pub, rugby's on." Clive's voice boomed down the phone.

"Is John with you?" I yelled, all my frustration, worry, nerves, fear and anger bursting through.

Jess winced slightly.

"No." Clive sounded bemused. "Should he be?"

"When did you last hear from him?"

There was a pause, punctuated with a scream of laughter in the background. I wanted to be carefree in the pub, you by my side. I took a deep breath.

"Er, actually, you know, not for a few weeks. He cancelled on me last week, said work was too busy, although I was going to call him tomorrow to get him out for a few jars. Why, is everything all right, Eve?"

Nearly every conversation that followed with your friends either continued the same pattern, or I was forced to leave a garbled message.

No luck. Just Sophie left. For the first time, I could feel tears sting the back of my throat. You had now been away for over seven hours. Your phone was switched off. None of the friends that I had managed to speak to had seen you.

Jess gently took my phone. "I'll call Sophie."

My gratitude was outweighed by the fact that for the first time Jess was displaying some anxiety. Eyes clouded, biting her lip, she hit call. I clasped my hands together so tightly they turned red.

Please be with her. Please.

All hopes faded when, after asking the question, Jess said flatly, "Oh. Okay."

Of course, Sophie wanted to hear what had happened. She was obviously not taking it well — I could hear her shrill voice through the phone after Jess had explained. It seemed to go on for a long time. She had a lot to say.

Finally, Jess hung up.

"Now what?" I said blankly.

Jess hesitated. "Maybe it's time we reported him missing."

"But you said you were sure there was an explanation and that he was okay, and now you're swinging the other way!" I exclaimed, my worry making me angry.

Jess touched my shoulder. "I still think he's probably all right, but I think we now need to act."

Probably.

* * *

Eight thirty in the evening. I was sitting in the local police station with Jess and her fiancé Jack. They sat on either side of me as we waited to speak to the officer on duty.

Seventy-seven per cent of adults who go missing are found within twenty-four hours, I discovered after surfing the web, and finding statistics from relevant charities. It should have reassured me.

It was a warm day, so why was I cold? I pulled my jacket tighter around my body as I waited for the summons from the officer. My foot tapped rhythmically on the floor. I wasn't even aware of this until Jess — kindly but firmly — clasped my knee.

A thin woman with large, tired eyes beckoned me through to a back room. "Inspector Kate Matthews," she said, gesturing me in. "Can I get you a tea or a coffee?"

I nodded. "Black coffee, please." My voice was higher-pitched than normal. The thought of clutching a warm mug felt comforting and would help me shake off the cold I felt.

Once I was seated holding a (lukewarm) polystyrene cup of instant coffee, Kate Matthews shuffled her papers together.

"I believe your fiancé has gone missing," she said slowly. Kindly. "Can you tell me what happened?"

Words poured from my mouth. At times I hesitated, at others I spoke fluently. I needed to get them off my chest to hear answers. I couldn't quite believe that I was sitting in a police station but a small part of me felt some relief. They would help me find you, wouldn't they? It felt a relief to hand some of the responsibility to someone else, someone infinitely more capable of dealing with this than me.

She listened, making notes as I recounted the events of the day, now and then asking a question.

"We'll check CCTV images at the Tube station, around Oxford Circus, and check hospitals."

My forehead was damp. I wiped it with a clammy hand and took a gulp of coffee, trying not to retch as it slipped down my throat.

"We'll check his bank account, see if any money has been taken, and his mobile phone record." She shuffled her papers together.

"Is there any reason why he might have decided to leave, to go missing on purpose?" She was probing for information. "Was he depressed or worried about anything? Was there anything going on in your life or his life that was a concern?"

The words came out in a rush. You had work worries and your manner had been quieter recently. I also spoke about your mother's illness. Jill had been diagnosed with stage three breast cancer thirteen months earlier and had had a mastectomy, as well as chemotherapy and radiotherapy. Happily, she had finally seemed to be on the road to recovery, the downy fuzz on her head and eyebrows seeming to signify a new chapter ahead. But it had hit you and Sophie very hard.

And the fact you had left your watch. I tried to emphasise how unusual this was. Inspector Kate Matthews merely nodded and made notes, her eyes expressionless.

At the end of my recollection of the day, a thought hit me violently, like lightning striking through grey clouds.

"Do you think he has harmed himself?"

There was a flash of sympathy in Inspector Matthews' large eyes.

"We will be looking into everything we can here to solve this," she said firmly. "I can't say whether he has harmed himself or not, but there is nothing from your account of events that would indicate he has." She leaned forward and said gently, "Most missing people return after a few days. Only a very, very small percentage of people don't."

I emerged from my interview room. To my shock, Sophie had arrived and was waiting with Jack and Jess. She was standing in the corner, tapping her foot. "What's happened to my brother? How could he just go missing?" She exhaled. "I was meant to be going out this evening. This has totally ruined my night." Sophie's voice had a whining quality that I had always found irritating. "I really don't need this."

* * *

The sound of a key turning in the door. I struggled out of my hot, twisted duvet. "John." My voice was loud, hard, longing. The door handle of the bedroom turned, and you were there. Hair stood on end, an apologetic look in your cornflower blue eyes.

"Sorry." You opened your arms. Tears of joy and relief poured down your cheeks. I tripped slightly as I disentangled myself from my bedclothes and flung myself into your arms.

"I thought — I thought . . ." I couldn't get the words out.

"I'm so sorry, Eve, it wasn't what you thought. I'm here now and I'll explain," you murmured in my ear.

When I woke up my cheeks and pillowcase were damp. Our wedding rings glinted on the bedside table. But you weren't there.

* * *

One day missing

You walked purposefully; your jaw was set. Your eyes were like rocks. That was all the grainy images allowed me to see as you moved through the barriers of the station. I leaned forward and touched your blurry face. I wished that I could walk through the screen, take your hand and lead you back to me and our home.

One of the officers shuffled uneasily as my hand slid down the screen.

"It's him," I confirmed, withdrawing my hand reluctantly.

Police had trawled through the CCTV at the Tube and caught your image. They rewound it and I watched it again. You looked like a man who knew where you were going. I didn't think you had missed the train by accident.

"He made the decision to not get on the train." I enunciated each word clearly.

No one in the stuffy room reacted. Inspector Kate Matthews busily tapped away on a computer. She told me you were not in any hospital and there had been no report of an accident. No money had been moved from your account.

She leaned forward. "Obviously we can't say for definite, but we think he decided to deliberately go missing." She added that it was unlikely you had come to harm. I knew only too well what that euphemism meant.

She said for the third time, "Most adults who go missing are found within forty-eight hours, with less than one per cent missing for longer than a month."

What if you were in that category? The thought of possibly not knowing where you were for forty-eight hours was unbearable, let alone a whole month.

They told me more information, but I was finding it impossible to take in anything. Inspector Matthews' voice came from far away, as though I had ear plugs in. I was lucky my mother, father, Jill and Sophie were with me. Mum was studiously taking notes.

We learned that if someone is reported missing and not found within three days, then the police must notify the UK Missing Persons Unit.

"But we're not at three days yet," Kate Matthews said quickly.

* * *

Two days missing

Like a record on repeat, I ran through the day: my chatter about the wedding, your subdued manner . . . Over and over until I emitted a wail, so guttural and animal-like I was shocked. *I'm sorry, John, I let you down.*

Then I fell into a deep, dreamless, but unsatisfying sleep. When I awoke, I didn't feel refreshed and perspiration clung to the ends of my hair, leaving my neck damp.

It was Monday. I was supposed to be at work but that was impossible, so I had been given compassionate leave. I sat in your mother Jill's house, on the borders of Kent, clutching what seemed like my tenth cup of tea that day, with Sophie and my mother and father. Jess had kindly taken the day off work and sat close to me. She looked drained, skin pale, with dark shadows under her eyes. It was getting to her now.

Inspector Matthews and a colleague had searched our flat. They had taken your computer.

Sophie was taking it badly. She was much more animated than I was. I sat silently, feeling dazed.

Sophie rocked slightly and loudly refused all offers of hot drinks. I was ashamed that even in the midst of my anguish Sophie riled me. I tried to be charitable. Your mother had been seriously ill with breast cancer. Your father had divorced

Jill when you and Sophie were small children, and neither of you had had much contact with him since. Such circumstances meant you were very close. You were three years older than Sophie and very protective of her.

I was jealous of your close relationship and had never really clicked with Sophie. We were resentful of each other. Her grip on you was all-consuming and claustrophobic. And you knew that, John. You knew how much it bothered me. I should apologise, I suppose, if that added pressure to you, if it was one of the factors that pushed you to disappear from our lives.

"I just don't know what to do with myself." Sophie sighed.

Abruptly I left the room, and stood by the open kitchen window, letting the cold air sweep over my face. I felt somebody touch my shoulder and turned to see Sophie's pink face, mascara leaving spidery stains under her eyes.

"What did you do?" she murmured. Hostility shone from her blue eyes. Almost the same colour as yours.

"What do you mean?"

"You put him under all this pressure." Those eyes narrowed. "You were on at him all the time: marriage, marriage, marriage. 'When are we going to buy a flat?' You didn't shut up until you made sure that you got that engagement ring on that finger," she snapped.

I slumped against the sink. That wasn't how it had been. Yes, I had wanted to move the relationship on but so had you. I pictured your eyes as you proposed on that windswept beach, shining at me, your cheeks pink, your voice slightly tremulous and bashful, the grin that stretched across your face when I said yes. You had spun me round on the sand, both of us laughing a little hysterically.

My phone rang, cutting her off. I hoped against hope that it was you, John, and went from hope to disappointment in a nanosecond. I had long since lost count of how many times this had happened. A withheld number.

"Eve, Kate Matthews here. We've been through John's computer and nothing major has been revealed except for one thing, which may or may not be significant. He has been on a lot of sites about Hong Kong. Tourist sites, expat forums about living out there and also job sites. The last time he went on one of these sites — a job site — was five days ago. Were you looking to move out there?"

I tried to make sense of what she was saying. "Never. No. Never." Then a thought hit me. "Do you think he might be there?"

"Well, no, because we found his passport in your flat," Inspector Matthews reminded me gently.

"Of course, sorry. His friend Mark lives there. He might know something."

Like a zombie I read out his mobile number. Then as soon as the phone was down, I was ringing that number myself, my fingers moving over the numbers of my mobile in a frenzy. I brushed off Sophie's loud demands to know what the police had wanted, swept past Mum, Dad, Jill and Jess to shut myself in the spare bedroom.

Luckily Mark answered after three rings. I got straight to the point.

Mark sounded confused. It took a while for him to understand what had happened. I went through the events for what felt like the hundredth time: the disappearance on the Tube, the loss of contact, the police. Then I told him about Hong Kong.

"Look, he isn't here but there is something that might be relevant," he said slowly. "About a month ago, John emailed me and said he was interested in working in Hong Kong and did I know of any jobs going?" He paused. "Did you know this?"

"No," I whispered.

Silence.

"What happened then?" I was glued to the phone, and ignored Sophie as she opened the door and peered in indignantly.

"I said there were currently no jobs going at my company, but I would keep an ear out," Mark continued. I knew he worked in a publishing house as a production editor. "Then I never heard anything back."

He paused.

"And?" His words felt unfinished.

"Well . . ." Short silence again. "I did notice that in both emails about Hong Kong, he only referred to himself."

I could almost see his face screw up in an awkward grimace. "I mean, it probably means nothing. Just thought I'd mention it."

You never said anything to me. Not one word.

Tears ran down my face as my mother stroked my hair. I couldn't bring myself to mention Hong Kong. The elephant in the room.

We were back at our flat. Dad had popped out to get a takeaway for us, even though eating was the last thing I felt like doing. I clung to my mother, feeling five years old again. *Take it away, Mum. Make it better.*

I went to bed straight after our takeaway, after I'd managed a few mouthfuls. It was only eight thirty, but all I wanted to do was lie there. Mum and Dad wanted to stay but I practically pushed them out of the door, back to their hotel nearby.

My phone beeped periodically with texts from well-meaning friends. I ignored them. Usually, I would grab my phone straight away. For the first time I didn't think it would be you, John.

Hong Kong. *Hong Kong?* Were you really going to move to the other side of the world without me? I texted Mark as it suddenly seemed very important to know the exact date and time of the first email. Despite the time difference, Mark responded almost immediately. He had received the email at about six, UK time, on 15 May.

I looked at my diary and remembered the day well. We had gone out for dinner straight from work, in Soho. We were both busy and didn't leave work until about seven, I recalled.

So, you had sent the email at work, just before we went to our favourite Italian in Soho, where we'd shared a bottle of red wine, eaten delicious pasta and talked about where we should go for our honeymoon. We both fancied going to South America and doing some proper exploring.

You were smiling, affectionate, yet at the same time apparently thinking of starting a new life on the other side of the world.

I reached out to the bedside table, fumbling until my hand touched the cool metal of your watch. I could see it glinting on your wrist as you tapped out a message on your phone, raised your hand to your mouth with a drink, chopped vegetables.

I was so confused. Things had been fine between us. Hadn't they? I lay on our bed and closed my eyes, exhausted.

We were in Northumberland, by the sea, staying in a cottage near Bamburgh. We were frolicking in the water. You dramatically splashed out of the sea and dropped to your knees on the beach. "Marry me!" you declared. But my joy turned to confusion as a dark shadow passed over your face. Without a word you jumped up and stalked from the beach. I followed you, dread building in my stomach.

The cottage door slammed and was locked from within. I turned my keys in the lock but to no avail. I turned and turned, desperately trying to open the door, the fruitless grind of the metal growing louder and louder.

Suddenly I was back in our flat. I heard the same sound of the key in the lock, except I wasn't holding a key anymore. Someone was trying to get into the flat. Every limb stiffened as I froze in bed, my heart thumping. A sudden silence, and then the grating and crunching started again.

Where was my phone? I needed to call the police. I felt sure someone was trying to burgle me, but my limbs felt so heavy. I froze in bed. Then a single thought filled my mind. You.

My eyes flew open. I jumped out of bed and made towards the bedroom door. Snapping on the light, I rushed down the hall and flung open the front door.

A gentle wind cooled my face as I stared into the night, hoping to see a flash of dark hair under a street lamp, a figure in the distance. A patch of grass and an empty street met my eyes.

* * *

I'm not sure what I was hoping to achieve by going to her flat. It was gone midnight and I couldn't sleep, couldn't stop thinking. I found myself on auto pilot, making my familiar way to her home. It felt funny approaching the front door, knowing she wasn't expecting me. Of course, I have been round before without her knowing. But this was different. The key felt smooth and cold in my pocket as I fingered it and took it slowly out. I peered through the peephole. Darkness. The key in the lock. I turned it and it made a scraping sound. I wasn't expecting that. But I persevered, turning the handle. I pushed again. I had forgotten about the internal lock. I heard a noise from inside and heart hammering I scampered down the street. I turned the corner of the street. Made it! I'd probably woken her up. I wondered if she just rolled over, half asleep, or if she'd properly woken and was lying in the dark scared, heart hammering like mine was. The second thought made me smile. Perhaps I would pay another visit.

CHAPTER 3

Dear shop owner,

My fiancé John Sullivan has gone missing. We are desperate to find him after he went missing when failing to get on the Tube with me at Oxford Circus. Please can you pin this up in your shop to raise awareness. John is thirty-two, 5 ft 11 in tall, and, as you can see from the attached recent photo, he has dark hair, blue eyes, has a slim frame and is clean-shaven with slight stubble. He was wearing a red Adidas zip-up jacket, blue T-shirt, slim-fitting Levi jeans and grey Converse trainers on the day he disappeared. If anyone has any information, please call Eve Jennings on the number supplied.

* * *

I went over and over the hours before you went missing, desperately searching for clues.

Nine thirty Saturday morning.

"Come on, you. We need to get up." I curled my legs around yours. "It's a lovely day and we don't want to waste it! The day we get our wedding rings." I happily sang out the words.

"Mmmm," you said sleepily. You opened your mouth wide and let out a yawn, before smiling. "I'm looking forward to it but I'm exhausted, work's tough at the moment, give me a few minutes."

I planted a sympathetic kiss on your cheek, which was warmed by the sun streaming through the blinds. You did not respond, just exhaled heavily through your nose.

You were a journalist on a shipping newspaper and the pressure was intense, particularly as there had been job cuts recently.

I was features editor at *Real Lives*, a weekly women's magazine. My dream job. A women's magazine journalist was all I had ever wanted to be, and I had my eye fixed on this as I headed up the university newspaper features section, completed my journalism course after university and worked long hours of unpaid work experience on any magazine that would have me. Finally, I won a staff writer job at *Real Lives*, before working my way up to features editor.

I loved the real-life stories we wrote about. The thrill of the chase, trying to get in there before a competitor magazine, trying to persuade the person to tell us their story. I lost myself in their stories, from the affairs, the weight losses, to the truly strange tales, and the desperately sad accounts of cancer and child deaths, where I found myself welling up. I loved the life-affirming ones best. Where the woman lost her partner but there was a happy ending.

I led a team of features writers and encouraged them to strike a balance between being hard-nosed, sniffing out, chasing and winning the story, to having empathy and sympathy. These were people's lives.

The irony wasn't lost on me that my own true story, of you disappearing, could feature in the magazine. *He was right behind me and then he was gone.*

It was through my job that I had met you, in the staff canteen of our mutual publishing house. We had sipped cappuccinos as we bemoaned the challenges of our respective jobs, the pressures, the competition, but also the immense satisfaction of winning a scoop, of a feature or news story well told.

Four years later, we were renting a flat together in Tooting Broadway. You had proposed to me six months ago in Northumberland, with Bamburgh Castle looming over the sand dunes, wind whistling through our hair and turning our cheeks ruddy as you sank down on one knee. Since then, I had been in a whirl of wedding plans.

"You okay?" I whispered, slipping an arm around you. "I know it's been tough recently. But it's not your fault. God, they are a daily! Fancy making five reporters redundant, ridiculous, then piling the pressure on you. So unfair!" My voice squawked in indignation.

You sighed. "Yes . . . can we not talk about it? I want to enjoy today."

"Of course." I pulled myself as close to you as I could and ran my fingers through your hair. No response. I stretched and pulled the covers back. "Come on! Up!" I ordered.

"Hey." You eventually rose, stretching your arms out. You pushed me back onto the pillows. "It's a special day and I'm going to make you breakfast in bed."

Strolling to the Tube, we chatted amiably about our weekend plans. "I'm really looking forward to Jess and Jack's dinner. It'll be nice to see the gang again, hear about their wedding plans and compare notes," I babbled.

You were silent. "Do you think they are happy?" you asked slowly.

"Of course, I . . ." My words were drowned out by the sirens of a passing ambulance and by the time it had gone, we had got distracted and the conversation moved on. I gripped your hand, fingers curled tightly around your palm. Your hand lay slack in mine.

Do you think they are happy?

* * *

Three days missing

I checked your Facebook page. Again. I knew that I would see no new activity, but still, I kept refreshing the page. Just

22

in case. The last time you posted was a month ago. You had posted a photo of the two of us with Jess and Jack, in the pub. Smiling, carefree. If I looked closely, I could see the faint dimple in your cheek. Your eyes were screwed up slightly as you smiled.

Do you think they are happy?

I wished I knew your password. I tried my luck with various names and dates of birth but no joy. My hands were flat on the keyboard with frustration.

Then I was going through your drawers. Frantically pushing and throwing objects — crumpled-up papers, old deodorant, a pen here, a reporter's notebook there.

I needed answers. It had been three days now. Your disappearance had been reported to the UK Missing Persons Unit, as the three-day landmark had been reached.

Both my friends and yours were taking the proactive approach. They wanted to *do* something. There was talk of printing and distributing posters, travelling to places that meant something to you to hand them out . . . and so forth. I knew we had to do this, but I was so tired. I slipped between exhaustion, disbelief and anger.

Mum and Dad were still staying in a hotel near me. I had sent them out for a walk and was now going through every drawer, cupboard, nook and cranny in the flat. I wanted answers and I wanted them now. It was a relief to be doing something, to be fired up and purposeful. Something to ease — however briefly — the grief and despair, panic and guilt.

My hands touched on what felt like a packet. I grabbed it, losing interest as soon as I saw it. An ibuprofen box, nothing interesting there. I was about to fling it to the side when I caught a glimpse of the inside of the packet. It did not look like ibuprofen to me. I should know as I was frequently taking them for headaches. The pills looked a different size. Smaller, smoother. I drew it out. *Citalopram*, I read. My mind buzzed. Maybe I was naïve, but I didn't know much about this medication. I grabbed my phone and googled. A type of antidepressant.

I felt cold, numb. I had no idea. My intermittent anger since I had discovered that you had been looking into living in Hong Kong disappeared. You must have been depressed and I had no idea. Yet I was your partner, and I should have been there for you. The pressure in my chest grew as I stared at the pills in my hand. You had gone to the doctor to seek help with depression with no word to me. I knew you were worried about work pressure and losing your job, but that was it. A bit of worry. It must have been more than I thought.

I knew what I had to do. I rang the police and told them about my discovery. They were already waiting to receive your medical notes from the doctors. But there was more urgency now. I could hear it in the police officer's voice.

* * *

I sat stirring my G&T slowly. Mum and Dad had insisted that I go out with Jess for a drink. *It will do you good. You've been cooped up all day. You need to talk to your friends.* In the end I capitulated. I had talked endlessly to them about what the antidepressants meant, and we were going round in circles. I wanted fresh input, and that was why I was sitting in a pub in Tooting with my best friend, a fire flickering in the corner.

"I failed him, Jess, that's how I feel. I never knew he felt like this. I never knew he went to the doctor to be prescribed pills. He didn't feel he could tell me."

I downed three quarters of my drink. "Now I feel like I don't know him, that the relationship has been a farce."

Jess took my hand. She was looking pale and had dark shadows under her eyes. "I think he loves you but is really mixed up and suffering from depression and felt like he needed to go away on his own for a while," she said quietly. "Your relationship wasn't a farce, he loved you."

Her voice trembled. All this was hard on her, too. The double whammy of having to support me while she was struggling in her own right. Jess, Jack, you and I often did things together and she and you had become good friends.

I noticed the past tense she used and stiffened. Had she secretly written off either him or my relationship with him?

Back at the flat, I fumbled for the light in the hall. Mum and Dad had gone back to their hotel. I put the kettle on in the kitchen to make myself hot chocolate.

I went to choose a mug from the cupboard and frowned. Something was missing. I stared at the assorted mugs and tea cups and picked out my Cath Kidston mug. I couldn't put my finger on it — then it came to me.

Where was your Maradona mug? I started pushing crockery out of the way as I scanned the cupboard. It suddenly seemed urgent to find it. The mug meant a lot to you. The footballer Diego Maradona was your childhood hero, and you loved that mug, using it to drink your tea nine times out of ten. You used to tell me jokingly that it was off-limits to me. His mum had bought it as a housewarming present when we moved into the flat, just before she was diagnosed with breast cancer.

Growing frantic, I opened every cupboard door. I went through the bin in case it had been broken and put there. I scoured the bedroom, the living room, but nothing. The sound of the key in the lock meant my parents were back.

"John's Maradona mug has gone! I don't understand it. He loves that mug. Have you seen it? I just wonder where it is. It might be significant . . ." I babbled.

Mum and Dad looked confused and weary.

"What was that, love?" Dad asked, shrugging off his coat and making his way to the sitting room. Slowing my voice down, I repeated the information, my mind racing ahead, trying to work out what it meant. I was halfway through when I realised what I wanted it to mean.

"Maybe he came back for it. Maybe that means he is alive, and he came back to the flat," I said. "That mug meant so much to him, he wanted it."

Mum and Dad exchanged glances. "Are you sure he didn't break it a few weeks ago and forgot to say?" Mum asked gently.

The police were not exactly overwhelmed by this information. Inspector Matthews sounded irritable. "We'll bear it in mind, but I very, very much doubt that it means anything significant."

Her words pricked my bubble. Even if you had come back to the flat, what would that mean? That you had chosen to come back for a mug. Not for me.

A mug.

A fucking mug.

Would there ever be relief from this awful waiting?

* * *

She's not the only one feeling devastated. I too need something to numb this dreadful pain. And the thing is, I look for this in the same things as her.

CHAPTER 4

"I really think I should be doing this." Sophie pouted. She planted her hands on her hips and stared at the reporter from *South London Echo*. "I'm his sister. She—" she waved impatiently at me — "is his fiancée. Not married." The sting in the tail.

Jake Jones, the reporter looked flustered, as well he might, confronted with Sophie's belligerent gaze. "Er, well, the police media officer specifically said that Eve would be doing the interview, so I think we'd better stick with that."

Thank you. I didn't have the energy to fight Sophie but knew I had to do that interview. Sophie muttered and grumbled under her breath but backed down in the face of the firmness of Jake's tone and the authority mentioned. One–nil to me.

The police media officer had arranged a series of press interviews for me to raise awareness, starting with the local newspaper.

"I'm sorry to have to go through this with you as it must be so painful, but I think we'd better start at the beginning," said Jake, as he settled himself at the table in Jill's dining room. Despite being fresh out of university and a new reporter, he had an empathetic manner. He waved his Dictaphone. "Mind if we use this?"

Sophie had luckily been persuaded by Jill to leave the room and go for a walk with your mother.

"How did it go?" Mum asked later. I was back in our own flat that evening. I shrugged. "Okay. The reporter had a courteous manner and was empathetic. Got a couple more newspaper interviews lined up. Though what use it'll do . . ." My voice trailed away.

Five whole days. It was hard to be positive. Seventy-seven per cent of adults that go missing are found within twenty-four hours. Not you.

"I'm not going to go back with you tomorrow," I told Mum and Dad after a pause where Mum stroked my shoulder and Dad looked on helplessly. "I know I said I would go back with you for a few days but I just — just need to be here. I'll only feel completely restless at your house so I might as well be here. I'm talking with John's friends about getting together and visiting places, putting up posters. I might as well get started."

There was Leeds, where you went to university, and Crystal Palace, as you supported the football team, as well as all over London, including the border of Kent, where your mother now lived. My mind raced.

Mum nodded. "I understand," she said gently. "Would you like us to stay longer?"

"No honestly, you should go home tomorrow still," I said firmly. Truth be told, while I really appreciated Mum and Dad being with me, I needed to be on my own. "I'll get in touch with Jess and tell her I'm not going home after all. I'm sure she'll keep me company."

I waved Mum and Dad off the next morning. There was a whole list of things I could do to make the search for you stronger, like galvanising your friends as I'd said, planning an investigation of the places I thought you might go, mobilising social media, even just ringing Jess to tell her I wasn't going back to my parents after all. I should let Sophie and Jill know I was staying in London — although I felt that I couldn't bear to see Sophie at the moment. But I just wanted to be on my own. The thought of any task, even just picking up the phone exhausted me. I sat staring at my hands in a kind of stupor in the sitting room when my mobile phone rang. The county code belonged to that of my parents.

"Hello, Janey from Janey Bridal Couture here, just phoning about your dress. We arranged the first fitting to be on the first of March, would you mind making it later that week instead? I do apologise, it is just that I realise I won't be in the shop then."

I froze.

"Hello?"

"Yes, that's fine," I heard myself finally say. "Can we say third of March instead?"

I hung up, hands shaking. Our wedding. Since you had disappeared, I had put it in a box and shelved it into the deeper recesses of my mind. No one had mentioned it, and I had put the wedding rings deep within my underwear drawer, covered by socks. I couldn't bear to look at them. *You will be back by then. You will be back by then.*

I heard the click of the letterbox. I went to collect the post as though on autopilot, still caught up in the phone call about my dress. A phone bill for me, and what looked like a bank statement for you. With a sudden spurt of energy, I ripped it open and scanned it, looking for any tiny clue, any small meaning. It was for the month before, before you had disappeared.

Council tax £80, Tesco £7.25, Starbucks £3.20, £12 for our local wine shop — my heart did a painful movement in my chest at that. Clear images filled my head, you smiling at me as I came back from work, leading me to the kitchen and gesticulating to my favourite bottle of Sancerre sitting chilling in the fridge. "I saw how stressed you were today meeting the magazine deadline," you said tenderly, "so I thought this might cheer you up."

Me smiling and hugging you hard, feeling so lucky to have such a thoughtful partner. Hard to believe that was only just a month ago and hard to tally with this secret you that

I didn't know, the one on antidepressants, who looked into jobs in Hong Kong behind my back, the one who took off his beloved watch.

It jarred me to suddenly find myself back in this silent flat, its emptiness pressing on my nerves. With an effort I continued scanning the statement. *Pret a Manger £3.50, British Gas £48, Emelda Boutique £42* . . . my eyes froze, the typed words seeming blacker than those around them. Emelda Boutique was a women's clothes shop in Balham. Had you bought me something?

My mind was sluggish, and I struggled to recall what you'd bought me recently, and whether it came from that shop. But I knew you had not — I only had one item from that shop in my wardrobe, a dress, bought about a year ago. Maybe you bought it for Sophie. That must be it. I whipped my phone out.

Hi Sophie, sorry if this is a strange question, but did John buy you a piece of clothing from Emelda Boutique recently?

If you did, it certainly wouldn't have been for her birthday, which was back in January. Still, that meant nothing, she had you wrapped round her finger. I pressed send on the message and scanned the rest of the bank statement.

Nothing. Restlessly, I paced the hall before turning into our bedroom. Your bedside drawers were the focus of my attention again. I had already been through them and knew they were unlikely to yield anything else, but still I rammed one open, feverishly digging my fingers into pens, scraps of papers, bills . . .

"You're wasting your time, you should be galvanising everyone to put up posters, get a strategy in place . . ." My internal voice continued to lecture me sternly, but I continued rooting in your drawer.

My fingers brushed against a pile of notebooks. Your reporter notebooks for work. I dragged them onto the bed. Five tatty-looking books covered in shorthand and scrawl. They were unlikely to yield anything, but I flipped the first one open and painstakingly went through page after page of interviews, occasionally noting small doodles of cars, triangles and scribbles. Page after page of quotes from shipping CEOs, analysts, consultants . . . My earlier ardour had turned to apathy as I flicked through the last notebook. I almost missed it as I flipped quickly through, but the doodle, with curly capital letters caught my eye as I moved to turn the page. *GEMMA.* The name was written at the bottom of the page, where you had finished writing your interview. And next to her name was scribbled: *Coffee at eleven.* Gemma, your journalist colleague who covered shipping finance for the paper. You had to mean her.

Studious, serious, and dare I say it, slightly dowdy. Whenever I saw her, she was squeezed into a badly fitting, rather cheap-looking suit that was either black, grey or beige, I seemed to recall. I mentally gave myself a shake; I was being shallow, but then I worked on a women's magazine where image was taken more seriously.

I knew you were friendly with her, and you had spoken admiringly of her news-writing skills. But plain old Gemma? Were you meeting her for a coffee at the café that you and I always went to? Could there really be anything more than friendship there?

My phone bleeped. *No*, read Sophie's text.

* * *

I climbed into bed at nine that night, not because I was tired, but because I did not know what to do with myself that evening. I had spent the day on my own, ignoring messages from well-meaning friends. I knew I just had to text Jess, or any of my friends or yours for that matter, to say that I had decided to stay in London after all and they would have come round or asked me round to theirs, but I couldn't face being in anyone's company, even though being on my own, with a constant inner dialogue stirring up blame and guilt within me was not something to be relished either. The item of clothing you had bought played on my mind for the rest of the day — I rollercoastered between innocent explanations to a secret affair.

I clung onto the fact that my birthday was in three months. Maybe it was a very early purchase for my birthday; you were very thoughtful about buying presents. I searched the entire bedroom for an Emelda Boutique bag or piece of clothing I didn't recognise, even tipping out your socks' drawer. Nothing.

I lay in bed expecting to veer between the terror of you being dead to living a new life in Hong Kong, but a dark curtain of sleep slowly came down and stilled my mind.

CHAPTER 5

One week missing

"I think it was him." Jess and I were sitting in the local Starbucks, clutching cappuccinos. A baby squalled at the table next to us, as I traced a finger around some stray sugar grains that had been spilled on the table. The rain spattered against the windows and bleakness settled on me, particularly as I saw the sceptical look on Jess's face.

"I guess . . ." she said slowly. "But why would he do that? I mean, what reason would he just come back to the flat and not let you know?"

"I don't know, it's a mystery." My mood deflated even further. I had felt so buoyed up that it had been you coming to collect your Maradona mug, that you were still alive and wanting to be in contact with me, that I had brushed aside such questions.

"But I still feel it is something to do with him," I argued. "I know it doesn't make sense, but I just think that added to the fact that his favourite mug has disappeared . . ." My voice trailed off. "I know people think I am stupid to attach any significance to that, but I know how much it meant to him. His mum bought it for him before she found out she had cancer, he used it all the time, and I just think the fact it's vanished means something."

I also told her about how I had been convinced someone was trying to get into the flat, despite seeing no one at the door and having just woken from my sleep.

"Look, please don't take offence, but you don't think you dreamt that someone was trying to get into the flat, do you?" Jess asked gently.

"No." I shook my head adamantly. But then a flash of doubt pricked at me. What did I know — I never thought you would go missing and leave both me and your entire life behind, but you did. I didn't trust my judgement.

"What if he's dead and this is his ghost coming back to haunt me?" I shook my head and took another sip of my lukewarm coffee. "Sorry, I'm being stupid."

Jess frowned. "There's no evidence to suggest that he's dead, and I really don't think what is happening is to do with the supernatural!"

She smiled at me. "Honestly, why would a ghost take a mug? I think that the key turning in the lock is either a dream or, to be honest, and I don't want to scare you, but an opportunist burglar trying to break in. You have a double lock on your door, don't you?"

I sighed. "Exactly the reaction from my mum. She just started fretting about burglars and asking about my locks. Her and Dad want me to get another one installed, even though it's a big strong door with a double lock already and a chain you pull over." I paused. "But I just don't think it is a burglar, I did at first but now — I know I sound crazy, but I just don't."

Jess didn't say anything, instead looked at my blueberry muffin. Its smooth rounded shape had only been broken by two bites. "Aren't you going to eat that, Eve? You're wasting away, look at you. You need to keep your strength up."

I shrugged. My throat had closed up and my stomach turned at the thought of anything passing my lips. My clothes were baggy on me. "I just have no appetite. Everything's an effort, to be honest, including food."

"I think it would help to do something positive to try and find John," Jess said, draining her coffee. "I've been speaking to Clive and Jack, and we thought we could gather all John's friends and get a plan of action in place, put up posters, get the message out on social media and get moving quickly on this. What do you think?"

I nodded, trying to harness some energy. "Yes, of course. Sorry, I should have been taking the lead on this."

"Don't be silly. You've enough on your plate and we want to help. We thought we'd do some stuff locally but focus on other areas too. Can you think of any areas he might go to?"

"Hong Kong?" I gave a mirthless laugh as my mind added, "Or the bottom of the River Thames."

Jess covered my hand with hers. "It must be awful knowing he approached his friend out there about work, but there's no way he will be there when his passport has been left at home."

I ruminated on places that you might go to. There was our little corner of Northumberland, where we had been on holiday three times and which we loved, where you had proposed to me, but I doubted you would go there. You had been looking to go to Hong Kong without me, so I couldn't believe you would go somewhere so closely entwined with our relationship.

It was a long shot, but one place I could think of was Leeds. You had been to university there and had loved it. You had started your journalistic career on a local newspaper in the area after graduating before moving to London. You still went to visit it regularly and had friends living there. You had taken me up there and mentioned that one day you would love to move back there if both of us became freelance journalists. Us. A future that once included me.

Jess agreed enthusiastically that Leeds was an area to target.

"And the other area I can think of is Crystal Palace football ground," I said. "He's a huge fan, as you know, and when his mum was diagnosed with breast cancer and he was in a bleak place, he took a lot of comfort from going to football matches. If he is in some kind of emotional breakdown, then maybe it's somewhere he'd go. That's if he is still around." Again, I skirted delicately around saying the words dead or alive.

Jess grasped my fingers. "He is still alive, Eve, there's no evidence to suggest that he has taken his own life. We have to focus on that." There was a fierce undertone to her voice.

I let myself back into our flat half an hour later. The silence that greeted me as I closed the front door felt almost physical, like an impenetrable wall. My heart sank. I didn't want to be with people, couldn't wait to get away, but once on my own the loneliness of being without you and my terrible thoughts consumed me, and I just wanted to be in company again.

Glancing down at the floor, I saw the post had arrived. *Mr John Sullivan* was typed in bold print across an envelope. A bill of some sort. I grabbed it eagerly, ignoring the junk mail addressed to me that had also arrived. Ripping it open, I saw it was your mobile phone bill. I scanned it. There was your mother's home number — she had a mobile phone but usually kept it switched off — and also Sophie's number popped up again and again. I instantly felt irritated. I could tell that she had been upset when we announced our engagement, her smile had been hard, brittle, fixed. I resented her constant presence and possessiveness over you. I tried to understand — but I could never warm to her. And since you had disappeared, our relationship had disintegrated further. It was obvious that she didn't think that I had a right to grieve, she had first dibs on that.

I looked at other numbers, I thought I recognised Clive's and your friend Rob's. Jess's was also there, there had been a phone call and a few texts, as well as her fiancé Jack's number. Neither of those were surprising, as you were close to both. I saw one number that came up regularly: there had been five phone calls, and also ten texts.

My stomach turned uneasily as I dialled 141 and called the number and there was no surprise when a woman's voice answered. "Hello?" Slight question at the end as she didn't recognise the number. As I hung up, I realised that I knew that voice. The scrawled *Gemma* on your old notebook crashed into my mind; I could distinctly see the blob of ink at the end.

Solemn, staid Gemma. Surely not. Surely, you could not be attracted to her? She didn't seem your type. But then who knew. I didn't know you were on antidepressants, didn't know you had looked to work in Hong Kong, had never imagined you would just effortlessly and easily vanish.

* * *

She was sitting in the café opposite our work place in Shoreditch. It felt funny to be near our office but not being there on a general working day. It had only been ten days since I was last at work, picking up my bag and gleefully heading to the door on Friday on the dot, you motioning that you would be another half an hour. How everything had changed. Everyone at work had been very sympathetic, shocked and very upset at the news; after meeting Gemma I was going to meet with my publisher Paul to discuss my job. A few people had tentatively suggested that it would be good for me to go back, to focus my mind, to give me a routine. I couldn't think of it. There would be your empty desk, with your sailor teddy bear perched by your computer, given to you by a shipping company at an anniversary dinner. You'd had it for years — for some reason thinking of that teddy sitting forlornly on its own, with no you made me want to weep. I couldn't face seeing the daily paper every day, with no familiar John Sullivan by-line on its pages — the by-line that every day I loved to see as I flicked through the pages.

Gemma was sipping some water. Usually, I loved to be in the café, with its lofty ceiling, interesting art on the walls and retro chandeliers. They also did some of the best coffee that I had ever tasted. You and I had liked to go there for our morning quick fix of coffee on our way to the office. We occasionally went there for lunch, when time allowed, which wasn't often with our pressing deadlines. Your scrawled *Coffee at eleven* flashed into my mind. Had you been meeting her here as well as me? My eyes smarted as I saw a quirky-looking man with a goatee, horn-rimmed glasses and skinny jeans sitting at the table you and I preferred, the one tucked away in the corner. I might never sit there with you again.

Gemma peered at me through her horn-rimmed glasses. She had thick, dark brows that could do with a thread or a wax and dark hair scraped back into a severe bun. She was intelligent, sharp, a quick-witted business journalist. I knew she had got some particularly good scoops and that you had admired her skill. Her face looked strained, her eyes darting around the café. She smiled nervously when she saw me but it didn't reach her eyes. I slumped into the chair opposite, not bothering to order a drink. I'd emailed Gemma asking to meet up with her, explaining that I knew she had a friendship with you, and I wanted to ask her about you as I was trying to piece together why you disappeared.

"I'm so sorry, Eve." Gemma's voice trembled slightly, and she gripped her glass tightly. "None of us at work can believe it. I am just praying he comes back."

I bet you are.

"It's been over a week, and I still can't believe it," I said. "I keep going over and over everything, trying to find clues that he was unhappy, depressed, that he would go off like this. That's where I thought you might help. I know you two were friends." I paused and decided to go for the jugular. "Obviously much closer than I thought. I looked at his phone and saw a number of phone calls and lots of texts to you, which I was incredibly surprised at to be honest."

Two red spots appeared on Gemma's cheeks and her mouth opened and closed quickly. "I can understand you'd be surprised but we've got much closer over the last few months — in terms of friendship I mean. Honestly, Eve, that's all it was." Her words tripped over each other.

"So, what were you talking and messaging each other about?" I asked abruptly.

"We've always got on well and recently we bonded over all the crap going on at the paper, you know, worrying about losing our jobs, the huge amount of work due to staff cuts." Gemma spoke quickly. "And, also, he has been supportive to me as I've been going through a break-up. Liam and I were living together, and it just wasn't working any more. It was a mutual decision but still very upsetting, having to also move out and find another flat. John was really sympathetic and a shoulder to cry on, I guess. We went to lunch a couple of times and for a drink now and again."

"Okay, I get that, but the messages, phone calls? Really — you actually got that close?" My voice was hard, rasping, I needed the truth. The red spots appeared on Gemma's cheeks again.

"Yes, he was texting to see how I was, checking I was okay. The phone calls were about the same kind of thing. He rang the weekend I moved out of the flat to my new flat share to check I was okay, and another phone call was about the stuff at work, the fact that Kieran had been made redundant, it worried both of us."

"Was there something going on between you?" My voice had taken on a separate life of its own, barking out questions. Even I was surprised at the abruptness of my question, but then what was the point of sugar-coating it? I needed to get to the truth.

A fraction of a pause. "No."

"Gemma, please tell me and be honest if there was, or even if nothing happened, but you felt something for each other. I do need to know, as I need to find out why he went. I can't tell you the awfulness of not knowing, not having a clue why he went. I knew he was stressed at work, but that was it, I thought he was happy otherwise. Then I found out that he contacted a friend in Hong Kong about jobs, without telling me. I can only assume he wasn't happy with me."

The words tumbled out. There was a flash of sympathy in Gemma's eyes.

"That's awful." She paused. "Nothing went on between us, nothing, but I will be honest with you, I do find him attractive, a really nice guy and if I hadn't been going through a break-up, and if he wasn't with you, I would have been interested."

"And him?" I held my breath.

"I think he did like me," Gemma said slowly. "I suppose there was a bit of a spark between us, but he never did anything but treat me like a friend. It was just something I sensed. I'm really sorry to tell you this, it must hurt, Eve, but I want to be honest." She took a gulp of water.

Her words stung, but I also felt a sense of relief. It did seem like Gemma was telling the truth.

"But actually, I think one reason that we got on so well was that we were both a bit like lost souls, he really understood how I felt," Gemma continued.

Lost souls. Desolation surrounded me. "Why do you say he was a lost soul, did he ever tell you he wasn't happy, with life, with me?" I forced the final question out, swinging between hoping she could give me some answers but dreading what she was going to say.

"It was just something I sensed at times. He said a few meaningful things at times about relationships being hard, that sometimes it is hard to know what you want, but honestly, he never said anything that was negative about you. In fact, he talked about you a lot."

Frustration welled up as her words gave me no clear-cut answers. Taking on the one hand with the talk of relationships being hard but giving on the other in that he talked about me a lot. I tried to derive some shreds of comfort from that, tried to banish the negativity of the other half of her sentence.

"Are you being honest?" I asked. "Don't just say it to make me feel better."

"He did really, Eve, he talked about things you two got up to, about your flat and how you both liked Tooting and plans to buy a place of your own," Gemma protested, looking me directly in the eye.

"Did he talk at all about the fact that we are getting married?" I stared at the table, feeling embarrassed and desperate.

"I'm sure he did in passing . . ." Gemma trailed off. "Look I just thought of something that may be relevant to his frame of mind. You mentioning him looking at jobs in Hong Kong has reminded me. He said one time, when we both felt low about work, about the redundancies, and I felt really bad about the break-up with Liam, he said, 'Sometimes I feel like jacking it all in and just going to Hong Kong.' I remember feeling surprised because he just blurted it out, and he'd always seemed so stable, it seemed a funny thing to say. But then he laughed it off. I think that's why I might have described him as a lost soul to you before. I thought it was a strange thing to say, from someone supposedly content."

I accompanied Gemma across the road, to the office building. I was dreading going in, having to listen to the platitudes of my colleagues, see their sympathetic looks and most of all, clock your empty desk. My mind burned with your throwaway phrase. *Sometimes I just feel like jacking it all in and going to Hong Kong.* Whether it was due to me or not, you can't have been happy, and guilt tugged at me. Why did I not realise? Why didn't I ask you if you were happy? I just coasted along, presuming you were okay. So stupid and naïve. I slammed the heavy door of the office block angrily behind me. Stupid. Gemma's admission that there had been a spark between you stung, but at least there had been no affair or a fling between the two of you. That's if she was telling the truth. I packaged that whole subject away into a recess of my mind, to be mulled over later. Right now, I needed all my strength to deal with work and speak to Paul, the magazine publisher.

I slowly climbed the stairs. I loved my job, usually loved to bound into the office in the morning, excited to see what stories we would be working on today, eager to have the daily meeting with my team to discuss the agenda.

41

I worked on the same open-plan floor as you, my magazine sprawled over half the floor while the shipping newspaper covered the rest. I resolutely kept my eyes away from the newspaper section as both my and your colleagues approached me.

"But he seemed so stable . . . He was such a great guy, so normal . . . He seemed so together . . . I can't believe it . . . Just goes to show you never know." The words washed over me. Lowered voices, awkward embraces, eyes pools of sympathy. Others hunched over their computers awkwardly, glancing over to me when they thought I wasn't looking.

Paul, the publisher of the women's magazines, ushered me into his office. He wore a sharply cut suit, with small specs perched on the end of his nose. He was usually quite a fiery man with a hard-nosed look, but his expression had softened, and his voice was gentler.

"I simply can't believe it," he said. "Such a dependable, talented journalist. I'm so sorry, Eve, we all are, and we're just hoping he comes back. I am sure he will."

Except you aren't, I thought, watching his eyes slide to the side as he said this. Suicide, that great unmentionable, reared its head to become the elephant in the room. Paul became brisker as he broached the subject that he really wanted to talk about.

"Now, of course we understand that you cannot work at the moment and are giving you the standard two weeks' compassionate leave. As even though he is not . . . er . . ." He stumbled. "The company has decided to give you this leave, fully paid, of course, as we do understand it would be very difficult for you to work in these circumstances."

The implication was that I should be grateful that even though you had not died — as far as we knew — I was getting compassionate leave. Paul expected me to say as much. When I stayed silent, he continued.

"While of course we don't expect you to tell us when you are coming back yet, HR will need to speak to you when this time is up to hear your plans, so we can make provisions. Your deputy features editor is taking over your duties for now, with a bigger freelance budget, but of course that can only be temporary."

He coughed awkwardly. The real question: "When are you coming back? We need to know, and don't expect more than two weeks' paid compassionate leave," was the second elephant in the room.

I loved my job. I lived it, breathed it, it had been my lifeline. But not now.

CHAPTER 6

Three weeks missing

"Plan of action," Clive bellowed. He was sitting at the front of the minibus and had self-importantly assumed the role of leader, a role I was only too happy to let him have. I pressed my nose to the grimy window and watched the rain fall as the bus made its way to Leeds. There were eleven of us on our way there to give out posters, make enquiries, give local media interviews, to try and find you.

Jack and Jess were there, sitting at the front of the bus clutching hands, as was Vicky, who made up a tight-knit quartet with Jess, me and our other friend Rachel, from university. Rachel was unable to join us as she was on a work trip.

Sophie was sitting on the other side of the aisle, her greasy hair held back in a ponytail. The grey hollows under her eyes, and the obvious weight she had lost made it crystal clear the way she was suffering since you had disappeared. Pete, Tom and Fiona, three of your close university friends who also lived in London, were also part of the troop. The final two consisted of Steve and Joe, friends from your journalism course.

We had posted on Instagram, X and Facebook and handed out leaflets and put up posters around London, concentrating especially on Crystal Palace and its football ground, I had done some more local newspaper interviews, and now we were on our way to Leeds on a cold, grey, early Saturday morning. I wasn't hopeful that it would lead to anything, but it felt better to be doing something proactive rather than wandering aimlessly around our flat, with memories of you everywhere. Three weeks in, and there were no leads, no new pieces of information.

I still hadn't gone back to work, was signed off due to stress. It had been easy to get a sick note from my GP.

Clive mentioned key areas to put up the posters and distribute leaflets, including some of your favourite pubs and restaurants, the main shopping centres, hotels and youth hostels. His voice dipped in and out of my consciousness as I stared at the traffic roaring past on the motorway. I wondered when the emptiness and hollowness would end. It stretched before me, as deep as a well, ending only when we got an answer to your disappearance. If there was never an answer, then I wondered how I would resume normal life, get up, go to work, smile, talk, laugh, be interested in the world again, watch TV, read a book, things I had always taken for granted, but which had been snatched from me.

When would I stop questioning, analysing over and over my relationship with you, everything you said and did, until my mind felt like it would topple under the burden? I found myself constantly, feverishly, raking through every episode, holiday, weekend, work day, trying to find answers.

Vicky sat beside me. I could see her pale blue eyes anxiously sweeping over my face. Her mouth opened and closed a few times, before she ventured: "You okay?"

I shrugged. "Obviously not," my mind screamed. Instead: "I guess. Sounds like Clive has got it all sorted."

"Yep. If John is in Leeds, we will find him," Vicky said determinedly.

I don't think anyone actually thought you would be in Leeds, that we would find you, but doing something was better than doing nothing, no matter how remote the possibility.

Vicky patted my hand before tugging her red hair. She was a teacher in a North London primary school, took her job seriously. She was cautious, thoughtful and quiet versus Jess's bubbly, hail-fellow-well-met, open character, but nevertheless we were all close.

"How's . . . um, Ian?" I asked to be polite. I struggled to think of Vicky's boyfriend's name; I was wading through quicksand at the moment.

"Yeah, actually it's good." Vicky's cheeks pinkened. She tugged at her red locks again. "I mean it's only been six months, but things are going well so . . ."

She trailed off and I didn't ask anything else. Vicky didn't like being quizzed about her private life. And, despite asking, I didn't want to know about how happy she was and how great her relationship was going.

I stared at the fields and towns flying by, fiddling with my phone. That reminded me — there was one thing that I needed to do. I made my way to the text that had pinged its way to me yesterday morning.

I hear that you and some of John's friends are going to Leeds this weekend to look for him. Would there be any chance that I could come along as well, to help? I totally understand if you don't want me there, but I wanted to ask as John's friendship meant a lot to me, and I'd like to do my bit in helping to bring him back. Gemma.

That unwelcome little note had opened the Pandora's box that I had tried to keep firmly closed as I was scared about where opening it would lead me. Again and again, I analysed the nature of your relationship, going over and over Gemma's admission that there had been a spark; each time it felt like I had been punched in the stomach.

No, I'm afraid I don't want you there, I can't handle it. I had typed quickly, fingers trembling. At least I had been honest. There was no reply.

The bus eventually drew up at the side of Leeds rail station. As we got off the bus, I saw the graceful Leeds Hotel at the side and there was a stabbing pain in my chest as I was flooded with memories: the first time you had taken me to

Leeds, we had stayed in that hotel. "I've always liked it," you said. "And it's so central, the perfect place to show you Leeds."

We had had a drink in the hotel bar, before visiting an amazing tapas restaurant down by the canal, had a glass of champagne in Harvey Nicks, visited the indoor market to have a wander and admire all the food on offer, before buying bags of sweets from an old-fashioned sweet shop. The memories burned themselves into my brain and I struggled to take a breath.

Clive's voice sounded like it was coming from far away as he barked out orders, handed out posters and arranged people into partners to hand out the posters and leaflets. I found myself partnering him. "Right," he said briskly. "You and I are going to focus on some of the centre of Leeds, starting with Leeds Hotel."

My heart sank. "Do I have to go in?" I asked, thinking how pathetic I sounded. I said as much, adding, "It's just John and I have stayed there, I'm going to find it difficult to go in . . . sorry, I will pull myself together."

Clive touched me gently on the shoulder. "I understand," he said softly. He singled out a nearby Caffè Nero. "Why don't you go there and order us two coffees to take away while I go into the hotel? We'll need the fuel. A cappuccino for me, please."

I smiled gratefully and as I queued for the coffee, gave myself a stern talking to. "You must pull yourself together, you must. You cannot let Clive and everyone here and most of all John, down."

"Pardon?" the man in front of me asked.

"Nothing!" My cheeks reddened as I realised that I had been muttering the words aloud in my determination.

Clive appeared in the doorway just as I had collected and paid for the cappuccinos. "All done," he said, slapping his hands. "Right. Now we are heading down to Bridgend." I reflected on what a nice man Clive was as I trailed after him out of the coffee shop. He was so different to you, both character-wise and in appearance. He was a strapping, broad-shouldered, public-school boy, with rosy round cheeks and a slight paunch that his fondness for beer had given him. He also had a high-flying financial job in the City and a penchant for both watching and playing rugby. You were tall too, but slim with a narrow frame and an angular face. You hated rugby and were creative rather than financially minded. Nevertheless, ever since you had met when your family had moved to Clive's road when you were both five years old, you had been great friends. Clive was a bit flash with the cash and could be a bit of a braggart, but he was a loyal friend with a great sense of humour and had flung himself into trying to find you.

The hours flew by as we entered pubs, cafés and shops to ask them to display posters and taped them to lampposts and anything suitable that we could find as we made our way slowly down the streets. I tried not to look at the posters as I handed them out, as the picture of you was too painful. It was a picture of me and you at New Year's Eve this year — I had been cut out of the photo, although if you looked closely, you could see my shoulder and arm in the photo — smiling, happy, leaning in together at a gathering at Jess and Jack's.

"We can stop for lunch in a minute," Clive said, peering at his watch. "Let's just go to the homeless hostel first."

I had been following Clive's orders blindly and obediently. We stopped at the hostel. Outside, a man sat on the step, eyes sunken, a small bit of dribble escaping from his mouth. He smiled vacantly. I felt suddenly sick — what if you were homeless, living on the streets? You who were so fastidious about showering and clean clothes, who was always so clean-shaven and fresh-looking, so full of plans and ambitions — you had wanted to get onto a national newspaper's business journalism desk, and were writing a synopsis for a novel you wanted to write. Could you have entered this shadowy underworld of no hope? Was your mental state so bad, you had taken to the streets?

"You don't think John is living on the streets, do you?" I asked Clive afterwards, as we trudged around trying to find a café for some lunch — although as usual my mouth was dry, and I had no appetite.

Clive shrugged. "On the whole no, Eve, but then, we never thought that he would just leave . . ." His voice trailed away.

Twenty minutes later I was picking at a sandwich in a café. "Do you really think he is in Leeds?" I probed.

"He's gone somewhere," Clive said diplomatically, tucking into his mozzarella focaccia with gusto. A sliver of cheese got stuck on his chin. "Leeds is as good a place as any, if not better."

"And you do think he's still alive?" I asked, playing with my food.

Clive swallowed a large mouthful. "Yes, I do, Eve. I really do. I don't understand why John's done what he has, it's totally out of character. But I've known him since we were five and he would never kill himself, never." His voice was gruff but sympathetic.

I flinched at the word "kill".

"Clive, were there really no clues at all to you that he was going to just disappear? Did he ever seem depressed or angry or . . ." My voice faded away. I had asked your friends the same questions over and over again.

"He just avoided seeing me the last couple of times," Clive said, as I knew he would. "Well, he may not have been avoiding me, but he cancelled a few times. The last time though, he was fine. A bit down about work, maybe. But upbeat that his mum's final chemo session had just finished. We had a good night watching the rugby and a few beers.

"I should have asked him more, got him to confide, but then blokes don't really talk about things like that." Clive took a deep breath then hung his head, and I thought I saw a glistening in his eyes.

* * *

I collapsed on to my bed-and-breakfast bed, exhausted. It was gone six and Clive and I had pounded the streets, popping leaflets and posters into every commercial property we could see, fixing them to lampposts, trawling the streets and handing out flyers. My feet and back ached. We had then met up with the others who were all similarly shattered. We had decided to stay over in Leeds, and the plan now was to meet for a few drinks at the pub down the road from the B&B. I didn't want to go, just wanted to curl up in bed and sink into nothingness.

There was a knock at the door and Jess appeared. I voiced my thoughts to her.

"Rubbish," Jess said briskly. "You can't just mope in your room; it will do you good. Plus, we have all had a good day, we haven't left a stone unturned even if I say so myself. If John is here, we will find him." She sat at the edge of the bed, a determined look on her face. "He's out there somewhere and he will either come back or we'll find him."

I wished I shared her conviction. I thought of the vast expanse of the UK, Europe, the rest of the world. Leeds was just like a tiny pebble on a huge stony beach that went as far as the eye could see. I was drained just thinking about it. But Jess was expecting a positive response, so I plastered on a smile before ruffling in my suitcase to find a new top for the night.

The pub was crowded, merry, bustling, with cosy nooks and crannies. We were huddled around a corner table, food finished, and now concentrating on wine and beer. What had started as a fairly subdued gathering was now typified by laughs and liveliness. We spoke proudly of what we had accomplished that day in Leeds and reminisced and talked about you at length. I was surprised: I was actually more at peace than I had been since you disappeared. It was good to be with your friends, people who cared about you, talking about you and discussing what had happened. The atmosphere was surprisingly upbeat, no mention that you were not alive, were not somewhere out there and the conviction that you would return was strong.

It was my first night out socialising, and it was a relief to feel normal again, speaking with other people in a busy pub, rather than moping around accompanied just by my fears. Also, the alcohol was having a nice effect. I had tried not to drink too much since you disappeared, worried about the depressive effect of alcohol, about losing control. But the wine was giving me a hazy, numbing effect, which I embraced. I reached for the bottle to pour another generous helping into my glass.

I noticed that Jess seemed distracted beside me. Vicky, Fiona, Jack and Clive were talking animatedly but Jess had shut herself off from the conversation. "What's wrong?" I asked.

"I was just thinking about my wedding next year and how horrible it would be if John hasn't . . ." She faltered. "Reappeared. Sorry, that is insensitive of me and not what you want to hear, when your own wedding is coming up first."

The thought of our wedding, anybody's wedding, was hard to stomach. Such words would normally have me sobbing heartbrokenly, contemplating not only the loss of you but also of my dreams of my own happy-ever-after with you. But the wine continued with its anaesthetising effect, dulling the usual stabbing in my chest that I would feel at such words.

"He might not be there, Jess. He might never come back. He might not even be back for our wedding, and I have to face that." Those feelings had been bubbling under the surface, but it was the first time I had said anything like that out loud. I tugged at the sapphire ring on my finger. It felt looser than before.

"I know we have all been so jolly today, saying that he will definitely come back, but even if he is still alive, he might be starting a whole new life, which won't ever include us."

Jess's eyes filled with tears, but before I could touch her arm, determinedly, she blinked them away. "Sorry. It's so much worse for you. But I got really close to him as a friend. And Jack is so upset too."

"It's not just me, of course his family, friends, are all going to be devastated." As I said it, I marvelled at how noble

51

I sounded, trying to quash an unpleasant little voice that piped up that Jess, our other friends, had no idea how I felt, had no idea how lucky they were to still have their partners and husbands.

"Sophie is certainly devastated." Jess cocked her head at Sophie. "Understandably. I think she needs help, maybe some counselling. She's just gone to pieces."

Sophie sat at the end of the table, not even attempting conversation with Steve and Joe who had given up all attempts after trying gamely for the last hour. She tapped aimlessly into her phone, eyes huge and vacant.

It's just as bad for me, I wanted to say churlishly. *It's not a competition*, my sober, sensible voice reminded me. I took another glug of wine.

"Trying to get attention, trying to make out it's worse for her than anyone else, makes me sick." My mood had changed in an instant. Jess's eyes widened.

"It's terrible for both of you," she said diplomatically.

Before she could say anything else, Clive loomed in clasping a fresh pint. "Coming to sit with you lovely ladies," he boomed, his mood improved since our lunch in the café.

As he squeezed in besides me, Jess turned to speak to Jack.

"How are you feeling, Eve?" He leaned in closer, and I could smell the beer on his breath.

"I was feeling better than I did, it's so nice to be out, with people, in a bar, with normal conversations." My voice sounded slightly slurred. I did my best to remedy it.

"But I feel bad again. Jess just mentioned her wedding, it just brings everything back. Now I can't stop thinking about my own wedding." I didn't even attempt to stop the slurring this time.

"No, Eve, you mustn't think like that." Clive leaned forward. "I honestly believe John will be back. This isn't it. And he loved you, Eve, I know he did."

"Really?" I eyed my wine glass; I had almost finished it again. "I'm not sure he did. I wanted to get engaged, married, the whole package, but I don't know if he wanted it."

I drained the dregs of my glass and nodded as Clive topped it up.

"With me, that is."

Gemma's face loomed in my mind, and I tried to banish her voice telling me about the spark between them. "Then he tried to go away to Hong Kong without telling me. I think a major reason he left was because of me, because he realised that he didn't want to marry me after all."

"No, Eve, he loved you, I know he did. Look, I was his best mate, take it from me, he did. He used to tell me little anecdotes about you, about the stuff you did, he never mentioned not wanting to be with you. He talked about the wedding — hell, he asked me to be best man!" Clive was fierce in his opinion. "You guys were engaged, he wanted to marry you."

He leaned forward. "I think his family is a major reason why he left. He was damaged by his dad walking out on his mum when he was young, then not seeing him, it screwed him up. And he was devastated about his mum's cancer and Sophie always put so much pressure on him, their relationship was so claustrophobic, I think he snapped."

"Really?" My voice wobbled as gratitude welled up in me for Clive. "I really thought it was me." The noise of the pub, and the sound of the voices around me faded as Clive's blunt features blurred in front of me. Still, I topped up my glass, not caring that the wine was lukewarm.

"You listen to me." Clive touched me under my chin. "John loved you. He was incredibly lucky to have you as well, and he knew that. Who wouldn't want a woman like you — beautiful, funny, intelligent, kind, I was always envious, to be honest, as were the rest of John's friends."

I let his words wrap around me like a warm blanket. It was such a welcome contrast to the rejection of your departure, winding its clammy fingers around my heart, the nasty little voice whispering in my ear that you didn't love me enough. As, if you loved me enough, you would not have vanished without a trace.

"Come 'ere." Clive enveloped me in a warm hug. I breathed in the musky smell of his aftershave, closed my eyes. It felt so good to be held by a man.

It was time to leave as the pub was closing. Still holding me, we stumbled to the door. The others walked ahead of us. The hit of fresh air cleared one or two drunken cobwebs in my mind, but I was still caught up in a haze of alcohol. I knew where this could lead, in fact I wanted it to lead that way, I wanted to be held and to forget, just briefly. Clive put his arm round me. We walked the five minutes to the bed and breakfast in silence and got to my bedroom door.

"Are you sure?" he murmured.

We stumbled into my room, collapsed onto the bed and kissed clumsily, roughly. His tongue probed hard in my mouth, a contrast to your gentle kiss. I went through the motions in a blur, dozily clocking that his chest was hairy, not like your smooth, baby-skinned chest. You used to feel embarrassed that you had only the smallest of chest hair, but I didn't mind, I liked it. Clive pawed at me as I wriggled out of my clothes.

"Shall I get a condom?" he whispered.

As he moved inside me, my warm glow disappeared, pushed away by emptiness.

* * *

I opened my eye a crack, my temple throbbing and a dry, acidic taste in my mouth. I felt the heaviness of a body beside me, and it all came back to me in a sickening thud, as Clive snored gently, his beery breath enveloping my face.

Close up, I could see the spider veins threading the sides of his nose, the slightly receding hairline that he tried to conceal. A smell of sweat mingled with the sourness of Clive's breath. I scrambled out of bed and made it to the toilet just in time. As I heaved and vomited, shame and anger swept over me.

"You're disgusting. How could you sleep with John's best friend, his best man, a month after his disappearance!"

I chided myself, almost welcoming the acidic bile I was spewing. I deserved it, deserved to suffer. I compared our drunken, clumsy sex, Clive's heavy, hairy body to your slim frame and gentle skill and heaved some more. I might never have sex with you again. It might always feel like this. I was being swallowed by the familiar empty void that I had lived with for the past twenty or so days as I contemplated a future of awkward, unromantic sex with faceless men.

There was a banging on the door.

"You okay?" Clive's voice sounded gruff.

I had to confront him. Inching to the door, I opened it and saw some of my feelings chasing across his face: guilt, embarrassment, awkwardness.

"It shouldn't have happened," I said stridently, as if I were in a court, answering to my actions. The blue of my sapphire flashed as I flung open the door, as if in reproach.

We travelled back to London on the bus at opposite ends, him at the front, me at the back.

CHAPTER 7

Six weeks missing

The smell of tomato and garlic wafted into the living room where I curled up on the sofa, clutching a glass of wine. "I won't be a minute, just checking the sauce," Jess called.

I was at Jess and Jack's flat for dinner. They lived nearby in Balham, had managed to buy their flat and get themselves on the increasingly hard property ladder a year ago. You and I had wanted to buy too, had been saving seriously for a deposit. Our parents had also offered to chip in and help us as well. I loved looking at property websites, browsing two-bedroom flats in the grottier corners of South London that we could afford. Then I corrected myself. Well, *I* had wanted to buy a flat. I had thought you did, but who knew whether you did now. I had certainly been more vocal and proactive about it.

"Right, all finished, just needs to simmer for twenty minutes or so." Jess was back on the sofa next to me. "How have you been?"

I shrugged. "Well, I have made the momentous decision to go back to work, so I guess that is progress."

Our Leeds trip had led to a big fat zero, despite all our optimism. We had appealed relentlessly across social media and continued to put up posters, including at the Crystal Palace football ground, areas of Kent, both near to your family home and out to the coast. We had extended our reach in London; I had done more media interviews but still nothing.

The incident with Clive had been tough to get over. I hated myself afterwards. But I hadn't told a soul and Clive had promised not to tell anyone either. A few times I was tempted to tell Jess or another friend but stopped myself — what would they think? I tried to draw a thick veil over it. I had been drunk and just wanted to feel comforted after what had happened.

It was sordid; I had showered and showered to try and cleanse myself. I was sad about the effect it had on Clive as well. He was still so helpful and fired up about finding you and participating as much as ever, but there was now an awkwardness between us that was hard to cut through.

"That is good, isn't it?" Jess asked cautiously. I snuggled more deeply into her sofa, wishing I could stay in her cosy flat forever, the flames from her fire casting shadows and blocking out the winter chill, and not go back to our place, which felt so empty by comparison.

"I just feel stuck," I tried to explain. "In all honesty, I don't want to go back to work, I almost can't bear the thought, but I also don't want to not work, I can't bear the long days, feeling like I'm in limbo, I just don't know what to do with myself, and it won't bring John home."

"But you also love your job," Jess said gently. "You were so passionate about it. I think it might be good for you."

I fiddled with the stem of my wine glass. A knot of dread formed in my stomach when I thought about work, but then I felt the same when contemplating long, empty days just waiting, for news that I was not sure was ever going to come.

I focused on what Jess said. "Maybe."

Jess continued as if I hadn't spoken. "Your job is amazing! Oh, wow, I used to want to be on a women's magazine so much."

Jess was also a journalist, but she worked on a business magazine about pensions. She was an editor, which was great.

But I knew she had wanted to become a women's magazine journalist and it hadn't happened. Her career had taken a different path. Still, despite her previous focus on getting into the women's magazine sector, she seemed content enough with her career.

I opened my mouth but didn't know what to say, so closed it again.

"It's going to be really hard," Jess said. "I won't lie to you. But you have to try and get on with life, and a routine will help distract you, make you feel better. It does for me."

I quenched a small stab of surprise at her words. "It's really affected you, hasn't it, John disappearing." I had always known that Jess and you had got on well but hadn't realised what close friends you had become.

"To be honest, John disappearing has really made me question stuff," Jess said slowly.

"Like what?"

"Like, if I should get married next year."

I put my glass down on the coffee table in shock. "Really? But why?"

Jess and Jack had always been part of our friendship group during university, but it wasn't until a few years after we graduated that they just clicked. They had a lot in common, both into music and films, and living in the same part of London. Both so social and hail-fellow-well-met . . . they saw each other in a different light. They had moved in together fairly quickly, bought their first flat, and then came the engagement, just a month before you had proposed to me.

I had been jealous of Jess, I admit, tears springing to my eyes when she rang to tell me of her engagement and ask me to be bridesmaid. I was pleased for her . . . but where was my engagement to you? I reminded myself that she had been together with Jack for longer and had been friends with him for years, but it still rankled.

Jess sighed as she saw the surprise register in my eyes. "Something like that just makes you question everything." I was about to probe for more, but she added quickly, "But that's natural. I'll get over it. I love Jack, I do," she said fiercely.

It was obvious that the topic was now off-limits as she added, "What I really wanted to ask you about was, are you still okay to be my chief bridesmaid? And I am so sorry to ask you, I know it's such a difficult time and topic, but I need to know as I need to start looking for dresses. I totally understand if you don't want to be a bridesmaid anymore."

I thought about our wedding. Jess, Rachel and Vicky were my bridesmaids. Their dresses had already been chosen after a shopping trip that involved champagne and cake and lots of laughs. Their lilac dresses were due to be fitted in March, in the same week as my first fitting.

I thought about looking for dresses for Jess's wedding, being all happy and bubbly.

"I don't think I can do it." My voice cracked.

Jess grabbed my hand. "I totally understand and I'm sorry to have to ask." She paused. "What are you going to do about your wedding, Jess?"

"John might be back by then," I said automatically. It had become my answer on demand.

My words almost echoed in the empty silence.

I let myself into our flat later, preoccupied by both thoughts of our wedding, and Jess's admission that your disappearance had given her doubts about Jack.

As usual, I couldn't settle, and paced the flat uneasily, letting the thoughts race through my head. I moved from the living room to bedroom to kitchen and back again, before entering our tiny spare room, which just about fitted in a sofa bed for when we had people to stay and a bureau, upon which you and I sometimes worked, finishing articles or carrying out the odd bit of freelance (not really allowed, so strictly under nom de plumes).

I was proud of the bureau; we had bought it from a second-hand store and had varnished and painted it. I stared at it now, frowning; it looked different, but I couldn't place my finger on how. The slight crack on the front was still there, the art deco ornamental telephone was perched atop of the bureau as was the 1950s style lamp . . . but where was the framed photo? Casting my eyes around the room, I swept the window sill, the sofa, the bureau again, there was nowhere else to look, and no framed photograph.

The simple silver frame had been a gift from Jess for my birthday last year. In it was a photo of you and me centre stage, surrounded by friends, Jess next to you, Jack next to me and the rest of the gang, around a restaurant table celebrating your thirtieth. I loved that photo, we looked so happy, we *were* happy, a smile stretched across your face and your hand covering mine.

Think. Maybe I had moved the photo and forgotten, in all the distress that I had been feeling over the past month or so. I walked into the living room, scanned the shelves built in on either side of the fireplace, rifled through our kitchen drawers, went through the drawers and cupboards of our bedroom. I knew I wasn't going to find anything, but I had to look. That photo had always been on the bureau, and it wasn't me that had moved it.

* * *

"Jill, you are going to think I'm crazy, but I do think John is still around, I think he is coming into the flat, and taking things that mean something to him." I stirred the sugar into the coffee that your mother had given to me, determined to tell her what I believed was going on.

"I know I never moved that photo, like I know I never moved the mug, and someone tried to get into the flat that night, I didn't dream it," I said fiercely. "I hope this isn't too upsetting for you, but I wanted you to know."

I desperately wanted her to believe me. No one else had; my mother had taken a patient, condescending tone when I told her.

Jess had just shaken her head and said over and over, "But why would he do that? You have to think about it logically."

Rachel wondered if I should go to the doctors and get referred for counselling. Vicky had asked tentatively if I had been taking any medication to help me get by after you went.

Jill's eyebrows and eyelashes were growing back after the chemotherapy. She had been declared in remission shortly before you left. Downy grey fuzz covered her head, a contrast to the sleek chestnut bob she had sported previously. Her face was pale, the skin paper thin, her mouth turned down and her eyes haunted. I had always liked Jill, motherly, kind and compassionate. I knew she approved of me and my relation-ship with her son and she had tried to intervene on occasions that she felt that Sophie was overstepping the mark in terms of her possessiveness of you.

"It has to be him." I took a quick sip of coffee.

Jill stayed silent for a few seconds. Her face was inscrutable.

"I believe you," she said at last. "And I agree. I don't know why he would come to the flat and not get in contact with anyone, but then, I never believed that he would just vanish without a trace.

"But it means he is alive, as long as he is alive . . ." Her voice trembled slightly.

It was tactless but the words tumbled out before I could stop them. "I hope it is him alive and that it's not a ghost — sorry, I sound ridiculous."

"It does not sound ridiculous," Jill said firmly. "But I feel that John is alive, I probably sound naïve, going on about a mother's instinct, but I know he's out there, I just do not believe he would take his life."

She clutched her hand to her chest.

"I think my cancer, the worry about me, the huge responsibility that he feels for Sophie, contributed hugely to him leaving. I think it all got too much for him." She shook her head. "I blame myself. I should have done more to be there for him."

"No. I blame myself," I replied. "Jill, it wasn't your fault. How could you help getting cancer! I know that John adored you. I thought John loved me; now I think he felt trapped by our engagement. I feel I forced him into it. And I let him down: I didn't realise how depressed and anxious he must have felt. He didn't even feel that he could tell me about going to the doctors and the medication they put him on."

I stopped, the familiar cold hand of blame and guilt squeezing my chest.

"No, Eve, John loved you. I have never seen him so content with a girlfriend. After his dad left me, I knew that when he became engaged, he would have to feel sure that it was right, and I feel sure that you were the woman for him. I saw the way he looked at you."

I buried my face against Jill's shoulder, my tears making stains on her jumper. We sat like that for a long time, her stroking my hair, with my tears and her taut, still face.

* * *

Eve thought it was John. What has happened until now is nothing. Just wait to see what I have planned.

CHAPTER 8

Eight weeks missing

> *Dear John, just in case you come back, I am at work today and will be back late, as I have a networking function (boring!). Please call me. Love you.*

I placed the hastily scribbled note on the coffee table. I had been back at work for two weeks, and every day wrote a note that I left out in case you came back. I couldn't bear to think of you, lonely and depressed, or whatever state you might be in, turning up to an empty flat. Grabbing my Oyster card, I slammed the door shut and walked briskly to the Tube. It was difficult to concentrate at work, I often found myself in a reverie, the words floating in front of my eyes on the computer screen. But being among other people, forcing myself to think of things other than you and being back into a routine was preferable to hanging about our flat or at my parents' or Jess's, just willing each second to pass.

I walked into my office, taking care not to look in the direction of your empty desk. Firing up my computer, I sipped my cappuccino as I waited for it to load, going through my tasks for that day.

I had a feature to write — "I lost seven stone and met the love of my life". I also needed to galvanise and organise my features team.

Today's copy of *Shipping Eye* had been placed on my desk. As usual, I dropped it into the bin. I felt the missing John Sullivan by-line as keenly as if a chunk of the paper had been ripped out.

"Good morning, Eve, I liked your news piece on that woman with alopecia on the website yesterday," my publisher Paul said as he passed. I could almost see the thought bubble pop out above his head: *Must be encouraging, make my poor employee feel wanted and pleased to be back at work.*

I gritted my teeth and plastered on a smile, like I did when Sarah, my features deputy editor, gave me her normal tentative, nervous smile of greeting as I took off my coat. I knew they only meant well, but it sparked jolts of anger in me. I slammed my empty takeaway coffee cup into the bin. Out of the corner of my eye I could see Sarah hovering anxiously, no doubt wanting to ask me a question about work. I ignored her. *Let her wait.* I was fed up with being treated with kid gloves and I didn't want their pity. I just wanted my life to be back to normal, with you in it.

Gemma walked past, clasping her mobile phone and a takeaway coffee. Hair scraped back as usual with her normal severe glasses perched on the end of her nose, she wore an attractive white blouse with black bows dotted on it. I sat up straighter. That was a glamorous top for Gemma to wear. Normally she looked dowdy and studious in baggy suits or heavy jumpers. I didn't care that I sounded cruel.

We smiled stiffly at each other. We avoided each other, apart from stilted pleasantries when necessary. The coffee shop meeting and the text she had sent me about asking to help in Leeds simmered quietly between us. I tried not to dwell on the spark between the two of you.

"All right, Gem!" Sarah said jovially. The nervous way she had greeted me had totally disappeared. "Hey, I like your top, it's gorge! Where's it from?"

Gemma flashed her a smile. "Thanks. It's from Emelda Boutique, not sure you've heard of it, no? It's a lovely little boutique, there are a few of them in South London."

Suddenly I was back in our flat, your bank statement in front of my eyes. *Emelda Boutique £42.* "Who bought you that top?" I know the voice was mine, but it sounded like it came from far away.

Gemma looked taken aback. "I bought it," she said. She exchanged a puzzled look with Sarah.

I stood up mechanically. "Come on, tell the truth, Gemma, you at least owe me that — tell me who bought you the top."

Rap rap rap. The words were staccato, said in one breath as I found my legs taking me one step at a time toward her. Gemma took a step back. A look of apprehension flashed in her eyes. "I don't know what you mean, Eve." She was doing her best to sound calm, but she knew she was hiding her dirty little secret.

"Eve, what's wrong?" Sarah asked.

Ignoring her I advanced further on Gemma. "John bought that top for you, didn't he? No point lying, I know."

We had started to capture attention from other corners of the office; I saw the production editors Dean and Chris looking over.

Gemma bit her lip and annoyance mingled with her nervous look. "No, he didn't, Eve, I don't understand or know what you mean by this. I've told you; we were friends and that's it. And please step away from me, you're intimidating me."

All my pain rolled into a tight ball in my throat. I grabbed the sleeve of her top, and yanked it as hard as I could, not caring that I was making a spectacle of myself. I looked into her face and loathed her, hated her spark with my fiancé.

"You had something with him, didn't you, it was more than a spark," I hissed, clenching her top harder.

"Get off me, you're mad!" Gemma cried, trying to twist away and dropping her coffee in the process. The liquid splashed down her trousers and onto my skirt.

"Tell me the truth." My voice was loud but I didn't care. With one last tug the seam of the top ripped, exposing the flesh of her shoulder. Suddenly hands were on me, pulling me away, still I clutched the ripped top until my fingers were prised off.

"Stop it! What are you doing?" shouted Dean as he and Chris pulled me away.

Gemma burst into tears, her hand clutching the exposed flesh of her shoulder. Sarah ran to comfort her as a crowd gathered.

"What on earth is going on?" Paul stood at his office door.

* * *

I rested my head against the seat in front of me. I watched the rain spatter on the windows as the train hurtled towards Nottingham, the nearest station to the small town where my parents lived. Everything felt heavy, like there were weights strapped to my body. I wondered how I would find the strength to get off my seat and walk to the carriage door, exit the station, get in my parents' car. Those simple tasks felt like climbing a mountain.

Somehow, I managed to put one foot in front of the other, negotiate the busy platform and slide my ticket through the gates to the main concourse of the station. It helped that I was unencumbered by luggage.

Mum and Dad stood by the ticket barriers; concern etched onto their faces. "Let's get you home." Dad took me by the arm and steered me through the station, Mum scuttling along beside us. After my confrontation with Gemma at work, I'd walked blindly out of the building and headed straight to Kings Cross, calling my parents to tell them I was coming home, and giving a garbled account about the Emelda Boutique top, your bank statement and my confrontation with Gemma. Mum's bewilderment travelled down the telephone wire. Clutching Dad's arm, I allowed him to guide me to the car.

After a silent journey I was in the sitting room with a steaming cup of tea in my hand. "Now, I couldn't really understand what you were talking about on the phone, what is going on?" Mum sank onto the sofa with me.

I looked at her kindly face, noting that the lines etched around her eyes seemed more pronounced and that there were more craters around her lips. She looked a good few years older than her sixty-five years. Your disappearance had affected her too, in her worry and concern about me.

I explained slowly, my jumbled thoughts had slowed down, and I started from the beginning, from seeing the little boutique on your bank statement and Gemma's number on your phone statement, to my meeting with her and the final showdown in the office.

"You just walked out of the office?" Dad asked, alarmed.

I nodded.

"What on earth are your work going to do? That could be construed as assault, Eve, I can't believe you just walked out as well, goodness you could lose your job over this."

I stared at my dad, anger starting to bubble. "I don't care about that — what about the fact that John has had an affair, he bought Gemma that top!" Tears stung at the back of my eyes and pricked my throat.

"Eve, you have no evidence that John had an affair, you must stop this."

I drew myself up, shocked at the harsh tone in my mother's voice. "I know you are going through the most terrible time, but there is no excuse for attacking this girl. What evidence have you that he bought her this top? Yes, yes, the bank statement," she said sharply as I opened my mouth. "But so what, that is *not* evidence that he bought her that. And if he did — still not evidence they were having a relationship."

"But surely it's too much of a coincidence," I said. "And what about this spark between them, the phone calls . . ."

"She has a top from a popular clothes shop that has several branches in London, just because she has got a top there and his bank statement shows a transaction there, is not definitive evidence that he bought her the blouse."

I shrank back from my mother's tone. This was the first time since your disappearance that she had been anything other than sympathetic to me.

A small cloud of doubt settled itself across my previous certainty that you had bought the top for Gemma.

"You must call your work, apologise, try and save your job," Dad continued on his theme, clutching his hands. "You need that job, Eve."

Paul was icy on the phone. The full severity of my actions was drummed into me. Words like assault, human resources, verbal warning wafted over me.

"We are very sympathetic to your ordeal, but we simply cannot have our employees subjected to that kind of attack," he said stiffly.

I braced myself for the words "you're sacked" or "gross misconduct", but Paul said that my job was safe, this time, as long as it never happened again. And I had to avoid Gemma once I was back at work, any approach or word to her and I was in trouble again. We both agreed that I needed some more time off to come to terms with your disappearance, and it was decided that I have a week off with a sick note, that I gained easily from my mother's GP.

But more doubts had crept into my mind about the nature of Gemma's relationship with you and about the significance of the blouse. I veered between certainty that you had bought her that top, that the spark Gemma mentioned had been fully lit, to believing that it was a coincidence.

Among my confused thoughts was one small flash of certainty that surprised me: I was pleased that I had kept my job. I decided to spend the week I had off before going back to work at my parents'.

"While you are here, Eve, there's something we need to discuss," Mum said one evening halfway through the week. Dad was out having a pint at his golf club.

I took my eyes away from the TV that I had only half been watching. "Yes?"

Mum twisted her handkerchief between her hands and took a deep breath. "What are we going to do about the wedding? It's been eight weeks since John went, and there's no sign as yet that he will come back . . . We need to make a decision before any more plans are put in place." She paused. "I know this is terribly painful, Eve, but I think we need to cancel it. There are only five months before it takes place."

I had tried not to think about the wedding, frightened about where that train of thought would take me. Whenever it reared its head, I repeated like a mantra, "You will be back by the wedding." It became something to cling to, even though I wasn't sure I believed it. If the wedding went too, I would slip faster through the quicksand threatening to submerge me.

"No," I snapped. "I'm not ready to cancel, he might be back by then."

Mum sighed. She took my hand. "But even if he is back, and I'm sorry I am going to have to say this, we do not know what mental state he will be in, what your relationship will be."

I stared at the sapphire glinting on my hand. I wasn't ready to let go yet.

"This Sunday, we have the tasting session, don't we? At the hotel, to choose the wedding menu."

I'd been so excited booking the lunch at the hotel for you, me and my parents. I had spent a long time poring over the menu options, enthusiastic about trying them. I think you were eager to see the menu options too, I couldn't remember.

"Exactly," Mum leapt in. "Which is why we need to let the wedding organisers at the hotel know that we are cancelling the wedding now, before that lunch, which we can't possibly go to."

"I want to go." The words were out before I was fully aware of what I was saying, and I realised that I did want to go very much indeed. Perhaps you would remember that we had the lunch booked on Sunday. Perhaps you would come back.

My mother's eyes widened. "But, but . . ." She was at a loss. "Eve, that is morbid, we cannot possibly, John is not even here . . ."

I tried to explain, as much to myself as my mother. "It's a milestone in our wedding plans, just like my future dress fittings, I just want to get to that point, just to see if it brings him back. Please do this for me. I want to go to the lunch, and if there is still no news about him afterwards, then I guess I will have to cancel, but please just do this for me."

It was suddenly essential that we went to this lunch. I would do it on my own if my parents refused.

The promise of cancelling after the lunch seemed to entice my mother. She was disapproving that I wanted to go ahead, but after a few seconds, she nodded.

"Well, okay then, I can't understand why you would want to put yourself through this, but there we go. We'll go. I am not sure what the hotel is going to think about John not being there, you can deal with that. But we have to cancel the wedding afterwards."

"If there is still no news, if there is still no progress," I interjected.

I saw the lack of hope in my mother's eyes.

I stroked the sapphire glinting on my finger.

* * *

Dad slammed the door as he got out of the car. "Come on then," he said stiffly.

We had arrived at the hotel, which was at the edge of the village in which my parents lived. You had been happy to get married here. "It's traditional to get married in the bride's home town. And I like it in Nottinghamshire," you said. We had looked at a few places in our wedding venue search. A large, slightly soulless hotel had been discounted. As had a stately home, too grand for the cosy, easy-going wedding we had in mind.

"And too corporate," I remembered your pronouncement. Not to mention too expensive. Then we went to this hotel. Small, friendly, cosy, with an old-world elegance.

"This is it," I had said to you, eyes shining, relieved that we had found somewhere. You had taken my hand, nodding and smiling.

"Let's do it."

We walked past where we had exchanged those words, just outside the heavy oak door.

"We have a table booked at one, the name's Jennings," Dad said in tones full of foreboding. He might have been attending a funeral rather than a prospective wedding lunch.

The waitress glanced at her list. "Ah yes, the lunch to decide your wedding menu. Congratulations." She beamed. Mum and Dad winced at her words.

"Unfortunately, my fiancé is not well, but as this has been booked for a while, we have decided to go ahead. He'll like what I choose." The words tumbled out of my mouth awkwardly.

I caught the slight raise of her eyebrows before she responded easily. "Oh, what a shame for you! But never mind, I'm sure he'll be delighted with your choices," she tinkled merrily as she led us to the table, which was in the nicest part of the room, tucked into the corner.

Families, couples, groups of friends occupied other tables, chatting lightly, enjoying their food and drink, revelling in a nice lunch in a lovely atmosphere with the people they cared about. Will I ever experience a relaxed Sunday lunch without a care in the world again? I wondered. We took our places without a word.

"Our wedding planner will be with you shortly with the wedding menu and will run through everything with you then," the waitress said briskly.

I looked outside at the dappled late autumn sunlight bouncing on the trees and wondered if you remembered that this was the day to choose our wedding lunch, and if you wished you were here, if it had made you think about me. If you were still alive. My fingers were tense, clutching my mobile phone. I had been staring at it hopefully all morning, willing a text from you to appear. An hour ago, I had rung your mobile phone for the first time in weeks, as I found it painful to hear your recorded voice message. As before, it went straight to voicemail without ringing.

"Hi, John, it's me, er, Eve. Um, I don't know if you remember, but it's the day we choose our wedding lunch. I am still going; I'd love it if you could join me. I love you."

The wedding planner, Pam, bustled forward, a polished smile on her face. She was holding a tray which contained three glasses.

"Hello, Eve," she welcomed with a smile. "Oh, what a shame the groom can't be here! I do hope he feels better soon. But we should celebrate anyway, so here we go — on the house, champagne!" She merrily handed over the flutes to us.

My father had turned a purplish colour and my mother sat frozen. I took the champagne glass and stared out of the window. I hoped that you would appear at the lunch to take your empty seat, that I would see your lean frame out of the window, the sun beams illuminating your usual lopsided grin and dancing off the black beanie you usually wore at this time of year.

I continued staring out of the window; you weren't going to appear at this lunch, just like you were not going to turn up for our wedding, for your suit fitting, for your stag do.

A splash of champagne slopped onto my fingers as I placed the glass I was holding onto the table.

"Let's go," I said, standing up.

"What? Is everything all right?" Pam asked.

My mother and father both stood up too, their lips clamped firmly shut.

"I'm afraid not. My fiancé is not actually ill; he has gone missing, and I am not sure if he will ever return."

We travelled back to the house in silence. I went straight to my room and took the engagement ring off my finger. It seemed to flash in reproach as I shut it in my bedside drawer.

* * *

Eve thought that blouse was bought by John for Gemma. I loved how wrong she was. I could understand why she did. So would I in that situation. But I know the truth. I hugged my knowledge to me. Unfortunately, things would not be getting easier for her. I was glad she was back in London. There were going to be a couple of surprises coming her way.

CHAPTER 9

The silence of our flat was oppressive as I let myself in. I had decided to go back to London on the Monday rather than the Tuesday as previously planned before I went back to work on Wednesday. I was claustrophobic at my parents' just hanging around the house, fed up with them veering between false jollity or being overly solicitous.

I hadn't told friends I was coming back — I knew if I had that Jess would have asked me over instantly, but I wanted to be on my own. I went to the kitchen to put the heating on and boil the kettle for a cup of tea. I reached for a mug and frowned. The room felt different to how I had left it. I was sure I had never put the tea towel on top of the bread bin. I looked around carefully, trying to note other changes, but everything else looked as I had left it.

I wandered into the living room. There was a cushion on the floor. I bent to pick it up. When I had left for work the fateful morning I attacked Gemma, the cushions had been neatly on the sofa, propped at each corner. Unless in my rush to leave the house on time I had knocked a cushion off. *Have you been back?* A feeling of unease washed over me, followed by tiredness. All of a sudden, I was exhausted. The mix of the Gemma incident, coupled with the wedding lunch and deciding to cancel it had meant that my sleep had been even worse than usual, and I had tossed and turned most of every night. I didn't have the energy to wonder any more about whether you had been in the flat or whether I was simply being deluded, so I headed to the bedroom to have a nap. Curling up in bed, I was careful to sprawl across the middle of the bed. I couldn't bear to sleep in my half, feeling the empty side of the bed beside me.

It didn't take long for sleep to come.

"I'm back." You dumped your rucksack on the floor, and the euphoria I felt turned to horror. It wasn't you as I knew you. You had lost so much weight you looked skeletal, and your lovely dark locks were gone, replaced with a completely bald head. A smile stretched your skull-like face.

I woke with a start. It took me a while to work out where I was. As I took in the familiar contours of the bedroom, and tried to put the dream from my mind, I heard the scraping of a key in the lock. Groundhog Day. But this time I hadn't bolted the door from inside, and the door opened. As if from far away, I heard the familiar creak of the door hinge. You and I had been meaning to oil it for months but had never got round to it.

The dull thud of the door closing, then silence. Fear coupled with exhilaration that this was you coursed through me. I wanted to get up, run to the bedroom door and catch you, but I lay as if glued to the mattress.

Tip tap. The sound of the footsteps sent doubts through me. Tip tap on the ceramic hall floor. They didn't sound like trainers, which you constantly wore, but like a small heel. I strained to hear, maybe I had misheard, but . . . *Maybe it isn't you.* Tip tap. Closer now, almost at the bedroom door. The handle moved.

"Who is it?" I shouted. The pitter patter of footsteps hurrying down the hall propelled me out of bed.

"John? Is that you? Wait!" I cried as I flung myself at the bedroom door, opening it as I heard a slam. I dashed determinedly to the front door, I wasn't going to let you get away this time but as I reached the door, I heard the key turn in the external lock. I was locked in. Whoever it was would get away as, by the time I found my keys to unlock the door, they would have long disappeared. I ran to the living room to look out of the window. All I saw was a little old lady, bent almost double and clutching a walking stick, walk by.

Surely it had to be you. Who else had keys to our flat? But I couldn't shake off the sudden doubt that I'd had that it was you. I had been so pleased at the thought that you were coming back to the flat, it meant that you were still alive, still felt ties to me, to our life. But now I knew I didn't want you coming back again. Not like that. I went to the door and placed the bolt and chain across it. My hands were shaking and my breath was still coming quickly. I was spooked and suddenly didn't want to be here, on my own, with the prospect of a return visit.

I called Jess.

"Hello," she answered cheerily.

I could hear the background noise of cars and people. "Where are you?" I asked.

"Out and about in Guildford, we decided to visit Jack's sister for a few days. Is everything okay? You're still at your parents', aren't you?"

"Oh." My heart felt heavy. "No, I decided to come back to London, I felt like I was going mad, cooped up in my parents' village."

I didn't want to go into the episode when she was out and about, busy with Jack and his family. "I'll call you when you're back."

"We're back tomorrow. Come round for dinner tomorrow night," Jess said promptly. "I hope you're okay?"

"Fine, fine." I attempted a laugh. "Great, thanks, Jess, see you then."

My chest was tight, and my back a knot of muscle. Kneading my shoulder, I wondered who else I could call. Normally I didn't like imposing on people. Even after your disappearance, I was hesitating about accepting people's invitations. *Call whenever. Come round whenever you want; it doesn't matter what time. We're always there for you.*

To be fair, often I felt a need to be on my own. Either I couldn't join in happy, carefree dinners or drinks round the pub, or couldn't bear the feeling of forced gaiety, people tiptoeing carefully round me, the worried glances. But even if this wasn't the case, I would be hesitant to impose myself and my grief on people's hospitality, feel worried that they didn't really want me to follow up their well-meaning words. But this time felt different. I was scared. I couldn't be here on my own.

I hit dial and called Rachel. She picked up promptly and without any explanation on my part, said she would come over immediately and stay the night.

Rachel was the fourth of our tight university group: along with Jess, Vicky and me. She was sensible, down to earth, practical, blunt to the point of being tactless, an opposite to my impractical, sensitive and nervier demeanour.

Her blunt persona hid a warm heart and steadfast loyalty to the people to whom she was close. We had clicked on day one at university, when she had popped her head around the door of my bedroom in halls of residence to introduce herself as having the room next door and asked if I fancied a coffee when I had finished unpacking.

I almost fell on Rachel when she arrived at my flat. Her warm, nut-brown eyes surveyed me with concern as I dragged her through the door and bolted it, just in case.

"How are things?" she asked, following me into the living room, refusing my offer of a drink. "Tell me everything."

I hadn't told her about the incident with Gemma at work, so there was a lot to catch up on. Her eyes widened when I recounted my attack on her over the top.

"Give me your opinion then, so do you think he bought that clothes item for Gemma?" I demanded.

I knew Rachel would tell me what she really thought. True to form, she did not mince her words. "This whole blouse thing — it's really quite flimsy evidence," she commented. "I am really not sure it did come from him. But I can see why it upset you," she added, showing a rare bit of tact.

I moved on to recounting that day's episode of someone entering the flat, adding that it had happened before, and explaining about the missing mug and photo.

"I was so sure it was him, I almost welcomed it. But, to be honest, it was horrible. Someone was here, and I don't think it was him."

Rachel frowned. "First thing I would be asking is: who else has keys to the flat?" she demanded. "And could someone have got hold of his keys?"

I closed my eyes. The option of someone taking your keys from your person was somewhere I didn't want to go, I didn't want to question how those keys ended up elsewhere, why you would not have them anymore, and what that meant about what had happened to you.

But the first question set off a lightbulb in my mind. "Grace!" I said sharply. "The woman upstairs. She has a spare set of keys to the flat. We gave them to her in case we ever lost them or in case of an emergency."

Rachel raised her eyebrows. "I think you need to get them back."

"But honestly, I can't believe that she would enter our flat unannounced. Would she?" I puzzled.

She was a party animal. Out most nights, and sometimes bringing visitors back. There was a regular smell of weed lingering outside her front door. Gym-honed, she had a tattoo of a tiger on her thumb. The few times I had seen her, I always noticed its flash of yellow and black, its teeth bared in a snarl.

"I barely know her. I mean, when John went missing, I knocked on her door to see if she had seen him, but she seemed quite dazed and out of it."

Although there was one thing — she had been grateful because one day, I told Rachel, when the tyre was flat on her car, you had pumped it up for her.

"You need to get those keys back," Rachel repeated. "To be honest, I think it's quite dodgy, someone entered your flat, it has to be someone who has keys, she has keys . . ."

"You don't think it's John?" I interjected, hating the hopeful lilt in my voice.

"Well, of course it could be, as he also has keys to the flat, but you need to eliminate Grace," was Rachel's politician answer.

"I'm going now." I stood up. "No — don't worry, Rachel, I'll go on my own. Stay here, make yourself a cup of tea."

Grace's doorbell didn't work so I rapped on the door. I heard footsteps moving behind it.

"Hi, Eve." Grace smiled at me, the tiger's teeth looming into view as she tapped her thumb on the door frame. The smell of stale smoke wafted out of her flat. "How are you? Is there any news about John?"

"No." I shook my head. "Unfortunately, there's been nothing, despite trying to raise publicity."

"I'm so sorry."

There was a silence. With an internal shake, I decided to get straight to the matter.

"Would you mind giving me back those keys that you have for our flat, Grace? My friend Rachel is staying for a while, and I want to give her some keys."

I had decided not to tell her the truth. Yet.

"Of course," Grace said.

I watched her closely, but there were no signs that anything was amiss. She was smiling sympathetically; her answer had been instant.

"Come in a sec, while I get them from the kitchen."

I heard Grace rooting around in the drawers. She appeared at the kitchen door a few minutes later.

"I'm so sorry, I can't actually find them," she said apologetically. "Sorry, this is embarrassing, I'm normally really organised. Well, sometimes. When I've had a drink it's another story, but I didn't even go out last night!"

She gave a bark of laughter.

"I was sure they were there . . . I will definitely find them; they haven't been out of the flat. I'll have a good look now and then pop them back to you today, as soon as I find them."

I stood rooted to the spot.

"Ah, okay," I said weakly, then gave myself a mental slap for not being more assertive. "I really do need them today, Grace, so that would be great if you could get them to me as soon as possible."

"Of course," Grace said promptly.

My gaze swept her over one more time as I turned to leave, envying her slender, muscley legs in skintight leather trousers. I noticed that she was wearing leather ankle boots, with small heels.

"Well?" Rachel eyed me over her mug of tea when I got back. She was stretched out on the sofa, her Kindle in her other hand.

I told her hastily what had happened. Rachel sat bolt upright, slopping some tea onto her leg.

"What! That sounds really fishy, Eve. Who misplaces someone's house keys? Irresponsible at best and at worst, well . . ." She trailed off, her unspoken words hovering in the air between us.

"But why would she be coming into my flat? And if she did, was it her that took the mug and photo, and why, why on earth would she do that?" I sank onto the sofa beside Rachel.

"We don't know that they are connected," Rachel said. "Are you sure that you haven't just misplaced them, that the mug didn't break before John went, that he didn't take them with him?"

"No, he didn't take them, they were there, I definitely saw them after he disappeared and then they vanished," I snapped, fed up with being asked the same questions, and being met with the same disbelief every time I told people about the mug and the photo.

They acted as if it was no big deal. And we loved that photo, it had never left the bureau. It was so frustrating that no one took me seriously or thought it was significant.

"Why would she come into this flat?" I asked again, my sense of disquiet flaring.

Rachel shrugged. "To have a snoop? Did she have feelings for John?"

I considered. *Could you have had feelings for her? That toned, tight body, those skintight leather trousers.*

"Well, could she have harboured a crush on him?" Rachel persisted.

"She was very pleased that he sorted out her car tyres for her once, but that's it," I said. "Some men would find her sexy," I blurted out.

"Could he have had a crush on her?" Rachel asked.

I was silent. "I wouldn't have thought he was her type. But what would I know?" I shrugged my shoulders. I never thought you would have such a connection with swotty, serious Gemma.

Rachel glanced at her watch.

"Let's give her an hour, and then if she hasn't come again, we go and ask her for the keys."

I nodded.

"I told her that I needed the keys for you as you were staying a few days," I said. "I didn't want to tell her why."

"Why don't I stay for a few weeks?" Rachel offered. "It must get so lonely for you. And I'm about to have builders in to get a new kitchen next week, so it would suit me too."

Rachel had been eminently sensible when it came to getting on the property ladder. She had bought a one-bedroom flat with some help from her parents just a few years after graduating from university, and the money she had made on it meant that she had recently been able to upgrade to a two-bedroom flat in Stockwell, a few Tube stops from Tooting, but closer to the city centre.

I almost fell on her. "Thank you, thank you," I repeated, tears of gratitude and relief welling in my eyes. I hadn't realised how isolated I felt until her offer, drifting around our flat with your ghost just around every corner. The thought of being on my own after someone had been in my flat was also frightening.

"If Grace doesn't return the keys, you'll have to change the locks. In fact, I think you should change the locks anyway, whether you get her keys back or not," Rachel added.

"Hmmm." I knew that was the sensible thing to do, but I couldn't bear the thought of locking you out of your own flat, as what if you wanted to return and after not being able to get in, you just went away and never came back again. I knew that I wasn't being rational, but I wanted to cling to any link that I could with you, no matter how tenuous. I decided not to voice these thoughts to Rachel though. I didn't think they would go down well, and also I didn't want to put her off staying with me.

There was a light tap on the door. I peered through the peephole and Grace's face loomed.

"I'm so sorry," she said apologetically, before the door had even been opened fully. "I found them in the end, they had slipped down the back of the drawers. I knew I had put them in there somewhere. I am so sorry though, and embarrassed!" She gave a half-hearted laugh.

I grabbed the keys out of her hand, filled with relief. "Don't worry, these things happen." I paused, wanting to say more, to ask her if she had been in our flat, to tell her what had been happening. Instead: "Thanks Grace, that's great."

"Do let me know if I can do anything," Grace added. "And let me know if you get any news. I'm just so sorry you have drawn a blank, it must be terrible." She shook her head. "Such a lovely man. I still can't believe it."

I looked down at her feet. She had changed her shoes and was wearing trainers.

Noticing my look, Grace said, "I'm just off to the gym. I'm on a health kick before Christmas — hence why I wasn't out last night!"

After a couple more pleasantries, I returned to the living room, waving the keys. "Here they are. I don't reckon that the person entering the flat was her."

"Good. But I wouldn't be so quick to say that yet — let's just see what happens now," Rachel said. "Do you think you should report the fact that someone is coming into your flat to the police?"

I shook my head. "I'm not that keen on telling them, they weren't interested when I said that his mug had gone after he had disappeared, and they'll just tell me to change the locks."

"Which you should do," Rachel added promptly.

I let her words fall silently.

* * *

Things were falling apart for her. John vanishing created a domino effect. I really should have laid off, given everything that had happened. Did she really need to be more miserable? But I couldn't resist. You could say I got my comeuppance, almost caught in the act. I got a shock; I had been careless. It wasn't going to make me stop though. I would just have to be more careful in the future. And plan other things. I had plenty of other ideas to get my teeth into. It took my mind off things.

CHAPTER 10

The first of December. The Christmas lights twinkled in the centre of Tooting as I hurried home from the Tube after work, wrapping my coat tighter round me. Looking at the lights felt like a slap in the face. You still weren't back. I couldn't face Christmas, and hated every mention of it, detested the happy faces surging past me as I headed home, and the gaudy decorations that were now up in the shops. Mum and Dad had tentatively asked what I wanted to do at Christmas, but I couldn't bear to think about the day.

I saw the lights on in the flat and felt cheered that Rachel was already back. The smell of lamb stew wafted into the shared hallway as I unlocked the door.

"Hello," Rachel called cheerily from the kitchen. She appeared in the doorway, wiping her hands. Rachel had been with me for two weeks now, and it was such a relief having her to stay. I was dreading her going home once her kitchen had been finished.

"Enough for two. Fancy some? And how about a glass of vino?"

"Why not?" I headed to my bedroom to dump my bag. One of the pillows on the bed was on the floor, and the duvet was rumpled; I was sure that I had made it that morning. And the pillow had not been on the floor . . .

"Rach, have you been in my room?" I called as I quickly headed to the kitchen. "Sorry to ask and it doesn't matter if you have . . ."

"No," Rachel said, flashing me a bemused look as she stirred the casserole. "Of course not. Why?"

"Because it's just not as I left it, the pillow is on the floor, the duvet is rumpled and I could have sworn that it wasn't like that when I left," I explained, flustered.

Rachel stirred the casserole. "Why haven't you changed the locks?" she asked sharply. "I thought that was the plan. I'm not too happy at the thought that someone is potentially roaming around with the key, letting themselves in."

"I guess I thought there was no point now that Grace has given the keys back," I said defensively.

Rachel stopped stirring and turned to face me. "She took an hour to return the keys. Has it occurred that she could have pretended to lose the keys, then once you left her flat, popped out and got some new ones cut for herself, before giving your keys back?"

"No," I said weakly, startled at the scenario Rachel placed before me. Disquiet mixed with anger coursed through me. It was not something I wanted to believe in.

"I just don't believe it," I said. "Why would she do that?"

"John's keys could also be at large," Rachel continued, more gently.

That was also an area that I didn't want to visit. I didn't want to cut through the questions that that single line suggested. Why, where, what, who.

Rachel handed me a glass of wine. "Sorry to sound harsh, but I just think not only is it a bit dicey not changing the locks, but psychologically it's not good for you either, to constantly imagine someone has been in."

"Imagine! You think this is all in my head?"

Rachel shrugged. "Not when you heard someone enter your flat, but today, when you say the duvet is crumpled,

85

well, don't you think it's making you over-imaginative? Why would someone come in and do that? Where is the other evidence that they have been in? Has anything been taken?"

"Let me check." I bounded out and went straight to the jewellery box on my dressing table. Our wedding rings were there, and your beloved watch was still in your sock drawer.

"No," I replied reluctantly, ashamed that I had almost wanted something to be missing so that I could tell both Rachel and myself that I had been right: someone had been in the flat.

My phone beeped then and I had the usual hope: let it be you. But the crushing disappointment that I had felt when it wasn't had started to lessen. I supposed that was progress, but even a lessening of that terrible feeling made me feel sad, that I was getting used to your being missing and that you would never be back.

The text told me that I had a missed call and an answer-phone message. "Hello, Eve, it's Inspector Kate Matthews. Please can you call me back on this number . . ."

I emitted a throttled sound.

Rachel was alarmed. "What?"

But I was too busy tapping call-back to reply. My hand felt clammy as I clutched at the straw of hope that it would be good news, while trying to brace myself for something bad.

"Hello, I'm glad you rang before I finished my shift," Inspector Matthews said.

She sounded inscrutable. She got straight to the point. "We've had two possible sightings of your fiancé. What is interesting is that they are from the same place and the same night. Two people reported independently of each other that they think they saw him two days ago at the Crystal Palace stadium, when Crystal Palace was playing Tottenham."

Her voice drifted over me, and I caught words about increasing awareness in the area with media interviews, putting more posters up in the stadium.

I felt suddenly light, like I was floating. She warned me not to get too excited, that often people raised their hopes when there were sightings which only ended up leading to a dead end. But she acknowledged that two people thinking they had seen you in one night was positive news. The next time Crystal Palace was playing a home game was next Wednesday.

"You could go and hand out posters, keep an eye out for him," she advised.

"Two sightings of him, Rach," I said, once I'd hung up, "on the same night. I think it's him." My voice was unnaturally high. "Almost three months of nothing and now this." I sounded like I was drunk or on drugs, I didn't care.

Rachel led me to the sitting room and sat me down on the sofa. I took a glug of the wine from the glass that she had placed in my hand. "It's wonderful news if—" Rachel paused, then added — "if it is him. Sorry I don't want to sound like a killjoy, I just don't want to get your hopes up and then have them dashed."

A flash of anger. I knew it was unfair, but I couldn't help snapping, "Please don't ruin this moment for me, Rach. I've been through weeks of pure hell, with not one hope, one lead. To have this is so amazing — and two people, Rach, two people! It has to be . . . Oh, I need to tell Mum and Dad and Jess and I have to book tickets to that match she said." I was gabbling again, my thoughts taking quick zigzags. I drained my glass of wine.

Rachel put her arm round me. "You go and call people," she said. "I will book the ticket for the match for you."

I smiled at her gratefully. "Thanks, Rach."

I didn't believe in God anymore, even though I'd been brought up going to church regularly. But I found myself clasping my hands, eyes closed, before getting into bed that night. "Please God, please God, let that be you, please."

CHAPTER 11

The phone rang out. I felt nervous and almost hoped that she wouldn't pick up. Sophie always made me feel like that. The gap between us felt even broader since you had gone. I knew she was struggling, was still on leave from her job in marketing and had moved back home to be with her mother. She appeared to be taking it worse than me, but — I felt ashamed to admit it — that angered me. I knew it wasn't meant to be a competition, but childishly I wanted first dibs at being grief-struck.

It was just as bad for me as for her, worse, I had lost my fiancé, my future husband, I thought churlishly, as I waited for her to pick up. Still, I was trying to build a bridge towards her, reluctantly I must admit. It had been Rachel's idea.

"I've booked two tickets for the match," she announced the night before.

"Oh, thanks Rachel, that's so kind of you to come too—"

She cut off my gush with a shake of the head. "Not for me, although you know I would go with you like a shot. No, I think you should ask Sophie. You two need to be on the same side, you both want the same thing, it seems crazy not to support each other."

I didn't want to do it, but I didn't protest. I knew she was right.

"Hi." There was barely a note of recognition in Sophie's voice, which fired my irritation as she had my number stored in my phone, so she must have known it was me calling.

"Hi." I paused and chose my words carefully. "I guess you know about the sightings of John . . ."

Sophie cut in, her voice high-pitched and irritated.

"Of course, I am his sister." She emphasised "sister" so dramatically that I pictured the word in huge fluorescent capitals.

"Let's hope it's good news, our first breakthrough, I am so hopeful."

I hoped that it would elicit some kind of positive response from Sophie.

"Yes," she said.

The hope and anxiety conveyed in that one syllable reflected my own feelings, where one minute I was high, light and happy, the next suffused with nerves and anxiety that this was a false sighting and not going anywhere.

"Sophie, I've booked two tickets to the next Crystal Palace home match, next Wednesday, will you come with me?" I said, wondering if she would reject my offer or embrace it. "We can look out for John and hand out leaflets about him going missing," I rushed on, to fill the silence.

"Yeah, okay, to be honest I was going to buy my own ticket, but I guess I might as well have yours if you already have it. How much do I owe?"

That was as good as I would get from her. Still, it was better than a rejection of my offer.

"You don't owe me anything."

* * *

A roar went up from the crowd as Crystal Palace scored. It was one–nil against Fulham. I wrapped my scarf more tightly around my neck to keep out the cold that seeped out of the hard seat beneath me. I made no effort to even pretend I was watching the game.

I whipped some binoculars out, courtesy of Jack. "Birdwatching?" I'd asked Jess.

"No, cricket, he uses them for cricket!"

I scanned every face that I could: my row of seats, the ones in front and behind, the sea of faces opposite, and further. A flash of dark hair, stubble, a black beanie hat, I grasped at any clue and homed in with my binoculars.

Sophie and I had started the night full of purpose to get the message out there: dumped piles of leaflets in the main area and at the foot of the stands; sticking up posters and handing them out as people filed to their seats. It was almost half time. I had been so hopeful that this night was going to lead to you, but the hope was draining out of me like air from a pricked balloon.

I studied the expanse of faces and wondered how I would ever find him. If he was even here. I stole a glance at Sophie and knew that she felt the same as me, her eyes darting restlessly around, anywhere but on the pitch.

I zoomed in on my binoculars again. Despite the fact that you were such an ardent supporter, I had never gone to a football match with you. It was something that I had always meant to do, but the truth was I wasn't interested in football. My heart felt like it was contracting as I remembered you saying eagerly how you'd love it if I came too.

That was another reason to add to the list of things wrong with me and our relationship that had helped to propel you into leaving me. I couldn't even be bothered to show interest in your hobbies. My throat tightened as I wondered if I would ever get the chance to attend a match with you in my life.

The start of half time stopped my train of thought. I turned to Sophie, opened my mouth to say something banal, but instead: "I just want to find him here, I am so disappointed we haven't. Silly really though, given the size of this place and number of people."

Sophie nodded. "I kept telling myself that I mustn't get my hopes up as I'd only be disappointed," she said. "But I did, of course."

I had been shocked at Sophie's appearance. She had lost even more weight since I had last seen her and her face was so thin and pale, her hair hanging in greasy strips. I wondered when she had last washed it. Still, I knew I didn't look great myself; my clothes hung off me and great bags had formed under my eyes.

We both braced ourselves to get through the second half. I wanted the match to end so that I could continue my inspection of the faces surging past me.

"What if he isn't here?" Sophie asked in a small voice. It was one of the first times she had opened up to me. Her words opened up a bleak chasm in me, but conversely, I welcomed them. For the first time we were in this together, her words had started building a bridge between us.

I reached over and tentatively squeezed her fingers.

The second half passed in a similar blur to the first half. I spent my time again scanning the crowds for you and giving myself motivational pep talks.

"Just because he's not here tonight, doesn't mean that it wasn't him last week." I repeated that tired little sentence over and over to myself.

There was a brief feeling of satisfaction when Crystal Palace scored again. Two–nil. You would be pleased. Wherever you were.

The match ended. I jumped to my feet desperate to leave, to blot out the crushing disappointment I felt.

"Do you fancy going for a drink?" I found myself saying. Recently my mouth was not connected to me.

Sophie hesitated. "Why not?" she said at last. We trudged out, caught up in the bodies leaving the stadium. One last time, I stuck the binoculars against my eyes, surveying the crowds ahead.

I spotted a familiar side profile. The hair was slightly longer than I remembered but was the same style. He was wearing glasses — I felt a jolt as you hadn't been wearing them the day you went, but of course you had them on you, you carried them everywhere and you always wore them to watch TV or sport.

They were wire-rimmed. The profile was the same, the slight tilt to the nose, high cheekbones and long lashes. I felt as if I was in slow motion. Dropping my bag, I sprinted over, pushing past bodies.

"Watch it, love!" shouted a man as I elbowed him out of the way.

"John," I shrieked. People stopped and stared.

My John, you were back. I had to hold you. I grabbed you by the shoulders, tried to stroke your face.

"Why did you leave?" My grasp tightened.

I was never going to let go.

You turned to face me. The eyes were a pale blue, not the turquoise blue that I was used to. The stubble was thicker than I remembered. My grip slackened.

"What are you doing? Who are you? Get the bloody hell off me," the man roughly pushed my hands away.

"Bloody psycho!" he moaned to his friend. The voice was the final straw.

Not your soft southern tones, but a pronounced cockney accent.

My hands fell slackly to my side. I had made an exhibition of myself. I didn't care.

* * *

We sat opposite each other in the pub. The happy chatter around us was not reflected at our table. Sophie toyed with the stem of her wine glass.

"Well, that was embarrassing," she said coldly.

"I'm sorry." I was annoyed as soon as the words left my mouth. Why should I apologise to her? "I thought it was him."

"It was obvious from a million miles away that it wasn't." Sophie pursed her mouth.

"You seem to think only you should be grieving and devastated about John. Well, I have a shock for you — I was his fiancée, he was my future husband, this has wrecked my life too," I hissed.

Sophie tugged a greasy strand of hair behind her ear. "He was my brother. You'll meet someone else, get another fiancé, get married."

She somehow managed to make the term sound throwaway, like buying a new washing machine to replace an older, dissatisfactory model.

"I will never get another brother." She paused, and her next words cut like a knife. "And as I've said, I think the pressure you put him under to get engaged was a factor in his disappearance." She picked up her wine glass, took a deliberate sip and twisted the knife further. "I was the closest person there was to him."

Rage pulsated through me.

"You are sick and twisted. Your neediness stressed him out so much, it's not normal to depend on a brother like that, you're to blame for his disappearance. John was my future husband; we were going to build a life together. I can't imagine meeting someone for an exceptionally long time, if ever."

Images of Clive rose. His hot, sweaty body, the hair on his back, the bile rising in my throat the morning after. The way it felt so wrong. A succession of Clives reared their heads when I looked into my future; you gone forever.

I drained my glass and stood up.

"You will meet someone, which will progress to a serious relationship and marriage. I've lost my future. You haven't."

Sophie stood up too. "Fuck you," she said in a tone that was almost pleasant and conversational.

CHAPTER 12

"I just think that's so sad," Rachel said as she flicked through TV channels.

It was the night after the football match. I stiffened. Not the response I wanted. Still Rachel was nothing if not honest.

"She's an evil witch and I want nothing more to do with her," I said.

The combination of the disappointment of no leads on you from the football match plus the nastiness between Sophie and me had brought my mood crashing down.

I spent the day at work dazedly staring at my computer screen, fighting back tears and taking eight hours to write an easy feature about a woman who had given up on love, but met her future husband on a cruise ship: *Thought I'd missed the boat — then met the man of my dreams on a boat!* My hands hovered above the keyboard after the strapline, my mind blank.

"You should be bonding over this, not fighting and saying such horrible things," Rachel tutted.

"It's her, not me, so I'm leaving it, I'm damned if I'm making the first move." My voice rose a couple of notches in indignation.

Just as I was about to pontificate about my position and how I was in the right, my anger bubbling away at Rachel, she leaned over and grabbed my knee.

"Don't give up, just because you didn't see John or get any answers last night, doesn't mean that it wasn't him."

My anger melted away. She was so honest that I knew she believed that, and it gave me a renewed spark of hope. But as I was about to thank her, she switched quickly to another topic.

"I've been meaning to tell you, my kitchen has been finished now. But I'm happy to stay here until just before I go back to my parents' for Christmas. But then I will go back to my flat in the new year."

Rachel looked strained, I could tell she had been worried about telling me and had psyched herself up to inform me. My stomach curled up in a knot. I'd loved having Rachel living with me, keeping your ghost at bay. I could barely bear to contemplate the long, empty evenings and weekends in our flat, not even including the fear of seeing and hearing things that weren't right — footsteps, misplaced cushions. I *would* change the locks, I thought uneasily.

Rachel opened and closed her mouth.

"Have you thought about moving?" she said at last. "It would stop all this worry that someone has . . . been letting themselves into the flat. And it would help you move on, help you to . . ." Her voice trailed off.

"I don't want to move on. That is accepting that he is never coming back, and I can't believe that. I can't accept it."

I clutched her wrist and watched as her skin turned white as I squeezed tightly. My nails were ragged, unkempt. Normally I had a manicure on a regular basis, proud of my smooth, gently rounded, gleaming nails.

Rachel pulled her arm away and nursed her wrist.

"I didn't mean it like that." There was a note of exasperation in her voice. "I don't think he is dead actually; I think he is out there somewhere, but you can't continue with life here, you're stuck in limbo, it's not healthy."

The word "dead" was jarring.

"If he is out there and wants to come back, then he will, wherever you are." Her voice rang out, confident in conviction.

Some light seeped into the darkness that filled my mind.

"Maybe." I clung on to the confidence in her voice. *You will come back.*

"Sorry for the interrogation," Rachel said, not sounding very sorry at all. "But I need to ask you something else. Where are you spending Christmas? Your parents', I hope?"

Christmas. You got me some beautiful amethyst earrings last year. I gasped as I saw their sparkle. They were to be worn "at our wedding", you said, holding them up against my ear. I remembered that you looked serious, your mouth tightened. Were you unhappy then, planning your departure? *No no no, I won't go there.*

"I'm not spending Christmas with anyone, I want to be alone here." I spoke quickly, to drown out the thoughts chasing themselves across my brain.

"And no, Rach, please don't try and persuade me not to." I rushed on as I saw Rachel's eyes predictably widen and her mouth open to intervene. "I just can't celebrate Christmas or even be present at it, if you know what I mean. I don't want to speak to people, to put on a face. I don't want to exist . . . on that day."

The words kept pouring out of my mouth, elucidating what I had been struggling to explain, even to myself.

"I know maybe you can't understand that, that most people want to be with loved ones, but I just can't, please don't try and persuade me."

Rachel closed her mouth, and I could see the effort it took not to rail, to implore me to spend Christmas with people, to tell me that no one expected me to celebrate.

CHAPTER 13

A huge Christmas tree towered over the reception hall of the Missing Association headquarters, a charity which helped missing people and their families. Its twinkling lights and brightly coloured tinsel seemed at odds with the headshots plastered over the wall, some smiling, some surly, some distant.

Some photos looked like a passport photo, serious, staring straight ahead, others looked like they were encased in the bosom of their families. One man, bald, sixties, smiling, had a hand on his arm. It looked like they were sitting at a jolly dinner. The person whose arm it was, was cut off. I looked at the unknown hand, saw the pale pink nail varnish and slight wrinkles and wondered who it was. Wife, sister, friend? A wave of sadness spread over me.

I took in all the photos again. Glum-faced teenagers jostled for space with wizened men, matronly women and men in their early thirties who should look like they didn't have a care in the world. Why did they all have a haunted look? I knew they didn't really, it was what I knew about them that made me think that.

My eyes landed on one particular photo. I read the short paragraph.

John Sullivan, age at disappearance: thirty-two, missing from: Tooting, South London, Missing since: 2 September, reference number: 17-00134523.

My eyes skidded over the face I knew so well, the deep-set, heavy-lidded blue eyes, the slight dimple in the cheek. I made myself stare at you. I stared so long that your face started to blur.

"Can I help?" the woman at the front desk asked gently.

"I'm here for the Christmas advert thing . . ." My voice faded.

She nodded briskly. "I will take you through."

She took me to a room off the main reception. Three other people were there already. I sat next to a woman who looked around forty. She tightly clutched a Manchester United football scarf.

The Missing Association had asked me to appear in a Christmas advert to try and raise awareness of people out there missing from their families at such an emotive time. *Ten Things I Miss About You*, it was called. We had to be filmed citing the things that we most missed about our loved ones. I was dreading it, but anything that brought awareness to you and helped to find you, I was willing to do.

The woman next to me was chatty. "My husband's been missing five years," she said in her lilting Liverpool accent after a few polite opening lines and after introducing herself as Julie. "He'd been down, as his business was going badly. He owned his own kitchen refit business," she explained. "He took the car one morning, was meant to go to the doctor but he never turned up at his appointment. He just disappeared. They found the car abandoned on a country road fifteen miles away. I've never heard from him since."

She clutched the scarf tightly. Seeing my glance, she smiled.

"You probably guessed, his favourite football team. I always wear this scarf at wintertime; I like to feel it keeps me close to him."

Five years. I gulped. I had just about existed for almost three months since you had gone, and I couldn't imagine the torture of half a decade.

"Are you still hopeful of finding him?" I asked.

"I am waiting for him to come back," she said. "Oh, everyone else has given up, they think he killed himself, but I won't accept it. Our house is the same: all his clothes are on his side of the wardrobe. I email him every single day. I won't give up on my George."

She clutched the scarf tighter. She tapped her chest. "I still feel that he is out there," she explained. "And I'm only forty-one, if he comes back in the next few years, I could still even have kids, you know?"

Hope blazed out of her hazel eyes. I swallowed hard, feeling the toast I'd forced down for breakfast rise in my throat. *That poor woman.* I wondered if people felt like that about me. I felt some fight surface in me. *I will never be like that. I will continue and make a life for myself.* Although nervous I was desperate to get out of that room, its hope versus despair sucking away the oxygen.

Another couple were telling me about when their twenty-one-year-old son went missing in 1995 — a cheery bye when he popped out to get fish and chips for tea and left their house and their lives forever — when I was called in.

As the producer and cameraman fussed with the equipment, I carefully took the paper with my reasons scrawled across it and read it carefully.

Ten things I miss about you:
1. The way your hair sticks up in tufts when you wake in the morning
2. Cooking spaghetti bolognaise together
3. Your passion about finding and writing a scoop
4. Singing along to Fleetwood Mac's "The Chain" in the car

5. *The way your eyes light up when Crystal Palace scores*
6. *The way you look at me at work*
7. *Eating takeaway pizza and watching British Bake Off together*
8. *The way your arms feel so strong and warm when wrapped around me*
9. *Walking hand in hand through Tooting Common*
10. *Everything*

* * *

Eve didn't want to become a Julie. But I was pretty confident that she would be, by the time I had finished. Unfortunately, I feared that I would be like her too, despite my best efforts. Anyway, Merry Christmas, Eve. There is a gift on its way.

CHAPTER 14

The knock on the door unnerved me. It was six on Christmas Eve and I wasn't expecting anyone. Not that you would know it was Christmas Eve. The flat was bare of decorations, save for the Christmas music blaring from the TV, which I had switched on to feel less alone. I tried not to think of this time last year, when our Christmas tree dazzled with lights and tinsel in the corner of the room, with a robin that you had made when you were eight perched at the top.

I headed to the door and my slight suspicion gave way to hope — could it be you, maybe you were coming home for Christmas. I forgot to peer through the eyehole in my agitation and I flung open the door to see Grace from upstairs. She clutched a plate and smiled at me warmly. Tiger-face slippers adorned her feet.

"Hi, Eve, you mentioned that you were staying here for Christmas," she began.

I felt like a brick had dropped into my stomach as I wrestled with disquiet and dismay that Grace had not gone away for Christmas. I had never felt comfortable with her since the key incident.

"I thought you might like some mince pies — home-made, of course."

I took them limply, my expression giving away the surprise I felt.

Grace laughed. "Bet you didn't think I was the cooking type! Baking's my guilty pleasure. I make a mean Christmas cake too."

The mince pies were still warm. Their smell reminded me of this time last year when you and I decided to make mince pies for the first time. We tucked into them together, pleased with our baking. "Deck the Halls" blared out from the television.

"Thank you," I said, still holding the plate at arm's length. Grace looked hurt. "Thank you so much, yum!" I added hastily, trying to inject enthusiasm into my voice.

"So . . . I guess no news?" Grace twisted a bright blond lock round her finger. A bead of perspiration glinted on her right temple.

"Er, no. Nothing apart from a supposed sighting at the football match at the start of the month, I think I told you about that."

"We Wish You a Merry Christmas" now blasted from the TV programme. I just wanted her to go.

"Oh dear." Grace sighed. "So upsetting for you. But maybe he needed a bit of time on his own. Christmas might make him think about things and come back!"

The forced optimism in her tone was in contrast to the sad look in her eyes. She might as well have grabbed a microphone and boomed into it, "He is never coming back, if he is even alive."

But despite this I felt a tiny sliver of hope that you might come back for Christmas. Surely, you would think about our wonderful day last year, the Buck's Fizz and smoked salmon in bed for breakfast, the walk through the common, our feet crunching on the frosty ground, arm in arm . . .

"Are you okay?" Grace leaned forward to touch my arm. I pulled away.

"Yes. Sorry, it's just I'm finding it hard — are you not going away for Christmas then?" I quickly changed the subject, to bat off any more questions.

"Well, I'm off out tonight, down the pub shortly, with a few mates. But it can't be a late one as I'm going away to my mum's tomorrow but just for the day, as it's easy enough to get there, she lives in Epsom. She's got dementia and she's becoming more and more forgetful, and I've noticed changes in her personality. It's hard as my brother lives in Australia . . ."

I zoned out. I didn't want to make conversation. One of Grace's tiger slipper-shod feet tapped on the floor. I didn't want to hear about the bleakness of her mother's dementia, I wanted to shut the door on it.

"I'm sorry to hear that, Grace, look I'm really sorry but I must go, I need to call my mum, I promised . . ." Before I knew it, I had shut the door.

I was shocked at myself, I was usually polite and sympathetic to people, even those I didn't much care for. I peered through the eyehole, and watched her mouth drop open slightly. Then it tightened. She slowly put her hand on the door before turning to go up the stairs, her tiger tattoo in sharp relief.

I sat in front of an *Only Fools and Horses* repeat, nibbled one of Grace's mince pies as I hadn't made myself any dinner and poured myself a huge glass of red wine. My phone bleeped with concerned, well-meaning messages — Jess, Rachel, even Clive, other friends, Mum, Dad, Jill . . . *Are you okay? Thinking of you. Please call us anytime. We love you. If you change your mind, please come over tomorrow.*

I didn't respond. The only movement my hand was capable of was lifting the glass to my mouth and taking glugs of wine.

It didn't take long for it to have the desired effect. The muddle of fear, panic and sadness was numbed by a red haze. I switched off the TV and turned on Spotify. Our playlist. I hit the Stone Roses' "I Wanna Be Adored". Foot tapping to the climactic build up, I spoke aloud. "We always loved indie didn't we, John?" The Stone Roses, Oasis, Pulp, Arcade Fire, Band of Horses.

As the haunting tones of the song took grip, I closed my eyes. I could see you here, feel your warmth next to me on the sofa, your foot tapping away, a glass of wine on the coffee table. We put the world to rights; we talked about everything. "Why did you leave, why did you leave not just me but everything? I think you're still out there. I think you've come back to the flat." My voice rose. My cheeks felt wet and my tongue furry.

I was sure my lips would be stained crimson from the wine. I took another huge gulp and the wine slipped down the glass between my fingers. "I need an answer. If you're dead I need to know." It felt surprisingly good. Letting it out to the four walls of our sitting room.

More songs wafted over me, until unsteadily once the bottle was finished, I weaved my way to bed. Blissful darkness covered me the minute I closed my eyes. The next thing I knew, there was someone in my room. It was you, John. I felt your presence so strongly. The steady, even tread, a warm, comforting hand on my arm. Your floppy hair touched my shoulder as you leaned over me, head bowed.

I woke abruptly to pitch black, the air pressing against me. I tried to make out your profile, hear your breathing, but nothing. I touched my shoulder, where I'd felt your hand. My skin felt cold. A dream. That was all. I realised why I had been so hell-bent on staying here at Christmas. It wasn't just that I couldn't bear to be around anyone. I wanted to be here in case you came back. Properly. Not fumbling around behind my back, taking things and being a sinister presence. I realised that underneath it all I thought there was a chance that you would come back for Christmas, and I wanted you to come back to me, not a cold, empty flat.

But you weren't coming back, were you, ever? The cold clarity of that thought brought my skin up in goosebumps. My head was muggy because of the wine. Despite the despair drifting over me, I closed my eyes and gratefully felt the darkness envelop me. Then I realised something. Your face in my dream, John, it wasn't yours. It was a woman. I couldn't make out the features clearly in my dream, but I knew it was female. The long lashes, the delicate jawline, curve of the chest.

I fell into another uneasy sleep until the steady thud of rain drumming against the window woke me. I tried to ignore the identical thump in my temples after all the red wine I consumed. I peered through the curtains. A heavy grey sky and a sheet of rain met me.

"Happy Christmas," I muttered. Thoughts of happy couples filled my mind, Jess and Jack, no doubt having a leisurely breakfast, curled around each other. I was shocked at the jealousy that I felt.

Last year, the sky was a cold, icy blue, so bright my eyes had felt dazzled as I had peered out. You were lying back in bed, smiling lazily.

"Smoked salmon and Buck's Fizz, perfect breakfast, hey?" you said. Happiness swirled around me like a cocoon, and I dropped the curtain, set on sorting our breakfast. "No!" You leapt up. "I'll do . . ." *Stop it!*

I padded to the kitchen. No fiancé to get me breakfast this time. Still, food wasn't on my mind anyway. A glass of Buck's Fizz was. Not that I had anything to celebrate. But Buck's Fizz was a — just about — acceptable form of alcohol to have on Christmas morning. I needed something to numb my emotions and still my mind. *This time last year, this time last year* . . . I realised that alcohol was going to fill this role.

"Happy Christmas, darling!" The desperate lightness my mum was trying to project travelled down the telephone line as clearly as her voice.

"Merry Christmas," I said. I opened my mouth to say more. I should say something, anything, talk about the weather, what I was doing (nothing), what I did last night. Nothing came out.

"Please let Dad and me come tomorrow, please, we want to be with you," Mum pleaded.

"Maybe. Can I let you know later?" My eyes fell on the little pile of presents addressed for me that I had stacked up in the corner. Stuff from Mum and Dad, Jill, Jess. I didn't care. I might as well get this charade over.

When Mum hung up, after I promised to ring her that night, I grimly rolled up my sleeves. I would open the presents, and then go out for a walk. I drained the last dregs of the Buck's Fizz in my glass. It didn't have the desired effect, but never mind, I had whisky and brandy in the kitchen cupboard.

I dragged my sad little pile into the middle of the room. Vouchers, books, I shrugged them aside, and then opened up a present to see a delicate, polka dot top from Rachel. Even I was roused from my sadness and depression to appreciate how pretty it was. "Nice." Then I saw where it was from. Emelda Boutique.

I chucked it away angrily. *I told her about the saga of the top and Gemma. Why did she do this? So tactless.*

Simultaneously I chided myself for being unfair. Rachel had been so busy moving from here to her refurbished flat. Emelda Boutique was a popular chain in South London. She had probably dashed in desperate to get me something without thinking about it. But I knew I would never wear it.

I picked up a nondescript brown parcel addressed to me in print. Probably a book from Amazon from one of my friends or family. I ripped it apart and saw, encased in a clear plastic covering, a slash of lilac. Puzzled, I pulled it apart, and there lay a tie, silky and delicate in my hand. You were going to wear a lilac tie at our wedding. The colour theme was lilac. My favourite colour. I grabbed the envelope it came in and examined the outside. No signs at all, apart from a London postcode. I shook the wrapper. No sign of a receipt, no label on the plastic wrapping.

I don't think that I told anyone other than my mum and dad about the wedding colour theme. Only you knew. Did I tell Jess, Rachel or Vicky, as they were my bridesmaids? My mind whirled. No. I was definite in this. I knew this because, although embarrassed to admit it as it sounded churlish, I didn't want Jess to get ideas about her wedding and copy me. It didn't make much sense as our wedding was three months before theirs, so she could still do that, but I still didn't want to give too much away at an early stage.

We hadn't gone bridesmaid shopping yet and I had planned to tell them about the colour theme when we went shopping for their dresses. Which was never going to happen now. Did you tell anyone? I demanded that you didn't, and you usually kept your word — although that was the person I thought I knew. Who knew if you actually did.

I coiled the tie gently round my fingers. *You would have looked so handsome in this*, I continued my monologue, not realising the significance of the past tense until my ramblings finished. It would have looked so striking against the charcoal grey suit we had picked out, your cornflower blue eyes and of course the lilac neck of my dress.

Someone had been in my flat and now I had been sent this 'gift'. The footsteps that I'd heard that night beat across my mind as my unease grew. I wanted so much for it to be a sign from you that you were coming back. A spark of hope so electric shot across my head and caused me to drop the tie. But my usual hollow feeling soon swallowed it up.

You're never coming back.

The hours had never gone by so slowly. I hooked the tie over one of the dining room chairs and watched it as I slowly drank my Buck's Fizz. I should get out, take a walk on the common, have some fresh air, but we walked on the common this time last year, we held hands and laughed and talked about our wedding and honeymoon plans, we stopped in our local for a glass of red wine. I couldn't retrace my steps.

My phone beeped with a text. *How are you finding today? Sophie.*

I hadn't heard from her since the disastrous night we watched Crystal Palace play. I was surprised, I never thought that I'd hear from her again.

Terrible. I feel lost without him. I stared at my message and wondered if I should sugar-coat it. As if on pilot my index finger pressed down, and it was sent.

Me too, was the reply.

That was the most emotion that I was going to get out of Sophie. I glanced at my watch. Only midday. The hours were going by torturously and there would be no reprieve with meals, I just wasn't hungry.

I wandered into my bedroom and opened the top drawer of the chest of drawers. Digging through your socks, I felt for your watch at the back. I'd pushed it back there after you had been missing a few days. I couldn't bear to look at it — the thirtieth birthday present that you had said you would never discard. My fingers felt nothing but fabric and the end of the drawer. I slowly shook and took out all your socks, boxers and a random pair of tights of mine, but was confronted with an empty drawer.

I knew I had put it in there. I didn't even bother to search anywhere else.

I slung on my coat as if on autopilot and headed out of the door. I didn't care if it mirrored last year's Christmas Day, I needed to get out among the living. I was going to head to a lively pub where Christmas carols blared and people jostled at the bar, red-cheeked and happy.

I slammed the front door shut. Rachel was right. I needed to leave that flat. I was going to rent somewhere else as soon as possible in the new year. I needed to get away from the whispers and shadows in there. I needed to get away from the missing objects, the tricks something or someone was playing on my mind, the presence of someone other. Even if it was you, I didn't want you like that, the dregs of the person I knew. Someone I didn't recognise.

I stormed to the communal front door and barged into Grace.

"Oh!" I gasped. "I thought you'd be at your mum's by now."

Grace was clutching presents and several bags. "Just heading there, I was running late," she said lightly. "I slept in longer than I intended." She winked. Behind her slouched a gangly fellow, with his head down and a baseball cap covering his eyes.

"Ah!" I said, feeling myself blush, to my irritation.

Grace's attire was more suited to a night out than to visiting her elderly mother. Mini skirt, and black tights accompanied a V-neck glittery jumper that gave a flash of her cleavage.

She was sexy if you liked that kind of thing. *Did you?*

Among her bags and parcels she was clutching an identical tray to the one she proffered last night. The same smell of mince pies wafted up and made me feel nauseous. I made a muffled sound, and pushed out the door, noting her shoes. Boots with a chunky heel.

* * *

Boxing Day

I peered through the eyehole in the door and was met by my mother's familiar face, anxious eyes darting about, with my dad looming behind her. It was hardly a surprise — yesterday evening I had arranged for them to come down and they told me they would arrive at around eleven. It was eleven on the dot. But still I checked to see who was out there through the peephole. I didn't want any nasty surprises.

It was seven last night when I cracked and decided to ask my parents to come. In the pub I was standing behind a glass wall, looking into everyone else's happy lives, big lively groups of families and friends. I realised that I didn't want to be on my own over Christmas any more. It had been a terrible idea. I dreaded going back to the empty flat with the lilac tie hanging mournfully over the chair and the spectre of your missing watch. And the person/thing/whatever it was circling me and getting closer. I was terrified of going to bed, of turning my light off. *What if someone comes into my flat again?* I rang my parents on the way back from the pub.

"I've had a horrible day, please come tomorrow." The tears started falling as I babbled about the tie I had received and your missing watch.

I fell on my parents as they walked through the door, I had never been so pleased to see them. I'd triple-checked that

I'd bolted the front door, and had kept every light in the flat on, but still I had barely slept.

Mum took a searching look around the flat as we walked through to the living room. Discarded wrapping paper lay in the middle of the room, and two wine glasses sat on the coffee table, with an empty bottle of Buck's Fizz. Mugs were piled high in the kitchen sink and the smell of meat that had gone off drifted from the overflowing food waste bin. Mum dumped her handbag on the ground.

"Right," she said briskly. "I am going to clean and sort this flat out and put some coffee on. Robert, please put our case in the spare bedroom."

Dad touched my shoulder before shuffling off. "We'll get you through this."

"Thanks, Dad." Tears were building up behind my eyes. "What do you think about the tie, and the watch going? I just don't know what to think, whether it's John or someone else. I feel so spooked."

Dad looked uncomfortable. No one seemed to want to hear my tales of things going missing and strange comings and goings into and out of the flat.

"Perhaps John ordered the tie before he . . . went," he said at last.

I considered the possibility. "I suppose so. But there was no receipt or anything, it was like someone personally sent it, rather than it coming from a company."

Dad shrugged. He didn't seem to want to discuss the subject.

Mum bustled into the room holding a tray on which was perched a cafetière, a milk jug and three mugs. The smell of fresh coffee filled the air and I was actually looking forward to a cup.

"This is the tie." I gestured to the flash of purple that still lay wrapped around the chair. "And his watch has gone missing. You know, I was telling you about it, last night."

Mum tutted. She put the tray down sharply on the coffee table and placed one hand on her hip.

"We've got to get past all this," she said through gritted teeth. "All these finding things going missing, hearing, seeing . . . 'things' in the flat . . . it's holding you back. You won't move on with all this in your head." She gesticulated at her forehead. "It's a symptom of your worry and stress and time you stopped concentrating on it."

"You don't believe me, do you? So, all this is a symbol of my imagination. Well, how do you explain the tie, and the fact his watch has gone?"

I was drained. Not a single person had believed me, and Mum and Dad had been hostile to these things happening to me all the way through. Why should it be any different now?

Mum shook her head abruptly. "I don't know," she snapped. "But there will be an explanation for it that is not—" she coughed and spat out — "otherworldly.

"I think the tie was ordered by John before he disappeared, and I think that watch is not missing, you'll find it, you probably mislaid it; it may have slipped somewhere, maybe behind the chest of drawers."

She bent to pour the coffee, her body language signalling that the conversation was over.

I pursued it. "I did wonder if it was the spirit of John, yes it sounds corny, but I couldn't help it and I do wonder if it is John, alive, doing this. But I'm starting to believe very strongly that it's someone else."

My words fell like a stone into water. The second option distressed and irritated my mum more than the thought of you, alive or not, having something to do with it.

"You believe someone is letting themselves into your flat, nonsense! How would they do that?"

I sighed. I had told them before, but it had fallen on deaf ears. Dad looked awkward, busying himself with the milk. My mum's face was pink; even the tips of her ears were rosy.

"We don't know what happened to John, therefore we don't know about what happened to his key, which was on him," I explained.

I hesitated and then decided to bring the Grace topic in. It would be as welcome as a taxman's letter, judging by my mother's face.

Thankfully, my dad intervened. "You need to leave this flat." His voice was quiet but authoritative. "It's no good for you, these memories and anxieties haunting you."

I interjected eagerly. "Yes exactly, I have been thinking the same thing and I'm going to go. I'm going to start looking for somewhere to rent asap as soon as we get to January."

Mum sat down looking triumphant and exchanged glances with Dad. She opened her mouth, but Dad got in there first. "We don't want you to rent. We want you to buy, particularly after all you've been through . . . we want you to have some security." Dad paused and blinked, and I was touched by a moistening of his eyes. "We are going to give you money towards a deposit."

He named a sum, and I almost dropped my coffee cup. "Are you sure?" It would be a scrabble to get a one-bedroom flat in Tooting but it would help me a lot. "Thank you so much."

A thought hit me, but I wondered uneasily if it would be immoral. "John and I have a shared savings account. We have around thirty thousand pounds in there. I can access it, but I'm not sure if I should . . ." I faltered. "You know, he is missing, should I take what is half his, if he comes back . . . ?" My sentence drifted off.

My mum's mouth set in a hard line. "Yes. All the way yes. What that man has done to you." She muttered, "Selfish." Then: "Bastard." But maybe that was my imagination.

I sipped my coffee, and I felt the best that I had since you had gone missing. A spark of hope. My own place. I could afford a one bedroom in Tooting if I used our savings along with my parents' money. I thought about that email you sent to your friend, about moving to Hong Kong, and welcomed the rise of anger in me. I harnessed it. Yes, I would use those savings. I was riding on that wave and refused to let any other thought crowd my brain. The only downside was that I would be in this flat longer by buying another place than if I rented again.

Never mind. I would definitely change the locks.

* * *

"You can go in if you want, you don't have to stay out here," the locksmith said politely, glancing up from the lock on our — my — front door. I could see the flash of annoyance in his eyes. He did not like me watching. I had called an emergency locksmith, did not care about the extortionate charge. I needed to know that someone, you, whatever, was not coming into my flat. I wanted to watch; I was buoyed up. I was doing something positive about my future. I tried furiously to engage with my anger. Hong Kong, Hong Kong, Hong Kong.

It was the day after Boxing Day. I had been to work, had volunteered to work as that had been preferable to being on holiday. It had been nice to know that Mum and Dad had been waiting for me at the flat when I returned. They were staying until New Year's Eve. That night I was going to a party at Rachel's. I suspected that she wanted to show off her new kitchen.

I had arranged earlier that day to view some flats to buy with my parents. The very first one we stepped into seemed nice. Refurbished by a property developer. Solid wood floors and a wood stove. High ceilings and a fairly spacious balcony.

"This is perfect for a single person or indeed, a couple, it's an excellent size," the estate agent said, straightening his tie and gesturing around the double bedroom. "Indeed, there was a couple living here before."

Dad cleared his throat and Mum leapt in with a question about the length of the lease.

Hong Kong and Gemma melted into deep recesses of my brain as I stared at the built-in wardrobes. You would have liked them. You were sensible when it came to looking for somewhere to live. Storage was important to you.

The estate agent took us out on to the balcony. You would have loved that. We had both wanted an outdoor space.

The estate agent took us into the bathroom, pointing out the power shower and generous bath. I saw Mum and Dad exchange eager looks.

I should be doing this with you, John.

I tried to shrug off my discomfort about using our joint savings. *But the flat will be yours too, John. You'll have a proper home to come back to.*

CHAPTER 15

The Rolling Stones blared out as I applied my blood-red lipstick. I surveyed myself in the mirror. It was meant to give my face some colour, but in fact drained my pale, dull complexion further and highlighted the heavy shadows under my eyes, which no amount of concealer seemed able to conceal. Still, at least I was trying. I was applying make-up, a first since you had gone missing. I was wearing Rachel's Christmas top. I had changed my mind about it. *Let's see what she has to say.* I wanted to know why she chose to buy me something from Emelda Boutique. I had to admit, it looked nice on me.

I had made an effort. I celebrated that tiny milestone with a glug of Prosecco. It was New Year's Eve and I was going out.

I was determined to be with people and socialise, a complete contrast to Christmas. It was a huge effort, I was dreading it, but I had to get on with my life again, not hide away in my living room staring into space. Another glug.

This time last year . . . No no no. Someone had taken control of my mind, popping out constantly at both expected and unexpected times, with the regularity of a cuckoo bird in a clock. *This time last year, when we did this, we were going to do this.* Chasing shadows.

I had never liked New Year's Eve, the sense of nostalgia and light bleakness as the clock struck midnight, thinking about times gone forever, the forced cheeriness and feeling that it should be a great night. I knew this new year was going to reach depths I'd never imagined. You gone. Facing the year of my wedding, the year that should have been my best yet, but would probably be my worst. Stop it, stop it. I pushed the cuckoo back into the clock.

Mum and Dad had gone that morning, walking to the Tube with me as I left for work.

"Thanks." I squeezed Mum's hand and hugged Dad. "You've been amazing."

Tears filled my eyes. My mum's eyes moistened.

"You don't deserve this," she muttered. Touching my shoulder, she said, "Put an offer in on that first flat that we saw."

"Yeah, probably, I need to have a think," I murmured, my stomach twisting.

We had been round seven properties, each one a seesaw of hope and a sense of future versus loss and longing.

Anyway. I wasn't going to think about it tonight. I slammed the front door purposefully, the bottles of wine and champagne that I'd dutifully brought clanging as I walked to the Tube.

Rachel was only a couple of stops away in Stockwell in a slightly shabby art deco block of flats.

"Come in," she called breathlessly through the intercom when I buzzed.

She met me at the door, cheeks flushed and slightly frazzled. Laughter and chatter blared behind her, along with the dull thump of music, I recognised "Gimme Shelter" by the Rolling Stones, which was going to be our song for our first dance at our wedding.

"You okay?" Rachel touched my arm. But she was already turning away looking behind her, wanting to mingle with her guests and be the hostess.

I followed her down the hall. "I'm wearing the top you got me for Christmas, thanks so much!"

I plastered a smile on my face.

"Oh yes!" Rachel swung round and smiled, then frowned. "It looks great, but a bit loose. You've become so skinny, Eve."

The words settled themselves between us. We entered the kitchen. "You got it from Emelda Boutique, good shop! What made you choose that place?"

I cringed at my try-hard casual manner as I handed her the wine and champagne.

"Oh, thank you!" Rachel took the bottles from me. "Oh, fab we have loads of champagne, practically everyone has bought a bottle! And, the top — I love that shop! Saw it and just thought of you!"

She crammed the bottles into her overflowing fridge. Why was I bothered, I knew that would be the explanation, and why should Rachel remember every single aspect of significance attached to your disappearance.

Rachel looked slightly put out herself, I suddenly realised.

"Well?" She gestured impatiently.

"Er." I stared round. Gleaming white quartz worktops, Karndean floors, an Aga cooker — of course, Rachel's new kitchen. "Oh, Rach your new kitchen is absolutely gorgeous!"

The chatter in the background came nearer and Vicky and her boyfriend Ian tumbled into the kitchen. I hadn't seen Vicky since the trip to Leeds to look for you.

"Vicky." I hugged her warmly and kissed Ian politely. I had only met him twice. "I hoped you'd come! How are you?"

"Oh good! Yep, all good, actually I have some news, Ian and I are engaged!" Vicky trilled, a beam spreading across her face as she proffered her hand, flashing a gleaming diamond solitaire.

Then she looked stricken. I clutched my now-empty ring finger. Rachel was very still while Ian rubbed one foot against the other leg.

Before Vicky could say anything, I grabbed her hand.

"Congratulations!" I should ask her: when are you getting married, where and how are you celebrating, are your family pleased?

"Oh, thanks," Vicky murmured. Her cheeks were pink. Irrationally, that made me angry. I didn't want to be treated differently. But I didn't want to hear details about her wedding either. She couldn't win. Vicky and Ian started speaking to Rachel, to ask her about her new kitchen.

Jess entered the kitchen and gave me a hug.

"I guess Vicky told you her news?" she asked softly.

"Yep." I opened my mouth and closed it again. I would sound bitter and mean if I said what I truly felt about that. But there was something else I wanted to query. "She's only been with him less than a year, I'm surprised she's moved so fast. Vicky is usually so cautious."

And private. Her announcement about her engagement was at odds with her closed personality, the way she kept things tight to her chest.

Jess shrugged. "Yeah, I guess so. But everyone gets excited and sparkles when they get engaged, don't they? And I suppose she has fallen for him hard, despite the short length of time. They must have just clicked."

Jess clutched a glass of champagne, her cheeks rosy. It looked like she had been here a while and had obviously downed a few glasses of wine. It suddenly felt like it had been a bad idea to come.

I put my glass that Rachel had poured for me on the kitchen counter and took a step towards the hall to retrieve my coat.

Then Jess grabbed my arm. "Come on, you! Let's go into the lounge. We need to talk; I haven't seen you over Christmas." I saw a hint of remorse in her eyes.

Deciding it was too awkward to leave, I grabbed my glass again — I needed it — and followed her into the lounge.

"How have you been?" She pulled me into a corner.

At least twenty people were in the living room, their talk and laughter so carefree. I wanted to unzip myself from my body and step into one of them, into their happy and contented lives. Pulp's "Babies" played in the background. I tried to ignore the sneaky little voice popping up in my head: *John loved Pulp, and this was his favourite song of theirs*.

"How have you been?"

"It's been really hard, to be honest. But Mum and Dad have been down and that really helped. And I'm going to get out of the flat and buy somewhere. Mum and Dad have offered me some cash towards the deposit."

I stared down into my glass. *Please don't ask me about other funds*. I was ashamed and worried about using our joint savings. I was never going to tell anyone, not even Jess.

She nodded and clutched my arm. "Very sensible decision," she said. Then took a swig of her drink. "Does that make you feel better? That you are planning your future?"

I paused. How could I explain that I wanted to cry every time I went round a new property, you chasing my shadow. Your voice in my ear every time we entered a new room. We had been going to do this together, how could it be that I was doing this on my own? But I couldn't stay in that flat, with my memories, with someone or something there too.

Jack appeared at Jess's arm. He touched her shoulder. The tenderness made me want to weep. "Hey."

"Hello." Surprisingly, Jess's voice was slightly cold.

"Eve, hi, how are you?" Jack moved quickly round and hugged me. His arms felt limp, and his kiss missed my cheek.

"I'm okay."

Jack nodded, but it only seemed like he was half listening.

"We're having a chat," Jess said meaningfully to him.

Jack threw up his arms in mock protest. "Ah, okay, I'll leave you to it." He gave Jess an uncertain look as he retreated.

"Is everything okay?"

"Yes, well, it's not been the best Christmas to be honest," Jess said slowly. "We were at Jack's parents, but, oh I don't know, we just irritated each other. My fault, I snapped at him a lot."

She tried to smile, but it didn't reach her eyes.

"But why?" I was surprised, although I recalled the doubts that she had expressed about him just a few months ago. "You're getting married in a few months." *And I would give anything to be in that position.*

"Oh, I'm going to marry him, *of course.*" Jess sounded irritated. "I don't know what's wrong with me, I think I'm just stressed, planning the wedding, and then all the upset and worry about you and John."

Her voice dropped.

Count to ten, count to ten. I took a deep breath but angry words rushed out anyway: "If you feel like that, imagine how I feel? Upset and worry? *Really*? I'm sorry for you but I feel a little more than that, I think. And I would give anything to plan my wedding."

My shock when I stopped speaking was mirrored in Jess's face. We never fought. The last time we had a cross word was when we lived out in the second year at university, and I was lazy about putting the bins out and tidying up the kitchen. Jess had been quite right in telling me in no uncertain terms that I had to pull my weight.

Jess blinked rapidly. "I'm so sorry. That was so tactless of me. I don't know what came over me. I didn't mean it like it came out. I mean I feel so awful for you and sad about John. Jack and I were close to him, and I guess it's made me think about things in my own life, but nothing, nothing compared to what you have been through."

"It's okay," I said slowly, trying to swallow the bitterness and jealousy that I felt about Jess's wedding. "Look, you said that to me before, about John making you think about things, have you got second thoughts about getting married, about getting married to Jack?"

"No, I don't think so, not really, I love Jack." Jess was emphatic. "I really don't know what's wrong with me, but sure it's stress, it'll blow over." Her guard was up, and the subject was closed. "But look, please forgive me."

I managed to smile. "Let's start the evening again."

I went to get some more wine. But I needed to pace myself. Too much drink and I would end up a crying mess on the floor.

A few people I didn't recognise huddled by the table in the kitchen. Then, I saw a familiar profile, with slicked-back dark hair, a booming laugh that shot through me.

"Clive!" I was shocked. "What are you doing here?"

Instantly I was transported back to that unfortunate night in Leeds, could smell his beery breath, see the slight spider thread veins lacing his cheeks. I suppressed a shudder.

We had only seen each other once since then, to organise leaflet drops to Crystal Palace stadium, and that had been slightly stilted. But then neither of us had had a drink to smooth the path. A beer was firmly clutched in Clive's hand now.

"Sorry, yeah you must think it a bit strange." Clive gave a nervous bark of laughter.

"Rachel helped me with the leaflet drop a lot, and she asked if I fancied coming here tonight. Nothing else planned. So . . ." He gave a shrug of his shoulders. "Rach is a laugh and I like a house party, and old Nige here was at a loose end, so I brought him here as well."

He slapped Nige hard on the back, who spluttered slightly on his beer. After a quick hello, he muttered something about needing the toilet and slunk out of the door.

"Well . . ." I was at a loss. "It's nice to see you," I said at last.

And it was. Despite the underlying awkwardness after our night together, I was glad to see him. My sadness was reflected in his eyes. He had been your best friend since primary school. I wasn't alone in my feelings. I didn't care what Jess said, there was no way that she felt like me. She had a future, a fiancé, was getting married.

"We were meant to be going on John's stag do at the start of February." Clive's voice was low. He stared into his pint. He did not like talking about his feelings. "I should've been planning it now. We were meant to go to Leeds. I had the restaurant that I'd booked for the second night of the stag ring me the other day. They were making changes to the set menu. I had to tell them that I was cancelling. I thought about saying nothing." Clive paused and his chin sunk onto his chest. "But I don't think he's coming back." He stared at the floor. "Not yet. I think he is out there and will at some stage, but not for a while."

His voice sounded hollow. I noticed his stubble, unusual as Clive was usually clean-cut. There was a dash of silver in his hair. Unusual for him, Clive had been dyeing his hair for years.

I took his hand. "I don't think he's ever coming back."

Clive's head sunk deeper, almost touching his pint. *You agree*, I thought. Half of me had wanted him to disagree, to boost my flagging hopes. He reached out and hugged me. I leaned in, forgetting about the beer breath, the pasty chest with patchy hair and the slight paunch hanging over the top of his jeans.

He understood. A hand on my shoulder.

"You guys okay?" It was Rachel. She looked stressed. Clive let go of me abruptly and lurched towards her.

"Fine, great party, Rach!" He boomed, back to the Clive that I knew.

Nige swayed towards us. Giving Rachel and me an unconvincing high five, Clive slapped Nige's shoulder and the two slouched off.

"Yeah, good party, Rach." I did my best to sound light-hearted.

"Come on, how are you really?" Rachel went straight to the quick.

"It's difficult, I can't believe this is happening and it's the worst Christmas I have ever spent." The words came out in a rush, relief lacing them as I did not have to put a good face on.

"And Rach, that weird stuff is happening to me again. I received a present through the post, a tie, a lilac tie, the colour theme of our wedding. Only John knew that. And his watch, the one I bought for his thirtieth, has gone missing."

I paused. "It was buried underneath John's socks and pants in a drawer. I don't understand. I never moved it. Someone came in and moved it. There is no other explanation."

Rachel's eyes darkened and she frowned.

I was confused. I had expected some sympathy.

At my raised eyebrows, she burst out, "So are you accusing me then, as I knew where the watch was?"

"I told you? I don't remember doing that," I said. And then it came back to me. Amidst all the worry about Grace having the key and the intruder, I had totally forgotten telling Rachel about the watch and where I hid it. I was sure I even said "John's sock drawer". Not just a vague reference. It was when I needed to get everything off my chest, tell her everything.

She repeated, "Well, are you trying to accuse me of taking the watch? That's how you're making me feel."

"What? No! I honestly didn't mean that. I just wanted to speak to someone about it. Someone who knew about these weird happenings."

But I haven't ever told anyone else about the watch's hiding place.

I parked that thought and concentrated on the present.

"Oh, okay." Rachel's already flushed cheeks turned even redder. "Sorry," she muttered sheepishly. "I went a bit over the top. I just feel a bit stressed, what with being the hostess." She flapped her arm around.

It's only a party, I wanted to scream. *My fiancé has gone missing. Try that for stress.*

"But Rach, why would you think that I would think something like that?" I pressed.

The question did not go down well. "Because you've been so preoccupied with the idea of someone coming into your flat," she snapped.

Rachel's usual measured calmness had disappeared.

"But you thought it was a possibility, you thought it might be Grace upstairs!" I was stung.

Rachel shook her head wearily. "I know. I did. Look, let's talk about this another time."

A tipsy guest I didn't recognise grabbed her; I gathered it was one of her work colleagues.

You knew where it was. The thought reverberated around my brain. *You lived with me. You had keys.* I shook myself angrily. I couldn't think like this. Why would Rachel do something like that? And things had been happening before she came to stay. Rachel was one of my best friends, loyal and kind. She knew you fairly well and was perfectly friendly and pleasant to you. She was acting out of character tonight but . . . *So what, stop it.* I tried to still my mind.

I was so lost in my thoughts, I didn't notice Jack standing in front of me. He looked at me through his floppy fringe, hand clutching a pint. I liked Jack. He was friendly and dependable, and I got on really well with him. He was a freelance graphic designer and friends used to joke that if he were any more laid-back, he would be horizontal. It was a contrast to Jess, who was so ambitious and worked so hard in her job. But they worked well together, he smoothed down some of those harder edges that came with her go-get attitude. He was a contrast to you too, with your quiet focus, your steely determination to get the scoop.

But today, Jack didn't look as laid-back as normal. His lips were thin and tight. He tapped his hand rhythmically on the kitchen top.

"How are you?" he asked.

I hesitated. "Bearing up," I said finally. I could tell that he didn't want to talk about me, that he had something on his mind. "Are you okay, Jack?"

Jack swallowed. "It's a bit difficult. Jess and I aren't getting on particularly well." He paused. "It was more obvious over Christmas. She doesn't seem to like me very much at the moment." His foot started tapping in rhythm with his hand. "I feel awkward asking but has she said anything to you?"

My mind was taken off you as I battled with my loyalty to Jess, versus sympathy for Jack and wanting to help him. I took the halfway house. "I think John's disappearance has really troubled her," I said.

Jack nodded. "It has definitely been in the months since John went that things have been difficult. I mean, I understand she's upset, I am, we both love John and she's been very worried about you, but . . ." His voice trailed off.

I touched his arm. "You're good together and you'll get through it. Jess'll be fine," I said gently. "It's just made her think about things, that's all. You're getting married and I know she is excited about it."

Getting married. Jess was getting everything I wanted. She was so lucky. It felt like everything was slipping away from me. The lilac tie glimmered in the corner of my mind.

"Thanks, Eve." Jack's words brought me back. He looked at me gratefully, the faint smile playing with the corners of his mouth but not reaching his eyes.

* * *

The TV boomed and everyone crowded in Rachel's living room. "Come on, it's countdown to midnight!" Rachel's friend Paula yelled. People started to link arms.

Ten, nine, eight . . .

I stood in the corner of the room quietly; no one noticed me. Not even Jess, she was smiling at Jack, her hand on his shoulder, I was pleased to see it.

Seven, six, five . . .

It was meant to be my year, the year we married, the year we bought our first flat, the year it all came together. My future spread before me like glittering city lights.

Four, three, two . . .

You took my hand and kissed me tenderly. I stared at the sapphire on my ring finger, feeling such peace and contentment. That was last year of course.

One . . .

The sound of fireworks on the River Thames blared out on the television. I saw Rachel and Clive embrace, smiling shyly but happily at each other. I felt my heart jolt a little. So that explained his presence at the party.

Vicky and Ian clutched each other tightly, beaming.

Jess and Jack hugged and kissed. The smile reached Jack's eyes as she whispered in his ear.

That had been me, just three months ago. No, I *thought* that had been me, I corrected myself. I didn't know what I, what we had been, now. All built on something that didn't exist.

"Auld Lang Syne, come on!" yelled a very drunk girl staggering forward. At the same time, I saw Jess move away from Jack, eyes darting about looking for me.

Grabbing my bag, I slipped into the hall, closing the front door quietly on all the merriment and happiness within.

* * *

Happy New Year. I mean, I knew it wasn't, but that's what people say. It wasn't a happy New Year for me either. But people weren't thinking about me or concerned, like they were for her. I just had to get on with it. Eve had a bad time last year and this year might not be a happy one for her either.

CHAPTER 16

"Ms Jennings, Happy New Year!" Theo the estate agent's voice was smooth and professional. I cursed quietly; I shouldn't have answered my mobile. I had answered on autopilot, thinking it was work related and hadn't checked the number.

"Happy New Year," I mumbled.

"Just wondered if you had any more thoughts about the properties that you saw the other day?"

"Could I call you back? I'm at work," I said quickly. It wasn't actually a lie, but there was hardly anyone in the office, and I could easily have taken the call. It was the day after New Year's Day. I was relieved to be back at work. I'd stayed in bed until midday on New Year's Day and then wandered aimlessly round Tooting Common. I declined all the invitations I had received to have dinner at various people's houses in the evening and was in bed at eight o'clock, staring into the dark.

"No problem," he said. "But yes, give me a ring. You seemed to like the first property and we've had a bit of interest in that."

Put an offer in. Mum and Dad's voices reverberated in my ears, Mum's shrill, Dad's low and persistent. I'd think about it tonight. Taking the step to put in an offer on a flat on my own, rather than as part of a couple, felt like taking a leap across a river.

* * *

The pizza lay in its box on the coffee table. I couldn't be bothered to put it on a plate. It was now cold, the cheese hardened, with greasy, soggy patches smeared around the edges of the box. I'd nibbled at one piece. 8.15 p.m. Was it too soon to go to bed? I'd told Theo the estate agent that I would call that evening, but I couldn't face it, just like I couldn't face answering my messages.

Have you put an offer in yet? Love, Mum

Hope you're ok, lovely, come round if you want. Jess xx

How have you been? Sorry about the way I was the other night. Rach x

Hi Eve, good to see you on New Year's Eve, I hope you are ok. Don't suppose you are free for a quick drink this week? Clive

I ended up going to bed at ten in the end. Lost in my own thoughts while I stared unseeingly at the TV. The start of a new year and all I wanted was to press forward, to get past all of this. But then to what. I just saw emptiness ahead. Unless you came back. To me. But I didn't think you were coming back.

I began to head to the bathroom to brush my teeth, but a noise stopped me in my tracks.

There was a slight noise from behind the front door. It was so faint that it could have been my imagination. I leaned to the peephole and peered through. An eye stared back at me, the black pupil clearly defined, the iris a pale green colour. I couldn't move, my legs so heavy I wondered how they supported my body. The eye didn't blink. Then it was gone.

I sank to the floor. There was someone after me and I didn't think it was you, John. Your eyes were a beautiful clear blue. It was my favourite feature. I loved the way they reflected your emotions — the blaze in them as you talked about going after a news story; or the way they darkened to a blue that was almost navy when you were being reflective.

I stayed at the door, heart pounding for fifteen minutes or more, I was too afraid to move. *They can't get in, they can't get in*; I repeated it over and over.

Eventually, I rose and crept quietly down the corridor to our bedroom, turning on every light as I did so. I never heard anyone leave the building, which begged the question: was someone still there, in the communal hallway? I lay on the bed fully clothed, staring at the ceiling. I have to get out of this flat. It only occurred to me then: I had never met anyone with pure green eyes; was there even such a thing?

* * *

"Hi, can I speak to Theo, please?" Tat, tat, tat, my voice was staccato. It was 9 a.m. on the dot, I had called the estate agent as soon as I got to the office. Sarah glanced up curiously.

"He's in a meeting, he will call you when he's out, should be in about half an hour."

"Okay." I was terse. "Can you ask him to call me right away." I hung up.

Please don't let that flat have gone. It was a bonus that I liked it. The way I was feeling, I would put an offer in anywhere I could afford, I had to get away from my current flat, you, *it*, my memories.

I am going to put an offer in as soon as the estate agent rings me back, I texted Mum quickly.

Then I got up restlessly to go to the kitchen and make a coffee that I didn't want. I just wanted to move; I couldn't stay still. I frowned at the kettle, waiting for it to boil. I had agreed to see Clive tonight. I expected it was about more plans to put up posters and the campaign to find you, and to sheepishly mention what was happening with Rachel. She hadn't mentioned anything herself to me. Normally that would hurt but I found I didn't care, I had more pressing matters. Like leaving that flat.

Gemma entered the kitchen, wearing an ill-fitting orange shirt that made her face look sallow. She glanced at me before looking away as fast as she could. Sweeping to the coffee machine she firmly pressed the button for a cappuccino.

I was a coffee snob and hated the coffee in the machine. Instead, I brought a cafetière in and used that to make filter coffee. You were the same. We used to share a double cafetière. But since you went missing, I couldn't bear to use it. Instead, I bought myself a single cafetière that made enough for one cup. I tried not to think about our coffee ritual: one of us walking past the other's desk, cafetière firmly in hand, eyebrow raised.

Gemma stared resolutely straight ahead, glasses perched on the end of her nose, hair scraped back into a messy, unflattering bun. *She just didn't seem his type.* I couldn't help comparing my stylish work outfits, freshly washed and blow-dried hair every morning (or it used to be) and manicured nails. It was shallow, but I thought you liked my put-together look, that I made an effort. You were obviously attracted to Gemma in other, more important ways, not based on the physical.

I watched her stubby fingernails manoeuvre her cup from under the machine and felt instant rage. My anger was a quick shot of tequila after a few glasses of heavy red wine: bracing, crisp and sour. It felt the same when I remembered your Hong Kong plans or the woman's top you had bought. Or when I thought about Gemma.

But this time the anger became laced with remorse. I flushed as I recalled how I had attacked her, the warning I received at work. So out of character. I still couldn't believe that was me and my actions.

"Nice Christmas?" The words were mine. They came out without me realising. My hand paused mid-air as I poured hot water from the kettle into the cafetière.

Gemma's eyes were like stone. "You are not meant to speak to me."

I was taken aback by her iciness. I had been totally in the wrong, but I hadn't expected that. I forced myself to keep looking her in the eye. They were grey, I realised. My mobile phone started ringing and I hurried past her.

Theo the estate agent jumped straight in after I gave him my offer. "I will check with my client and get straight back to you," he said.

I crossed my fingers under the desk. I hadn't offered the asking price, despite the fact that the London market was so hot. The asking price would be a struggle, and I just hoped that I wouldn't have to go even higher.

It was hard to concentrate while I waited for the call. I aimlessly proofed a feature that had come in that morning from a freelance journalist.

Theo rang back half an hour later. "Right, well I spoke to him . . ." He paused, not giving anything away.

"And?" My heart was in my mouth. It was a relief to think and feel about something other than you.

"I'm afraid it's not enough. He wants the asking price. There is good interest in the flat and he is confident that he will get that price."

My heart sank. "I'll need to speak to my mortgage adviser," I said. As I hung up all my optimism broke into pieces. My dreams of escape, of starting afresh now seemed far away. I shuddered as I thought about our flat, the memories, the other thing coming and going. I had to get out. I picked up my mobile phone to ring my mortgage adviser but found myself automatically calling my parents.

"They want the asking price!" I moaned, embarrassed and awkward at my blatant hint.

"We'll give you five thousand pounds more," said Mum instantly.

My head was light with relief. "Are you sure?" I murmured, my escape once again within grasp.

"I want you out of that flat," Mum said firmly.

I needed to summon my team to discuss the true-life stories that we were focusing on that day, but that had to wait while I called Theo. I gave the asking price, my voice firm and strong.

"Well, I'll call him and see if that's enough, there's been interest . . ."

Anger shot through me. I couldn't afford more than the asking price. If that was the case, then I would lose the flat. Maybe if everything was going over the asking price, I wouldn't be able to afford anything in Tooting.

I gathered my team half-heartedly, and tried to concentrate on my notes, to recall the passion I used to feel for my job.

I was finishing up when the estate agent's number flashed up. Hurrying out, I stabbed at my phone.

"He says yes. Congratulations!"

For the first time since you had left, I felt a shot of happiness course through me. It even managed to block out the inevitable sadness that we weren't sharing this moment together, that we weren't celebrating, hugging and sharing triumphant looks.

I was getting away from that flat. I hung up, smiling. But amidst all the thoughts about contacting a conveyancing solicitor and what to do next, it popped up. *What happens if you return?*

Well, you'd have a brand-new home to move to. The fairy-tale would be that you came back, had just needed time away on your own, wanted to pick up where we left off, were delighted with the flat.

Another option was that you came back and didn't want to pick up where we left off . . . And wanted half of the savings invested in the flat. I firmly closed the curtains on that thought. *Don't go there.* Or you never came back. With a sense of astonishment, I realised that I was more ready for that option than the former.

CHAPTER 17

Clive stood up to greet me. We hugged slightly awkwardly.
We were in a pub in Balham, all shabby chic and cosy corners. It was where you and I used to go whenever we went
out in Balham and where we liked to meet Clive. In fact, I
had never met Clive on his own without you before. Another
unwelcome first since he disappeared.

"Thanks, Clive, you know me too well!" I smiled as I
spotted the glass of white wine that he'd bought for me.

"You're welcome." Clive collapsed onto his seat and
took a glug from his pint. "You seem in good spirits," he said.

"I had an offer accepted on a flat in Tooting today,"
I said, a smile spreading over my face as I sipped my wine.

"Congratulations." Clive clinked glasses. Tactfully, he
didn't mention you, and I was grateful. "Tell me about it."

We chatted and I was pleased to note that the awkwardness between us since the one-night stand had disappeared.

"Look, there's something I want to tell you," he said,
shuffling about in his chair. "Me and Rach, well . . . we got
on well when we met before Christmas to sort out more
poster plans for John and . . ." He cleared his throat.

I put him out of his misery. "I know, I guessed at Rachel's
New Year's Eve party."

Why wasn't Rachel telling me this? Apart from the text that she sent me the other night apologising, I hadn't heard from her. Was she avoiding me?

"Ah right." Clive smiled clumsily. "I suppose you thought it was weird that I was there too. Look, we got on well, I asked her for a drink, it is very early days, we've only had a couple of dates. I just want to check that you're okay about it?"

"Why wouldn't I be?" The words came out more abruptly than I meant them to. I mulled it over. It did feel slightly odd that Rachel was getting together with your best friend, only in that there was no you to gossip with over it, and to do cheesy double dates with; the four of us would have got on so well. An ache started in my chest and spread up my throat.

"Of course I am," I added more gently. "I just feel sad that John isn't here to be pleased by your news, to do a cheesy double date."

Clive grabbed my hand. "We still all might do that," he said quickly. Too quickly. The "will" had changed quietly to "might".

"Nothing might develop anyway," he said. "But I wanted to let you know . . . and er, about that night, um, ah, in Leeds." He paused, grimacing and staring down at the table. "I mean, you won't tell her . . ." His voice trailed off. His cheeks flamed a maroon colour.

"Of course not, I haven't told anyone. I'm so ashamed," I shot back indignantly, then too late realised what that sounded like. "Oh God, sorry, I didn't mean it like that! I just mean that I can't believe I did that so soon after John went missing and with his best friend, I've been beating myself up."

It came out in a rush. My earlier happiness about having my offer on the flat accepted had disappeared.

Clive nodded. "I do understand," he said. "But no one needs to know, we just wanted to comfort each other."

I was surprised at this level of emotion from laddish Clive. I nodded quickly, fighting back tears that flooded to the back of my eyes.

"And it's been awkward between us," Clive ploughed on. He drained his pint. "I don't want to lose your friendship. It's important that we stick together for John."

It was strange hearing these words come out of Clive's mouth, but I was grateful.

"Yes, Clive, I agree, we must. Thank you for bringing this up." I too finished my glass.

Clive rose to repeat the round. "No, I— my round!" I leapt up.

"No, no." Clive gestured for me to sit down and headed to the bar.

Rachel. I was surprised she had gone for Clive, I must admit, but he had a certain charm and confidence that some women found attractive, and they were both in finance. The hurt that I felt magnified as I went over the fact again that she hadn't told me, that it was Clive telling me not her.

Your watch appeared in my mind, so clear and solid it was almost as if I could reach out and touch it. I banished it quickly, shaking my head. Rachel was my friend.

I grabbed my phone and quickly typed. *Just heard from Clive that you two have started seeing each other.* I deliberately left off the usual kisses and pressed send before I could change my mind. I was grateful that Clive appeared at that point.

He plonked himself down and drew out a notebook with a flourish. "Right," he said determinedly. "Let's make a plan of attack about where we can go and what we can do to find John."

He fumbled in his pocket and pulled out a biro. "You impressed, Eve? It's more like you to have a reporter's notebook."

He chuckled and seemed chipper. I guess he would be. While it was his best friend who had gone missing, he could still continue with life; he had met someone, could happily develop a relationship. I couldn't. Everything had frozen in time for me. I tried to banish the bitterness and changed the subject tack on impulse.

"Clive, I haven't told you, but has Rachel said about these weird things that have been happening to me, someone trying to get into the flat, someone actually getting in, things going missing." I eyed him. Clive was an open book when it came to emotions. I saw on his face he had heard all about it.

"Er yeah." Again he shifted in his chair. "Rachel's concerned."

"I think people are finding it hard to believe me."

"No, Eve, it's not that." He leaned forward earnestly. "Rach does, she reckons that neighbour of yours upstairs has something to do with it. But we worry that the mind can also play tricks, particularly when you are so vulnerable." Those were words straight out of Rachel's mouth.

There was no way Clive would produce that on his own. "Vulnerable" was not in his vocabulary. I fought down irritation.

It's not in my head. Count to ten, count to ten. I had been about to give Clive a list of all the things that had happened. But I decided on another approach.

"Clive, the last thing that happened is that a lilac tie arrived over Christmas. I thought it was a present, I opened it and there was no message, nothing. Lilac was the colour theme of our wedding, and you and John were going to have lilac ties." I paused to let the significance sink in.

"Yeah, I know," Clive said casually. "John said we were going to have lilac ties. Could it be that the shop sent you a tie John had ordered?"

My mouth hung open. "John told you about the colour theme?"

We weren't going to tell anyone until much near the time. Our secret. You'd promised.

Clive raised his eyebrows. *No big deal* might have been emblazoned on a traffic sign above his head.

"Yeah, but what's the problem? He mentioned it in passing as I asked whether we had any colour themes we needed to adhere to."

Clive was the archetypal best man. He loved the pomp and circumstance of weddings and had been a best man three times already.

The way he described it made sense. Maybe I had over-reacted.

"It's just that we said we weren't going to tell anyone the colour theme for a while," I explained slightly sheepishly.

"Yeah, well, he probably assumed you meant the girls, not us lads," Clive said.

"So, who sent me the tie?" I probed.

Clive knitted his brows together. "I think John may have ordered it and it arrived at a very unfortunate time . . ."

That came straight from Rachel. I was disappointed, though not surprised. She thought the same as my dad. But I wasn't having it. I ploughed on.

"What, three months after he went, not three days, three months, Clive!"

"Maybe they were out of stock . . . so sent it later than planned . . ." Clive shifted about uncomfortably.

I raised an eyebrow. "And all the other stuff, did Rachel tell you all that? Things going missing, things related to John — someone has been coming into the flat while I was there. I heard them, footsteps, I was in bed, it was awful." I shuddered. "And then someone rattling at the door trying to get in, and then the other night I saw an eye in the peephole."

"John wouldn't do that." Clive's voice was soft. "I don't know what's going on but it's not him."

"I don't think it is either." But I couldn't be 100 per cent sure. "But I never thought he would just disappear, forge the relationship he did with Gemma, not tell me that he was taking antidepressants." The words came out like a chant, I was so used to repeating them over and over. I didn't know you. I suddenly felt weary.

"It's not him," he repeated insistently. "You need to go to the police." Typical Clive. Pack it up nicely in a box.

"It's not that simple," I explained.

"Why? Someone is getting into your flat," Clive cut in.

"Yes, but—" I was floored, but pushed on — "when I told the police about the mug they weren't interested."

"There's a bit of a difference between you hearing some-one trying to break in and indeed breaking in, and a mug going missing," Clive pushed back.

I shrugged and continued, "Not only did that tie arrive in the post, but also John's watch has gone missing, the one I got him for his thirtieth. So, a bit of a crap Christmas for me." I gave a shaky laugh.

Clive's eyes widened. "I know that watch, he loved it."

"Don't you know it went missing? I would have thought Rachel would have told you, I was very shaken up about it on New Year's Eve."

Clive shook his head. "No. But she told me about the other stuff."

"Well, I guess there's such a long list of stuff." I gave an unconvincing laugh. Why did I feel I didn't know Rachel at the moment?

As if on cue my phone buzzed. *Yes we are! I'm sorry I didn't mention it. Can we meet up this week? R xx*

"It's not him." Clive shook his head sharply. His pint clanged as it hit the table. "This stuff is creepy, man; John's just not like that."

"Did you think that John was capable of leaving, just . . . walking out of his life? Of looking at living in Hong Kong without me? Of . . ." I stopped and exhaled. "Do we really know him." A statement not a question.

Clive shifted about in his seat. "He wouldn't do that," he said at last. Confident and clear. But the last syllable shook slightly.

"You're right, I don't feel in my heart of hearts it's him either." I traced my finger around the place mat, agitated.

Clive changed the subject. He produced a map, and with a chunky finger and thumb, prodded at places. "Kent, where he comes from — where we come from, we need to look at more . . . go to every match in Crystal Palace . . . get more posts on social media and go to Northumberland, where you got engaged . . ."

The words drifted over me. I should be engaged, enthusiastic about finding you. But I couldn't believe that we were going to find you. You weren't out there. Or if you were, you weren't to be found.

My third glass of wine. I'd had nothing to eat, so it was going to my head.

Clive had stopped prodding his stubby fingers at his map. Instead, they were clasped firmly around my hand.

"John was so lucky to have you," he said. "Something bad must have been happening for him to do this. And it wasn't to do with you."

CHAPTER 18

The dress was beautiful. It cinched my waist, already so tiny after the lack of eating since you went. The sparkling pale lilac of the neckline glinted as I made a few twirls in front of the mirror. It brought out the blue of my eyes. I had never looked more beautiful, I thought dispassionately, despite my pallor and loss of weight. In fact, the loss of weight looked good, I thought. One good thing to come out of you going.

"You look absolutely stunning," said Janey, the wedding shop owner. She smiled, her eyes sparkling. "This is why I do the job, to see you brides so glowing and beautiful and happy."

I was surprisingly composed. My eyes were dry, my mouth firm. I stared at myself hard. All my hopes and dreams for my future were symbolised in this dress. They weren't meant to be. I wouldn't be standing in this dress again.

People would say I was mad to torment myself with a wedding fitting, when there was now no wedding, and no you. But I wanted to do it. A final goodbye.

"Wait until your other half sees you in it." Janey smiled. "Now, will you be collecting it three days before, as planned and for one final try-on?"

I nodded, not trusting myself to speak. I would never collect this dress. Janey would soon realise that, even though my parents had paid for it. One day it would go to a bride who was actually going through with her wedding, not a bride that was never to be. I hoped that would be the case actually. It was a beautiful dress that deserved to be worn and part of someone's big day.

As I left the shop, I almost collided with another bride-to-be, accompanied by either a friend or sister. Her face was expectant, excited, her cheeks a healthy red and eyes lit up. *Should've been me.*

The tears didn't start until I was halfway down the road. My phone beeped as I took the train back to King's Cross.

We bought the bridesmaid dresses for my wedding this morning. Wish you could have been there, but totally understand. Jess xx

It would have to be today, wouldn't it, the day that I went for my final goodbye to my wedding dress, that Jess bought her bridesmaid dresses. Full of excitement, hope and promise. Whoever was up there was enjoying twisting the knife. Jealousy stabbed me, entwined with guilt and shame. Jess was a really good friend. It wasn't her fault that you had walked out of everyone's lives and left mine like a bombsite. But I couldn't help comparing her future, marrying the man she loved, a future peppered with companionship, a family compared to my emptiness and loss.

I ignored the little voice reminding me of the doubts that she had recently. I wanted to wallow, throw myself a pity party. Once at King's Cross I reluctantly trudged among the crowd of people to the Northern Line Tube platform that would take me to Tooting Broadway underground station. Since you went missing at Oxford Circus Tube station, I hated taking the Tube. I felt the tunnels close in on me, the panic rearing at me from the fly-by trains, the sense of confusion following me up and down the escalators.

I waited on the platform for the train, watching the people around me, the woman in her twenties listening to music, tapping her foot, at ease with the world, the man linking arms with his heavily pregnant wife. Two weeks until D-day, wedding day.

* * *

"I'm really sorry I've been distant the last few weeks." Rachel traced the beer mat distractedly. We were in a pub in Clapham, halfway between our respective homes. I waited.

"It's two things." Rachel took a deep breath. She was as straightforward and pragmatic as I was used to. "First, Clive. Are you okay about that?"

I thought for a second and answered honestly. "Of course. I'm pleased for you both. Clive is lovely. The thing that hurts is that John is not around to know you are together, for us to do stuff all together . . . and the other thing that upset me is that you never told me. I heard it from Clive."

"I'm sorry." Rachel sighed. "I didn't want to say anything at first as we were just dating, it might have fizzled out. I'm superstitious like that, and also, I was worried you might be upset, you know, John's best friend."

"I understand." I took a gulp of wine and realised that I had almost finished the glass. Rachel had only taken a few sips. I was drinking too much and too fast. I had to stop. It was making everything worse.

"And we might do some double dates one day." Rachel sounded strained. I looked into her warm eyes and they shifted away. *You don't believe that.* I didn't say it aloud. I was too drained to get into the subject of the possibility of your coming back.

"And about the watch." Rachel's body now shifted. "Sorry I was weird, I thought you might think it was me that took it, because I lived with you and because I knew where the watch was. Which is crazy, but then all these things happening to you are so strange. And you are so focused on it."

I waited.

"I still think that Grace had something to do with it," she added.

"Of course I don't think it was you." My voice was loud and clear. But she'd started something. Drip, drip, drip at the back of my mind. "But why would Grace be behind it all? I don't see how she's doing these crazy things."

"She had your keys."

Even though I doubted Grace was involved, she gave me the creeps. I would be glad to get away from her and that strange tiger tattoo.

* * *

The day that was meant to be Eve's wedding. It was not a good day for me either. We were both suffering a loss, which is why I believed my gift to her, to mark this day, was appropriate.

CHAPTER 19

Ten o'clock. A hairdresser was curling my hair into soft ring-lets. I was having a coffee, nerves and excitement rolling over me.

Let's start again. I wanted that with all my being, but that was not my reality. Instead, on the day that should have been my wedding, I awoke on my own in a B&B bedroom in Bamburgh, Northumberland. The place where you pro-posed. Where I was so happy, I thought my heart would burst, where I was giddy every time I looked at my engage-ment ring. I had to acknowledge the day in my own way and say goodbye to you. I just couldn't believe you were coming back. If you meant to, if you were out there, surely, you would have by our wedding day.

I stared at the ceiling as I lay in bed. I needed to get up. The sun streamed through the curtains. A beautiful day for a wedding. If my life had continued on the course I had hoped for, I would have been thrilled with the good weather. The ceiling looked old and tired, the paint peeling slightly around the light fitting. I had deliberately chosen a cheap, slightly frayed B&B, to contrast with the beautiful boutique hotel we had stayed in when you proposed. I might be thought of as strange going back to the area where we had got engaged, but even I couldn't have stayed in that hotel or something similar. This wasn't a celebration. The tatty paint, windowless bathroom and tired, dreary green blanket on the bed suited the way I was feeling. I forced myself out of bed, my feet like lead.

I would now have been finishing with the hairdresser at this time, nerves and excitement bubbling through, looking forward to Prosecco with Jess, Vicky and Rachel as we got ready.

I'd missed the B&B breakfast, but you wouldn't know it, the smell of fatty bacon and black pudding wafting into my room. I gulped hard trying to fight the nausea as I grimly washed my teeth. Pulling an old sweater on and frayed jeans — a contrast to my graceful wedding dress with its shimmering neckline — I headed out of the door, head down. I didn't want eye contact with anyone.

"Excuse me." The woman at the reception desk leapt up as I stormed past. She had bright red nails and a sparkling solitaire diamond on her left hand. "You've had a delivery."

I paused, confused, as she dashed into a poky back room, returning clutching a bouquet of flowers. I stared as she thrust them at me. Something jarred, wasn't right. I automatically took them, staring at the velvety flowers, wrapped in beautiful paper. Black. They were black. I had never seen black flowers before. Black roses. I didn't realise that it was even possible.

"I am very sorry," the receptionist bowed her head stiffly.

"Why?" The flowers' sickly smell enveloped my face.

She pointed at the roses. "Oh, I'm sorry, I might be probably jumping the gun, but you know, black . . ." Her voice faded away and she looked up at the ceiling and down at the ground before determinedly staring at her computer screen, her cheeks pink. "Sorry." So quiet I could barely hear the words.

I carried the flowers back to my room. They felt like they weighed several dumbbells. I deposited them on the bed. Their black stood out sharply against the crumpled bedspread.

I tapped out black roses on the internet on my phone and words leapt out at me: mourning, grief, death.

It was only then I noticed the note tied to the main stems, a garish display of flowers on its cover: *I am so sorry for your loss.*

My heart beat so hard it felt like it would burst out of my chest.

The words were printed, their blackness matching the colour of the roses. Funerals, graves with flowers sitting sadly at their ends filled my mind. Your face, the dimple on your chin, your beautiful blue eyes, filled my mind.

Eleven thirty. Slipping into my dress, sipping Prosecco and enjoying admiring glances from Jess, Vicky and Rachel. My glimmering future out of my grasp.

Instead, I was on my knees clutching the bedspread. An unsightly brown stain lay under my fingers. I stared at the roses. I had only told a handful of people where I was. How had these flowers arrived then? And their message was right. It wasn't a wedding that I was celebrating today, it was a loss. I had come here to say goodbye.

I walked along the beach, legs aching as the rhythmic sound of the waves lapping on the beach soothed the frayed edges of my mind. I just had to get past today. I couldn't look at the future or the past, today was my focus. If I could just get past today, I felt things might become better. Not great, but more tolerable than my present.

The day of my wedding felt worse even than facing the anniversary of him going missing. I glanced at my watch. Again. Three o'clock. I should have been walking down the aisle, Dad holding my arm, so pleased and proud that I was marrying you. Mum would have been dabbing tears from her eyes. She was always emotional, and the wedding of her only child marrying a man she liked and approved of so much was bound to set her off. And as for me . . . I would have been nervous, excited and happy. My heart would have been beating slightly fast. My cheeks would have been a bit rosy. They always flushed when I was the centre of attention.

The coarse shriek of a seagull dragged me back reluctantly to my present. I had walked for over two miles, and I

146

realised, as I bent to examine a rockpool, that I had done the right thing coming here. I had only told a very few people and their reaction had not been exactly positive.

"Oh, please don't do it," Mum begged.

Dad looked pensive. He didn't say much but his mouth set in a thin straight line of disapproval. He thought I should be getting on with life, not "deliberately making myself feel one hundred times worse".

Jill looked at me with empathy and understanding and angst written all over her face. I didn't tell Sophie, but I was sure Jill told her.

Jess's eyes were inky pools of pity and astonishment. She was too tactful to say, but a speech bubble might have been wobbling above her head with "Why are you doing this to yourself?"

Rachel was less tactful. "I think you're mad. Why torture yourself?" she said bluntly.

To everyone else I just said in the vaguest possible terms that I was going away.

A crab scuttled out of the rockpool and cautiously inched its way along one of the rocks. I watched it dreamily. Wherever I spent this day was going to be torture, as Rachel said. At least here I had the sea and nature and the fresh air. It did me good. And I needed to say goodbye to him, to what I thought my future was going to be. And then I was going to continue, make a life for myself. Julie, the woman with the Liverpool football scarf that I had met at the Christmas charity advert, was always at my shoulder, her pale face, bright red scarf and determined hope haunting my days as well as nights. *I won't be that person, waiting forever, I won't.*

I took a deep breath and closed my eyes, willing Julie's face to cover my entire mind. As much as it depressed me, I needed that push, that jolt to get on with my life.

Couldn't she see that her husband was most probably dead? I chided myself for the frustration and incredulity I felt. People probably felt like that about me.

I rose to my feet and reluctantly left the rockpool and its inmate, the crab.

* * *

The lights were dim as I sat in a quiet corner of a pub nestled in the shadows of Bamburgh Castle. I nursed a glass of wine while a plate of chips sat untouched at my elbow. Eight o'clock. The speeches would have begun, you would have been saying I was beautiful, cracking a joke about my hypochondria . . . my hands were covering my ears, even though that couldn't quell the day that was meant to be, in my head. I picked up my pen and dug it into my notebook.

> *Life after*
> *My new flat*
> *Get into fitness again*
> *Join a running club*
> *Do yoga*

I stared at my little list. Was that my future? It was so empty compared to the list-that-should-have-been: buy a flat *together*, have a baby, have a honeymoon in South America, plan my future with the man I loved.

The usual pain in my heart started, the heavy ache whose fingers stretched out to squeeze my stomach also.

As a distraction I made myself consider the bouquet I received earlier. Who could have sent it? Someone didn't like me very much; this was for sure. Whether that was you or someone else. The sense of unease I'd felt since the delivery of the flowers started to grow, filling my mind. Perhaps I needed to call the police when I got home.

I picked up my pen and ruminated on who else it might be. It would most likely be someone who knew me. *Grace*, I wrote. But I frowned. She didn't know enough about my life surely to do that. Did she even know the date that we were getting married? She knew we were engaged but I couldn't recall mentioning the marriage date. But two things made her a contender. *Keys*, I wrote in stern upper-case letters. And: she lived above me. Location was important as someone had been coming round at all hours and I hadn't seen or heard any evidence of them leaving the building. Of course, I could have just missed sounds and they could have been too quick for me to spot them out of the window. But still.

Gemma. That blouse. Their texts. Her admission there was something between them. Her total rejection of me. *But who can blame her? You attacked her.*

My hand ignored the small but resolute voice in my mind. And it kept on writing. The hatred and coldness in her face when I bumped into her in the kitchen at work. My hand hovered, desperate to find more clues but nothing came to mind except — she had texted me about looking for you in Leeds. It was weak but I wrote it down anyway.

Who else, who else? I finished my wine and before I ordered another one, I rested my pen on my notebook. As if it belonged to someone else it wrote one more name, so familiar and lovable it looked out of place on my little list. *Rachel.*

I took a sharp intake of breath. Everything that I had been trying to bury came to the fore as I wrote swiftly: *John's watch*. She acted strange when I said it had gone missing. She knew its hiding place. She was the only person who did. She lived with me. The top she bought as my Christmas present — from the same shop as Gemma's blouse.

I was trying to process my alien thoughts when my hand started moving, writing another name: *Clive*. My fingers smudged the C, so the black blob covered part of Rachel's name.

"Don't be ridiculous." I snorted aloud. But still I wrote under his name: *Rejected him after our night together (a man scorned?).* BUT THE WEIRD THINGS WERE HAPPENING TO ME BEFORE THAT, I added in capitals. *John's wedding tie.* I wrote it quickly. Clive knew about our colour wedding theme, and I had been sent a lilac tie for Christmas.

I paused to chew on my pencil. Something was bothering me.

I then wrote: *Sophie*, underlining it firmly. Then it came back to me. "John was so lucky to have you." It was meant to be a lovely sentiment, but the undertones of longing, of held-back emotion in Clive's voice had made me uncomfortable. I hesitated but wrote it down anyway. I didn't really think it was Clive, but I was determined to write down any doubts I had.

Ah. Sophie. Seemed obvious. *She was jealous, possessive of her brother. Didn't like me, we didn't get on.* My hand flew as I wrote this down. And yet . . . and yet . . . she was so consumed by her brother's disappearance, would she really have the energy to conduct this kind of thing, to sneak about, entering the flat . . . that was a point: *Did she have a key, could you have given her one?* I wrote it as a question, underlining it so hard that the paper tore. I needed to find out.

The key was the key to this mystery. I smiled thinly at the tired pun. I couldn't totally believe it was Sophie, despite everything.

I didn't really believe that it was any of these people, if I was honest.

I wrote down everyone else who featured strongly in my life. *Jess, Jack, Jill, Vicky,* other friends, but I drew a blank.

There was one other name. The elephant in the room. *John.* I made myself confront it. Your name made all the others fade. I stared at it. John. The name should have been entwined with mine, would have been at our wedding in another life. Eve and John, on the front of our wedding service programme, on our menu cards. Eveandjohn. I rolled it together as one word.

Key. I wrote simply under your name. The pub was more crowded. Two couples sat at the table next to me, around my age. I noticed the rings on their left hands. The one with the blond hair placed her hand lovingly on her husband's arm. The other one laughed, pointing out something on her phone. A normal Saturday night for them. I used to be like that. The music playing in the background was racked up a couple of notches. "Go Your Own Way", Fleetwood Mac. That was on our music list for our wedding. I glanced at my watch. Nine thirty. The dancing would have started. We would be dancing to this now. I remembered driving across the Scottish Highlands listening to this with you. Turned up high as we sped through empty roads with mountains and grey skies, the purple of the heather standing out brilliantly at the side of the road.

After *key*, I hesitated, then it came out: the things that had happened related to objects of significance that only you would really know. *The watch, the photo, the mug. Your personality had changed: Hong Kong, not telling me about the antidepressants, your friendship with Gemma, buying that item of clothing.* I listed each point. Perhaps you were angry with me, which explained the flowers today, the missing watch, trying to go to Hong Kong. Could you have a mental illness that had changed your personality and caused you to go missing? I raised the question on my scruffy sheet of paper and resolved to find out. I wasn't sure how but Google was my friend here.

I read the paper very carefully and drained my glass. I wanted another, but that was a bad idea. None of the names rang true. Deep down I didn't really believe that it was any of them. But it was all I had. I slipped the paper into my bag and rose. I left the happy, cheery pub with its cosy candles and walked out into the dark. I could hear the sea lapping in the distance. I could walk back to my bed and breakfast along the beach. It was so dark I couldn't see my hand in front of my face. I didn't mind; the sound of the waves felt like they were lapping over my mind, erasing it of my torturous thoughts. I enjoyed the sensation and bent to take off my shoes, to feel the sand between my toes. It was only spring, but the night was mild.

I heard a rustle in the bushes at the side. Then it was silent again, apart from the waves. There it was again. Probably an animal. Still, I started to walk briskly. A woman, on her own late at night on a beach, maybe it wasn't such a good idea. A low murmur. It sounded like a voice. I strained to hear, but nothing more. I broke into a trot. I reached the pavement where the B&B was located and pounded onto it thankfully. But something stopped me from dashing straight in. I crouched behind the wall separating the beach and the road, my breath rasping. I clutched the stone and waited. Nothing. Just the rhythmic sound of waves hitting the beach. Perhaps I imagined it; I had started to doubt myself in the face of so much scepticism from family and friends.

Then the low murmuring sound of voices continued in the wind, getting stronger as their bearers moved closer. A man and a woman. My heart started thudding again, but I dug my feet into the ground; I was staying put.

"She didn't see us, thank goodness, and she's definitely gone," I heard a whisper as feet slapped onto the pavement. A voice I recognised. But I was still shocked when I rose and confronted them.

"What are you doing here?"

Rachel and Clive were like rabbits caught in headlights. Their arms were entwined. Clive's colour deepened until it was almost purple, while Rachel's had paled, from what I could tell from the muted light of the street lamp.

"You and your bloody idea!" Clive boomed crossly to Rachel, letting his arm drop.

"I know you must be shocked, but we meant this with the best intentions," Rachel said to me rapidly. "And we didn't mean to scare you."

I was still trying to process my thoughts. "But how did you find me?"

"It wasn't difficult, you said you were coming here so I rang round the bed and breakfasts," Rachel explained. "I was really worried about you being on your own and wanted to keep an eye on you. Clive and I are staying in the B&B opposite."

I was incredulous. "So you were in the pub with me? I'm surprised I didn't see you."

"We sat out of sight, and you looked in a world of your own," Clive muttered, looking embarrassed.

"So, listen, I know it looks strange but you're my best friend and I felt so anxious — we all have — that, well, you wouldn't be okay." Rachel, usually so calm, sounded emotional. "And your mum and dad and Jess know," she added. "Your mum and dad wanted me to come."

"Ok, I get you had my best interests at heart." My fear and surprise had waned. "Did you think I was going to wade into the sea and drown?"

Rachel took my arm, and we walked back to my B&B. I could barely put one foot in front of the other. My legs were like water.

"I told you this wasn't a good idea!" Clive repeated huffily.

I tried to smile at them. "Don't worry, it's a nice gesture, I'm glad you're here."

And it *was* a lovely gesture. It was so kind, thoughtful, I had people who loved me, I should be grateful. My notebook, which contained my accusations against Rachel and Clive, felt like a dirty secret now. I felt it bouncing around my bag and guilt raised its head.

"Please come up to my room with me," I said. Black petals filled my mind and my eyes and my mouth. At the very least they would at last see that I was telling the truth, that it wasn't in my mind; something nasty was happening to me.

I unlocked the door and fumbled for the light switch. The fuse was gone. I was grateful for Rachel's light touch on my shoulder and Clive's heavy breathing as he switched on the torch on his phone and we made our way up the shadowy stairs.

Luckily, the light worked in my room. The first thing I saw was the bouquet of flowers on the bed where I had left them. Its stems seemed to stretch across the room, covering it in a black shadow. But when I glanced at Rachel and Clive, they seemed oblivious. Rachel kicked off her heels.

I cleared my throat. "Notice anything?" I aimed at casual, but the staccato syllables were the opposite of that.

"Not the nicest room, and where's the telly?" Clive seemed outraged. "Oh, it's that box in the corner. They need to move on from the nineties."

I walked over to the bed and touched a petal. "I got sent these today." I picked up the accompanying card and threw it over to Rachel. "Lovely wedding gift, isn't it?"

Rachel grabbed the card and read it. She looked at the flowers, at the card and back again.

Clive peered over her shoulder. "Bloody sick," he pronounced loudly. I suspected that he'd had a couple of pints.

"I'm sorry." Rachel's voice was so quiet that I wondered if I'd heard correctly. At last, they realised that it wasn't just in my head. I waited for the relief, but there was just emptiness.

Once they had gone back to their B&B, I carried the flowers into the bathroom and shut the door firmly. I didn't want their dark presence in my bedroom, their stems stretching out towards my bed.

Eleven o'clock. We'd have been dancing in each other's arms, giddy and happy. My hair would have been coming out of its updo, my cheeks flushed, my lipstick no doubt smeared. My eyes would have been shining with happiness.

I lay stiffly in bed. My hair was smooth and flat, and I knew my cheeks were pale. I wasn't giddy and I most definitely wasn't happy. I closed my eyes. At least today was over.

You looked so handsome in your wedding suit, your cornflower blue eyes almost popping from your face. You were smiling. The woman in the wedding dress clung to you. Her hair was in soft ringlets; my hair was meant to be up. She wore the same dress as mine, but the diamante neck line was not mauve, it was black. I was watching them dance in a corner surrounded by the guests.

It wasn't me; it wasn't me, but it should be. Who was this imposter? I began to fight my way through the guests, but they surged around me thicker than glue. I couldn't get near them. Then the bride saw me and moved towards me. Gently her hands were around my throat. Her face was in shadow as they began to squeeze.

"John!"

I opened my eyes. I struggled against the bedclothes as I felt sweat trickle down my back. Had my shouting woken anyone? My heart thumped. It was natural that I would have distorted dreams about my wedding, I told myself. I shifted as I realised that I needed to go to the toilet. I snapped my eyes shut, thinking of those roses, inky dark in the bathroom. I didn't want to go in. It would have to wait until morning.

CHAPTER 20

I pushed open the door of my flat and dumped my bag onto the post that had arrived in the two days that I had been gone.

It was over. I slammed the door shut. The flat felt so empty. I stiffened slightly, my hand on the door, but the locks had been changed so no one could get in. You and I had decided to go somewhere in the UK for a week after our wedding, then take an exotic honeymoon later in the year. We were still in the planning stages of where to go when you went missing. I was glad we hadn't decided on somewhere concrete, although South America had been a major contender. At least I couldn't torture myself with that.

I picked up my bag and on top of the junk mail lay a crisp white envelope with my name and address written in capitals. I picked up the envelope, a sense of foreboding creeping over me. I didn't recognise the writing. I opened it slowly. A card covered in roses and *wedding regret* printed on it. All I could see was the colour of the roses. Black. I opened it.

In it was printed: *I regret that I cannot attend your wedding.*

The card was just addressed to me. Not you. I suddenly felt so tired. My brain was enveloped in a fog. The questions and analysis felt beyond me. Apart from one thing. I checked the postmark. It was too blurry to make out.

I knew I had to do something. There was a police telephone line that I could go through directly, due to what had happened to you. My hand shook as I told the woman who answered my call about the black roses, and now this card. She logged the incidents and told me to call again if anything happened.

I fumbled in my handbag and took out a single black rose. I carried this and the card into the living room and flinging open the built-in cupboard door, extracted a plain shoebox. In they went, to join the wedding tie. I was gathering evidence.

London Daily Eye newspaper wanted to interview me about you going missing, to coincide with what would have been our wedding day. It was me that approached them. I knew how important it was to garner publicity, and the wedding was a strong hook. "The day of my wedding and my fiancé is still missing." I could see such a headline in my mind's eye. It was the kind of thing we would run in my magazine.

But the thought of it left a sour taste in my mouth. I didn't want to do it, but if there was a one per cent chance that it could lead to you, I knew I had to.

I was at work when one of the news editors had rung me to arrange a date to be interviewed, which led me to give short, clipped answers. But I needn't have bothered. No one even glanced my way when I put the phone down. It rang again twenty minutes later. This time the news was more cheerful. My conveyancing lawyer said we were on course to exchange on the flat in ten days, with completion a week later.

No need to feel I was being watched. No need to feel someone was going to enter my home. Take things. Send me things. The relief spread over me as I hung up.

* * *

"It must be dreadful." Ethan the journalist looked sad as he smoothly clicked his Dictaphone on. "Can I just say, before we start the interview, that by doing this article, you have a great outreach, the whole of London and Home Counties. We can help you."

I pulled a sickie at work. The interview would take a whole afternoon. If I had explained the real reason, they would have had to let me go. But I was too tired to explain.

He leaned forward eagerly.

"We'd been choosing our wedding rings," I began. I could feel the heat rising from the train as it hurtled towards us, the smell of bodies and stale sweat emanating from the pushing crowds as we waited. The gap I felt behind me when you didn't get on the train. The panic I felt that day, rising like a slow cooker.

I thought Ethan was going to be second-rate with his cheesy introduction. But his skilful questioning drew me out. I found myself blurting out about the presence of someone in my flat and of an unknown person trying to get in, the tie, the missing watch, the black flowers. He laid down his notebook.

"I'm not sure I can report that," he said gently. "We really need to focus on the disappearance of John, I think, to raise awareness."

"It's okay," I said. And I meant it.

"One last thing," he said. "Do you believe he is going to come back?"

"No." The surprise on his face mirrored mine. "No," I repeated. I meant it.

"We can't put that in the piece," he explained. "Well, we can, but we want leads for you, so it would be better for you to express hope."

I fixed a smile on my face. "Then, absolutely."

He pushed across his number. "Take it in case you think of anything else, or just want to talk," he said.

That was nice. I took his number.

I walked towards the Tube after the interview, enjoying the fresh air, trying to ignore the knot of panic as I contemplated the underground. The feeling of your body pressed against me, then just nothing. The glimpse of your dark hair as the train set off, the faces pouring down on me on the platform, none of them yours. My breathing quickened as I took the escalator down into the depths. Sweat trickled down my forehead as I tried to control my rising panic.

Stop it stop it stop it.

The feature was out the next day. I picked up the newspaper on my way home from work, from Victoria overground station, a lengthy way for me to get home, but it meant that I could skip the underground. I was pushed up against other commuters on the train to Balham as I flicked through the pages to find me. My story. A briefcase from another passenger rubbed the backs of my legs.

My wedding day — and no groom. The headline was big, black and bold.

She should have been in a beautiful dress, clutching flowers, celebrating the best day of her life. Instead, Eve is lying on a grotty duvet cover in a dreary B&B, tears running down her face. Her fiancé has disappeared. I never said that the bed and breakfast was that grim, did I? And the duvet cover, well it did have a nasty brown stain on it, but it wasn't that bad. I found myself smiling. As a fellow journalist, and a women's true-life feature writer at that, I thought he had done a good job. I would have written it like this.

I engrossed myself in my story. My loneliness as I travelled on the train towards Bamburgh. My escalating despair. The article was well written, but I felt more keenly what was missing than what was included. The black roses lying on that grotty duvet cover.

I focused on the bodies and their bags around me. Anything was better than the faceless person or persons skirting around me. I wanted to touch a man's damp shirt in front of me, to feel connected to the present and ward off the nasties.

I got home and went straight to my computer, ignoring the stillness and stale smell that had come about since you went. People made online comments on these features. I had an urgent desire to know what they thought about my situation, did they think you were out there and coming back? I clicked on the article, cringing at my face, the dark shadows under my eyes, lines tracing my down-turned mouth. I was thirty-three going on forty-three. My heart beat fast as I saw that there were already 133 comments. The paper only came out today!

I started reading.

"So sad — he obviously killed himself. She is deluded."
Anon, London

"I can't comment on whether he is dead or not (although my money would be on a suicide), but either way he is not coming back. I feel very sorry for her, she needs to move on."
Pete, Hampshire

"My granddad did the same thing. Disappeared off the face of the earth one day. My grandmother was devastated. Forty-five years later a knock on the door. One of his grandchildren. He had died but the grandchild was trying to trace family. He had gone off to Australia to make a new life with another woman." *Joyce, Manchester*

"He's left her for someone else and is too cowardly to say it."
D. Ritchie, Dorset

"Very sad story. The fact that he approached his friend in Hong Kong speaks volumes. I think he is still out there. Sadly, he didn't want her, or his life anymore. He wanted to start again." *GogiRL, Surrey*

"I know both John and Eve. And he had his reasons, believe me. Eve's been through some nasty events since John left. These will continue, I think. I'm still here." *BlackRose80*

I froze. My heart pounded in my ears as I re-read slowly, the words swimming in front of my eyes. Here it was in black-and-white. Someone was out to get me. *Somebody I know.* Should I go to the police again?

My throat was suddenly bone dry. I went to get a glass of water.

When I came back the comments had jumped to 200.

"Blatantly dead at the bottom of a river. He is never coming back." Nathan, W 32

"Sounds like a very troubled young man. I think he wanted to leave his life, run away from it. She shouldn't blame herself." Tabby, Dorset

"You hear about cases like this in the media and there is rarely a happy outcome." JB, Bristol

I scanned each new comment, each one puncturing the little bags of hope buried away in the depths of my mind.

I looked again for BlackRose80's comment, scrolled through, but couldn't see it. I went through the list again more carefully. It had gone. I saw the sign at the top of the page of comments: *Comments moderated.* Previously it had said the comments were unmoderated. The comment must have been deemed unsuitable and deleted. I let out a cry of frustration. I wished I had taken a screen shot with my phone, as now I had nothing to show the police.

I know both Eve and John. BlackRose80's words reverberated continuously round my head as I paced the sitting room. *Who is it?* Our friends, acquaintances and work colleagues all filed through my mind.

They said that the nasty events would continue. My throat was dry again and I grabbed my glass of water as I jumped up to check that I'd bolted the door. They were warning me.

* * *

"Come in." Paul waved me through abruptly. He looked tense. Probably worried about what I was going to fling at him.

"I want to talk to you about John," I began. He stiffened and pushed his laptop away.

"A journalist interviewed me for a feature about John the other day, because it was when we were meant to get married. It got me thinking — why should someone else write my story? I am a journalist, on a well-known magazine, so why don't I write a column about it? It would raise awareness of him, and also help other people going through the same thing and bring awareness to the topic of missing people."

Paul's face relaxed. "I think that's a brilliant idea."

I walked out of his office, my creative juices flowing more strongly than they had done for months. I was meant to write about a woman whose boyfriend had been tortured. Instead, I started tapping: *I thought you were right behind me. But you weren't.*

CHAPTER 21

The grey buildings and vast urban landscape that had been flying past had been transformed into lush green fields and small sleepy towns. I should have been excited at getting away from the grime of London and out into the countryside. The others were. Rachel was beaming, her shoulders were slumped against the train seat. Jess had stretched right back in her seat, a dreamy expression on her face.

It was all right for them. A bubble of jealousy and anger rose within me and took my breath away. Them and their partners, their dreams.

I gave myself a mental slap. They were my best friends. It wasn't their fault I had lost you. I focused on the bubbles fizzing out of the champagne bottle that Rachel had popped.

"Cheers!" she yelled.

Did she have to be so enthusiastic, so carefree and happy? I plastered a smile on my face as she slopped champagne into our plastic flutes.

Jess's hen weekend. We were heading to a cottage on the outskirts of Brighton. Jess, Rachel, Jack's sister Suzie, me and Vicky had caught the train from London Victoria late Friday afternoon and were sitting in first class on our way to the cottage. The other hens were joining us there.

"Here's to a wonderful hen!" Rachel continued. Her cheeks were flushed a delicate pink and her eyes sparkled. She was in the first throes of romance with Clive. Probably thinking of her own future hen do and wedding, I thought sourly, shuddering as memories of Clive's beery breath and octopus hands enveloped me.

My hen do would have been in Bath. I had always loved Bath since I visited it once with you. Even though it was early days, Jess had already planned it when you went missing. I had never wanted to know the exact details after you went.

Jess took a huge gulp and then spluttered, bringing me back to the present sharply.

"Ah thanks." She smiled, dimples appearing. So happy. Just so happy. I closed my eyes so they wouldn't see the tears.

Jess reached over and squeezed my hand. I forced my eyes open and plastered on a smile.

I had always known Jess's hen do was going to be a struggle. I just had to get through it. It wasn't her fault. I squeezed her hand back.

My phone buzzed with an incoming work email and I clicked on it quickly. I saw Paul's name flash up. *Hi, Eve, your column about John is doing brilliantly! I have seen the Instagram figures and we've had so many comments there. It's really striking a note with people. It was a great idea. I realise how hard it must be for you to write this, so well done again. Looking forward to the next column.*

I smiled involuntarily, pride flushing through me. Even now, my job could give me some solace.

"What's that you've seen?" Jess asked, somewhat nosily.

"I've started writing a column about John going missing for my magazine. It's to help others going through the same thing, raise awareness of the issues of people going through it and those who are missing, and I've just had the first one published. It's gone really well! We've had loads of reposts and my boss has just congratulated me!"

I hoped I didn't sound boastful, but I couldn't contain my pleasure. Something positive had come out of something so negative. I loved my job, and it was so good to have a reason to pour my soul into it again. I could help others, forgotten people like Julie, and raise awareness of your disappearance. Maybe it would help me find you.

"I've had forty thousand likes, I've never had so many," I said in amazement, clicking on my Instagram app.

"Wow, well done!" said Rachel. "That's amazing. And just from one column? Imagine the impact when you write even more."

"Yeah, it's going to be a weekly thing, for the magazine." I was already thinking about what my next column would be. Maybe our search through Leeds, the football match, my Christmas appearance for the charity . . . I zoned out.

"Well done! Despite what you're going through you're writing about it. A true journalist," Jess said. "Bit different to my work this week — an in-depth look at why pensions should be a priority!"

"But it's important stuff, Jess, you're dealing with critical issues that affect people," Rachel said earnestly. "Although yeah, no denying it sounds dry, especially compared to Eve's job!"

"I'm just happy that I've been given a platform for what I'm going through," I said quickly. My mind was off again. I'd thought of something I needed to get into my next column. Grabbing my phone, I tapped: *A man sat on the step, eyes sunken, a small bit of dribble escaping from his mouth. He smiled vacantly. A sick feeling came over me — what if you were homeless, living on the streets?*

That was it. I would start with our fruitless search for you in Leeds . . .

"Earth to Eve!" Rachel's bellowing turned my thoughts reluctantly back to the present.

* * *

"Oh wow, this is amazing!" Jess flung down her case and did a little jig in the kitchen. An old-world cottage with exposed oak beams and huge kitchen diner confronted us.

A stab of guilt went through me. I should have been involved in organising Jess's hen event. I'd done nothing since pleading that I couldn't be a bridesmaid.

The bell rang. Rachel slapped her hands together. "Great, Sainsbury's delivery!" They delivered champagne and Prosecco, white wine and red, chorizo and paté, smoked salmon and fresh bread, as well as five different types of cheeses.

Before the guilt could take hold, Vicky led me off to my room. "We thought you might like the room on your own," she said grandly. *Because you are sad and lonely and a Terrible Thing Has Happened to You*, she might as well have added.

It was the loft room. I felt grateful I didn't have to put up with the others' mindless chitchat and snores.

"Thanks," I said simply.

Vicky twisted her hands, sighed, stared out of the window, looking anywhere but me. "I hope you're okay, I know the hen must be difficult," she burst out quickly. She meant well.

I took a deep breath. "I'm fine," I said firmly. "It's Jess's hen do, and I want her to have an amazing time. That is all I am trying to think about." So noble and brave. So untrue. I should be polite and ask about her fiancé Ian, about how her wedding plans were going, but my mouth wouldn't open.

"Okay that's good," Vicky said formally, trying to smile. "Right, I think the plan is to have a dip in the hot tub before dinner."

"Great!" I made a display of rooting through my suitcase for my bikini.

* * *

"Oh, this is brilliant." Jess lay back in the hot tub, sipping her flute of champagne. She looked amazing. She had lost weight for the wedding. She was in a bikini too. I commented that I had never seen her in a bikini before. Usually she was in a plain, black, all-encompassing swimsuit.

Jess's eyes narrowed slightly then she laughed. "Yeah, I'm not overweight for once!"

"No, I didn't mean it like that!" Flustered, I took a large sip of my champagne. The bubbles were spreading through my body, building a coat of armour.

Vicky and Rachel clambered in. Suzie was already in, a beatific smile spread across her face. Jack's elder sister, she was married and had a nine-month-old daughter, Maria. "Oh wow," she said with a smile. "This is bliss, I can chill out, no little one running me ragged!"

I zoned out as all the others chimed in eagerly asking questions about babies, Maria, food, milk, sleeping patterns. Suzie expounded upon her experiences with messy, food-throwing babies. Jess was leaning forward, engaged and nodding while Rachel had a dreamy smile playing on her lips. No doubt thinking about little Clives running around.

I used to think about babies; hazy thoughts of nappies, breast feeding, a happy, smiling family, 2.4 children, all the time with you in the background. I'd always imagined having a son, with your blue eyes. I twisted my left finger, still feeling the empty patch my engagement ring had left since I had put it away.

"I reckon we'll start trying quite soon," Fiona, Jess's friend from home, said, her voice sounded like it was reaching me through the roar of cars on a motorway. "I know it'll be a massive life change, but you know, we'll be in our mid-thirties and time is ticking on."

"Yep, we feel the same, no time to lose." Jess's voice was sing-song, she sounded tipsy.

I wanted to smash my glass into their faces, grab my case and get out of there. They were rubbing my hopes and dreams in my face. Their futures were full of cuddly babies, happy husbands and family homes while mine felt like some lonely, empty Russian steppe. I had to count to ten before I did or said something silly.

* * *

Nine o'clock.

I stood up. I had timed my moment carefully. Rachel had gone to the toilet, Jess was looking very drunk, Suzie was helping herself to more ice cream in the kitchen. Fiona was pouring herself another glass of wine. Other hens who I vaguely knew — Jess's colleagues and home friends — were dancing to "Macarena". Vicky was sitting at the dining room table, fairly alert. Never mind.

"I'm going to bed now." I sounded like I was speaking at a posh university formal dinner. I pushed on. "I hope you don't mind, but I'm saving myself for tomorrow."

I am leaving you to talk about your futures, your hopes, dreams and wonderful men. Men that would never walk out on you and your life, leaving you like a fish out of water gasping for air.

Jess jumped out of her seat and embraced me fiercely. "You okay?" she whispered. Eyes full of concern.

"Yes, honestly, I want to be fresh for tomorrow." I cringed at the sing-song girly tone.

I could feel all their eyes on me as I slowly traipsed up the stairs. They might as well be screaming "poor thing, horrific". And then the relief would be flooding through them that their husbands/fiancés/boyfriends had not done this. They could be depended upon. They had a rock behind them. I had an empty space.

I got to my room. And noticed that I was still holding my wine glass.

I raised my hand above my head and flung it at the wall. It smashed into pieces. I paused. My only worry was that they had heard down below.

I needn't have concerned myself. An eighties song wafted up the stairs. They were dancing and enjoying themselves. I left the shards of glass on the floor.

The next thing I knew, it was dark, and I was curled up in bed. The pressure in my bladder and dull ache in my temples were simultaneous. Too much champagne. I needed paracetamol and to go to the toilet.

I got out, one hand rubbing my temple and gingerly felt my way to the light switch. I flicked it down. Nothing. I irritably flicked it on and off a couple more times. Nothing. Just my luck the bulb would go. Clutching the wall, I made my way towards the stairs.

A piercing pain in my foot made me yelp. Warm wetness seeped through my toes. The glass. My own damn fault. I soldiered on regardless. One foot on the stairs, clutching the banister. Then I heard something. I paused. A slight breath being inhaled, then exhaled. A creak of a floorboard, someone, something moving their foot on the landing. Then a heavy breath. That night at my flat flashed through my mind; footsteps, rustles. How could it be happening here? I placed another foot on the next step, wincing at the sudden sharp pain from my cut. The sudden suffocating silence felt worse. My bravery disappeared in a flash; I didn't want to face what was waiting for me below.

I rushed back to bed and pushed the covers up around my face, ignoring the pressure on my bladder. It threw everything into confusion. I had thought there was someone in my flat, but how could that be the case here, on my friend's hen night. My mind was playing tricks on me. I pulled the duvet over my head, trying to take deep breaths to still my pounding heart. There was no one at the foot of the stairs. All in my mind, it had to be. I couldn't hear anything from downstairs now. My foot was sodden. There would be blood everywhere.

* * *

The chirrup of birds woke me up. It should have been a nice awakening, a feeling of being at one with nature and the countryside. But their beaks were pecking at my brain, mirroring the dull thump of my wine-induced headache. I groaned inwardly as I thought of the day ahead. But I had to put on a cheery face. Clenching my fists in anticipation I pushed back the covers and planted my feet on the floor. The sheets were splattered bright red. I let out a gasp, my stomach lurching, until I saw the caked blood shredding in between two toes. It all came flooding back, especially as I saw shards of glass and bloodstains on the carpet.

I heard the light tread of steps on the steps. "Hey. You up yet? Fancy a bacon sarnie?" Rachel called. Glass, blood — I did not want her seeing this.

"Um yeah, don't come up I'm naked!" I yelled out desperately. Oh God that sounded odd. It worked though. The footsteps stopped halfway up the stairs.

"I mean I'm getting up and dressed — not a pretty sight." My forced laugh sounded like I had the shards of glass embedded in my throat.

"Okay!" she sang out.

I pulled on my jeans and a T-shirt that had a stain on it. I remembered spattering my baked beans against it the other night. My hair looked wild. But I didn't bother running a brush through it.

I scrubbed with a J cloth and soap at the red stains, hoping that they would fade enough. I'd have to somehow secretly wash the sheet, unless I could get the blood out with soap.

I regretted my appearance when I went downstairs. Vicky had lipstick and mascara on. Rachel was rosy-cheeked, clean and fresh-looking in a gingham top and skinny jeans. Jess was in a summery floral dress, showing off her newfound slimness. Suzie's hair was washed and squeaky clean. I stepped back slightly. I looked grubby and I might even smell. Mental note: take a shower.

The smell of bacon filled the air. My stomach turned.

"Mmmm yum, I need this." Suzie plonked herself down at the kitchen table. "Soak up all the wine." She gave a bark of laughter. "Oh, the bliss, the lie-in, a bacon sarnie, you don't get this with a baby!"

Okay, okay, we get it, you have a child, congratulations. I clamped my mouth firmly shut in case the words escaped. I focused on my breathing, trying to control my anger. *It is not her fault, it is not her fault she is happy and has what you want, it is not her fault your fiancé left.*

"Sure you won't join us for the water sports?" Jess sidled up to me and placed a hand on my shoulder.

"No, I just don't like the water much," I said feebly, trying to ignore the stab of guilt. I had foregone being a bridesmaid and got out of the first proper hen activity. Truth be told I couldn't summon the energy to jump about in the water, clinging to kayaks, falling in and screaming with laughter. I just wanted to walk on the beach or grab a coffee in the village. On my own.

* * *

"Sure you're okay?" Rachel asked as we left the cottage.

I plastered on a smile that made my ears ache. "Oh yeah, I can't wait for tonight," I proclaimed as we marched past the reception. The layout was very quaint; eight cottages on a small, pretty complex with a reception to deal with all enquiries.

"Let's leave the keys at reception." Rachel swung into the wooden cabin. "Ah, 53?" The young woman — no doubt a student working in her holidays — got up. "Post for you. Eve Jennings?"

"Me." I didn't give myself time to think about who it might be that was sending me post and how they knew such a temporary address. I pocketed it quickly. I would open it later.

Jess took my arm. "Probably someone checking you're okay," she murmured. "I know it's not easy for you."

I couldn't look at the big pools of sympathy her eyes had become.

"Uh huh," was all I could manage.

The sand of the beach stretched out to the gently lapping waves. The only person in my radar was an old man walking an excitable dog. It was beautiful. I sank onto the sand and allowed myself to play out my parallel life: I was just married to you and loving the landscape and the fun. I would have been dashing down to the waves to lap them up and bob about on my board. I would have been messaging you about how great it was.

Instead, I slowly took the envelope out of my bag. The writing was in capitals, written in spidery biro. I didn't recognise it, but then I never did. Usually, it was printed. Maybe they were growing careless. I squinted at the postmark. It looked like it said Croydon, but I couldn't tell as it was so smudged again.

I knew what was coming. I opened it slowly, not wanting to shatter the peace I felt in my surroundings. The honey-coloured sand, the deep blue sea, the lazy lapping of the waves. For a brief moment they massaged and numbed my torment.

I pulled a card out. It looked harmless — just lots of women clutching glasses of wine. One had an L-shaped plate strapped to her head. A hen do. Suddenly my body was flooded with relief. I slumped forward with a new appreciation of the sea that stretched as far as the eye could see. The soft sand between my fingers. It must be meant for Jess, and someone had written my name by accident. Then I saw the hens' faces.

They were wizened, wrinkled with huge hook noses and hooded eyes. One wore a black pointed hat. The champagne bottle held by one particularly horrible witch, whose front teeth dangled over her bottom lip, was smashed.

I opened the card and read:

It should have been you.

The beautiful beach before my eyes splintered into a thousand pieces, like the champagne bottle on the card.

* * *

The sun beat down as we crouched on a blanket on Brighton Beach, fish and chips and rosé wine spread out before us. People crowded on the beach; another hen do was near us, I noted, cracking open the Asti Spumante and already sounding tipsy. The cafés and restaurants spilling onto the beach were full of people. Happy, carefree, beaming people. I clutched a chip and stared at it. I couldn't put it in my mouth, the thought made me want to vomit.

171

"Right!" Rachel plonked a huge bulging bag of presents on the sand, causing it to fly up. "Some pressies for you, Jess, and you have to guess who they are from!"

I cringed at my present. "Buy Jess something that means something for your friendship to her," was Rachel's stern instruction. I couldn't think of anything; I didn't want to think of anything. Instead, I came up with a bland idea: a wine glass. A nice wine glass that had cost me fifteen pounds but it could have been from anyone, it didn't evoke a special memory. Who didn't go on a night out and drink with their friends?

Jess unwrapped each present amid shrieks of laughter and fond reminiscences — a tea towel plastered with a map of Gran Canaria to remind Jess of a last-minute getaway with Rachel. A framed photo of our gang of friends from our university graduation, the DVD of *Jaws* because that was what Jess and Suzie had watched together shortly after Jack introduced them. And so it went on, until Jess came to mine.

But she smiled and gave me a warm hug, no sign of annoyance. "Our legendary drunken nights." She laughed.

Her cheeks were flushed pink, her eyes were bright. I was sallow and pale and washed-out beside her.

"You okay?" she murmured as we headed back to the apartment. The air felt fresh and salty, seagulls cooed, and groups of people wandered happily. It was so vibrant, and I always loved the sea. I wished I could just lose myself in the atmosphere and really enjoy my best friend's hen do. I gripped her arm and stared her in the eye.

"Yes," I said as firmly as possible. "I'm really enjoying it."

It wasn't a total lie, a very small part of me was soothed by the sea. I wished I could forget the witches' faces. I had always been particularly scared of witches, since I read Roald Dahl's *The Witches* when I was eleven years old. The card, which I had stuffed in my jacket pocket, pressed against my side. Something else to add to my collection.

* * *

"What does Jack like most about you physically?" called out Rachel, donning a beret and a little black dress. The theme for tonight was a little black dress and a hat — a nod to Jess's love of hats, she collected them and had lots of them, from vintage to modern.

"My eyes," replied Jess with a sweet smile.

"Yes!" yelled Rachel to hoots of derision and cries of "Ah, so cute!" I joined in automatically.

"What? With those boobs — is he mad?!" shouted Louise, Jess's workmate. Everyone laughed like it was the funniest thing ever. Jess was well-known for her substantial chest. The wine was also flowing.

"Okay, more serious — what does Jack think is the most irritating thing about him to you?"

"His indecisiveness!"

"Yep!" Rachel shrieked. "Wow, you're getting every question right — we're never going to get you drunk at this rate!"

A line of shots had been lined up by Jess in anticipation of the Mr and Mrs questions that she had got wrong. So far, every single one had been right.

We were in an underground private room of a tapas bar in the Lanes of Brighton. Twelve of us crammed around an oak table with dim lights and candles. Rachel and Vicky had done well, I acknowledged. Brighton was great, the cottage was amazing and the bar that we had gone to for cocktails before the dinner had sea views from the heated terrace.

What did you like most about me? My eyes too, didn't you. I feel the sadness seeping in that I had automatically used the past tense. You always used to say that my eyes were navy-coloured and like marbles. But then again maybe you didn't like my eyes best, maybe it was my arms, my lips, my hair — I never thought you would disappear, and you did, so how much did I really know you? Maybe you liked nothing about me.

I was aware that there was a break in proceedings as Jess went to the toilet. Rachel slopped more white wine in my glass. Her face was flushed, she was drunk. She was annoying me and I tried to fight back a spark of jealousy; she was happy and in love, her eyes sparkled, dreamily gazing into the distance at various times.

"Just off to the loo too," I muttered, to get away from Rachel's joy. They were quiet, I noted with relief, splashing my hot face at the basin.

Jess opened one of the toilet doors and slunk out. Her eyes were watering. As soon as she saw me, she scrubbed fiercely at them.

"Jess! What's wrong, are you crying?" I jumped forward and wrapped an arm around her.

Jess smiled weakly. "Oh sorry, I just feel overwhelmed with it all, the wedding, the hen do . . . I am happy, I am, it just — oh sorry I'm really embarrassed — it just suddenly all felt a bit much."

I hugged her, my sympathetic smile masking sadness at my own situation.

After Mr and Mrs, it was time to tell funny stories about Jess. I had forgotten about this part of the night. My mind went blank, as Fiona told a story about how when they were teenagers, Jess got so drunk she staggered off the train, her trousers around her ankles. There were so many things we had been through, since university onwards, and I couldn't think of a thing.

"Your turn!" Rachel ordered me.

"Um, how do you think Jess is linked to a comedy TV programme?" I blurted out.

Instant laughter. "Oh, it was for that slot about quirky media titles," giggled Vicky. "They don't do it now, but do you remember they used to name a niche magazine or newspaper title?"

"Yep," laughed Fiona. "Wasn't it for the first magazine you worked on Jess, about forklift trucks, or something like that?"

Squeals and snorts of laughter around the table. I was relieved that I had done an okay job, coming up with something and making everyone laugh. Tick, tick, tick.

I glanced over at Jess, expecting her to also be laughing but her cheeks were crimson, her mouth in a straight line. "We can't all be as lucky as you and land a job on a women's magazine, Eve," she said. "Forklift trucks are an important part of the construction and logistics business."

"Oh, Jess . . . I didn't mean to upset . . ." I was flustered, but Louise interjected, "At least our magazine is slightly better than that, eh Jess — just! You've gone up in the ranks. From trucks to pensions!"

And then Jess was laughing, her eyes crinkled.

Everyone hit the dancefloor. It was eighties night — my secret guilty pleasure but I knew that I had to get away when Tiffany's "I Think We're Alone Now" made my eyes well up. Mumbling my excuses and giving Jess a fierce hug, I pushed past sweaty bodies and headed to the waiting line of taxis.

They would be relieved anyway, I thought sourly as I gave the driver the address, the wretched soul raining on their happiness parade.

The cottage was pitch black and I fumbled quickly for the light, relieved when it blared on, even though it made me squint. I hesitated at the kitchen bar, filled with bottles of alcohol of various stages of liquid and quickly poured myself a finger of gin. I couldn't be bothered to find tonic water.

I ran up the two flights of stairs and closed the door of my attic room with relief. I got through it. I could cross it off my list tomorrow and focus on my flat move next week.

The room looked different, but I couldn't put my finger on why. Shrugging it off I quickly got into my PJs and took a swig of gin. And then I saw the configuration of the pillows on the double bed. Three pillows piled up on one side and on the side that I had been sleeping on last night, just one pillow. Just as you and I always slept. It was a running joke between us — I only liked one pillow and you piled up as many as possible. Since you'd been gone, I always slept with two.

I had not left the bed like this.

"Are you here?" I spun around the room frantically. But then I paused. Maybe it was me. On autopilot. I couldn't remember making the bed, and I was in a fluster cutting my foot, so I could well have made the bed up like that without thinking. That had to be it.

Still, I downed the rest of my gin quickly and left the bedside light on when I eventually lay down.

A creak pierced my foggy, sleep-addled brain. Then another. Instantly my limbs tensed, and my eyes snapped wide open, alert. There it was again. Someone was coming up the stairs. I had no idea what time it was, if the others were back, I might still be on my own in this huge cottage. There was a silence, punctuated by the blood pounding in my ears. Then again, a stealthy step. Whoever it was, was almost upon me. Yet still I couldn't move. The door opened and my mouth opened in a silent scream.

It was Vicky. She was dressed in cute flowery pyjamas, her eyes wide open but unseeing, black mascara smudged underneath. Relief made me shiver all over. She was sleep-walking. My limited knowledge meant I knew I shouldn't just wake her so I took her hand to guide her into my bed, but she shuddered and gasped.

"Sorry Ian," she mumbled.

"Vic, it's me, Eve, you've been sleepwalking, are you okay?" I asked softly.

Vicky's unseeing eyes slowly became alert. "Oh sorry. Sorry, Eve."

"No problem." I drew her into my bed and lay the covers over her as I snuggled in, limbs weak with relief. "I didn't know that you sleepwalked, Vicky."

"Oh, I do, only very occasionally but since I was little, it happens when I'm upset or worried." Vicky spoke slowly. She looked shocked herself.

"What are you upset about?" I might as well go for the jugular.

"Ian." Vicky didn't miss a beat, but she still didn't seem 100 per cent awake. "I was so happy when we got engaged, but we'd only been dating for a few months, I wasn't in a good place and I was so happy to meet someone, to make me forget. But now I think we rushed it; I don't think we know each other well enough; I don't think I want to marry him."

Tears rolled down her face. She was properly awake now.

"Oh, Vic. I'm sorry. Why weren't you in a good place?" Truthfully, I wasn't surprised. Vicky getting engaged to Ian so quickly had seemed out of character for someone usually so cautious and used to weighing things up and agonising over the smallest decisions.

"Because I'd met someone and had a brief thing and he finished it, I was so upset and I don't really want to go into it to be honest. I fell head over heels. So, I couldn't believe my luck when I met Ian, there was an instant attraction and I felt comfortable with him. But we don't have a lot in common, I've now realised; he doesn't want to go to the theatre, isn't particularly interested in walking, and you know I love walking and rambling. But it's not just that — he doesn't make me laugh, not like others have."

You loved the theatre and walking, and your droll sense of humour made me laugh so much. I could end up with an Ian too.

Vicky being devastated over a "brief thing" also didn't sound like her. She kept her emotions close to her chest and I had never known her so upset about a boyfriend. She didn't usually deploy dramatic vocabulary like "head over heels", so she must have felt a lot for the one-before-Ian. I opened my mouth to probe about him, then closed it again. I must admit I was curious about what happened, but it wasn't fair to question her when she had made it clear she didn't want to talk about it. And I knew how private she was and how she hated being questioned about her personal life.

"You don't have to marry Ian." I wasn't sure what else to say.

"I think that seeing Jess so happy this weekend has really drummed in these doubts and I think that's why I sleep-walked," Vicky continued as if I hadn't spoken. "I haven't done that for years."

"I heard some strange noises last night — sounds like breathing and movement on the landing. Was that you?"

"I'm not sure. But it could well have been. In the past I have occasionally got out of bed sleepwalking and managed to make my way back, still in my sleep," Vicky said.

I was relieved. Out of nowhere a true-life feature I once wrote flashed into my head: *My fiancé caused me to sleepwalk.* Now wasn't the time to mention that.

"Lie down." I laid a comforting arm around her. Another thought occurred. "Vicky, my bed was laid out in a weird way today. Do you know if anyone has been in this room?"

Vicky looked surprised.

"A cleaner comes in to tidy and make the beds," she proffered weakly.

* * *

Eve always has to get one up on me. Despite all the sadness, she still comes up trumps with her shiny new column for the magazine. I notice she hasn't talked about the other side of John vanishing. Me and . . . well let's call it my 'work'. I'm aiming for a mention in that super column of hers.

CHAPTER 22

"Right, that's the last of it!" Matt the packer slammed a grubby hand on top of one of ten boxes in the living room. Your life and mine had been reduced to sterile containers throughout an empty, musty-smelling flat. My sadness was tinged with relief. No more memories clutching me round the throat in every room. The packers had saved me the tedious job of packing, but they had also saved me finding things and rooting through your belongings. My earlier desire to raid your stuff for clues had been drenched. Maybe that was a good sign. *I won't be Julie, I won't be Julie.*

I wanted a normal life, a chance of happiness, a flat that didn't make me think of loss every time I entered it.

I'd only just thanked Matt when the doorbell rang. I flung it open expecting my parents, who were coming down to help me move. Instead, Grace stood there. Her hair was more platinum blond than ever — she must have just had it done.

"Oh . . . hi," I croaked, hoping I didn't betray the fact that I would rather she was anywhere but on my doorstep.

Rationally, I couldn't believe that she had anything to do with your disappearance now. But I still felt uneasy. Skintight jeans showed off her toned muscular thighs. Her sexiness made me question you and what you were attracted to. Maybe you liked her overt sexuality. That made me uncomfortable, as did the sadness of her mother's dementia.

I was admonishing myself as she said, "I just wanted to say goodbye." She shifted from foot to foot (sunshine yellow slippers adorned her feet). "And I want to wish you all the best. You've been through a terrible time."

Guilt ripped through me as I recalled her mince pies and my lukewarm reaction.

"Thank you so much." I tried to inject as much warmth as possible into my voice. "I appreciate your support, I really do."

"Don't give up, I think he is still out there." Grace smiled then turned and thudded away. I closed the door quietly.

"Right then, we'll be back at nine tomorrow morning to start loading," Matt informed me as he and fellow packer Mike pulled on their coats.

No sooner had they gone than my parents arrived. Mum had a look of grim determination on her face. "Don't worry, the packers have done everything, there's nothing left for you to do," I said reassuringly as I took their coats and bags.

"Robert, put the kettle on, please." Mum stared meaningfully at Dad, and he scuttled off to do her bidding.

"What's wrong?" I followed Mum to the sitting room. She sank onto the plastic covered sofa.

"I'm starting to get quite angry at John," Mum said aggressively. "I felt so bad for him at first, but then I look at what he's done to you." She gestured in my direction. "What he did was cowardly." Her eyes turned to steel. "You can't let him ruin your life, you can't. Please use this move as a fresh start, to build your life up again, to be happy, please."

"I will, Mum. I will." My voice was hollow.

* * *

"That's the last of it." Matt laid his hand on a random box. The wooden floor was golden and gleaming, and the glass doors stretched invitingly to the balcony. The walls were a crisp white. The move had finished — my parents and I had about twenty boxes to unpack but I could cope with that. I wanted to focus my mind firmly on the present, moving my hands to unpack and rip open boxes, no time for other thoughts to come in.

My mother loved to get stuck into tidying, cleaning and unpacking — anything to do with the home. I waited for her to get going.

"Come on, Robert, let's get this underway," she said dramatically.

Mustn't be sad, mustn't be sad. I watched as they disappeared to my new kitchen to start putting my crockery away.

I was celebrating my new flat and new beginnings, but you were hovering, John, just out of reach. How could I ever move on and put it behind me when I didn't know what happened to you and if you were gone forever?

* * *

It came the next day. Of course, it would. The address was printed this time, the envelope crisp and white. Such a nice card, with a picture of a cosy house atop a hilltop. *Happy new home* was emblazoned in red letters just above the smoke rising from the neat black chimney. I opened the card slowly, steeling myself for the hit.

You can run but you can't hide

A cliché, but it panicked me none the less. How did they know my new address . . . I had signed up to the postal redirection service but the envelope bypassed this with my new address printed on it. It had to be someone who knew me.

"Here we go," Mum squawked as she jogged into the room brandishing a bottle of champagne, Dad following her. In her eagerness to pour, she slopped champagne down my glass stem.

"Cheers," she bellowed. "What a fabulous flat! Here's to a happy, fresh start!"

She gulped her drink, her eyes beseeching. She wanted this to be the truth and so did Dad and I. But you might as well have been standing in the middle of the room. I hastily hid the card under a cushion, until I could move it to my box of 'evidence', when my phone beeped with a message.

I hope your move went well. Mum wants to see your new flat. Any chance we could pop round tomorrow? As Mum is staying with me in London this weekend, so it would be easier. Sophie.

Friendly and chatty as usual. The blunt ending of "Sophie" was a dig. I tried to shake off my rising anger.

"Jill and Sophie want to come around tomorrow, but we'll still be unpacking probably and sorting this place out, it's not very convenient," I grumbled.

Mum's face softened. Despite her angry words about you, she was desperately sorry for Jill, no doubt imagining herself in her shoes.

"Well, you must have them over," she said. "We can pop out if you want."

"Oh no, the more people the better," I said quickly. "You know I've never really got on with Sophie. She's been even more horrible since John went."

Mum patted me on the arm. "Nevertheless, you must make them feel welcome," she repeated.

Sighing, I tapped out a curt message. Two could play at that game.

"We're treating you tonight," Mum continued. "Dinner at that lovely little Italian down the road."

The card was burning a hole through the cushion.

I mustered a smile.

* * *

"Well, this flat is really quite something!" Jill weaved her way through some boxes and sank down on to the sofa. The joy and admiration she did her best to inject into her voice did not hide the hollow undertones. Her hair had grown in nicely since I had last seen her, grey curls tumbled round her face. Her hair had been a rich chestnut colour before she lost it through the chemo. She must have decided to stop dyeing it. Her face was pale, with strong grey circles under her eyes. I wondered with alarm if something was wrong again with her health, if the cancer was back.

"Such a lovely flat, I had always hoped you would buy something like this with John." Her health wasn't behind the way she looked, I realised. It was grief.

Mum and Dad bustled in with tea and a cafetière. "Now, let me put this down." I cleared an assorted pile of books, papers and letters off the coffee table.

Dad put the mugs down. "I'll just go and get the biscuits."

"No, no, we'll get that." Sophie jumped up and beckoned me. I followed reluctantly. Sophie never actively sought out time with me on my own. I wondered what she wanted. I knew it wouldn't be good.

Sophie closed the kitchen door and took the plate of biscuits Mum and Dad had prepared.

"Very nice flat," she said conversationally.

"Yes," I murmured, noticing that Sophie looked better than when I had last seen her. She had put on a little weight, and she had some colour in her cheeks.

"You must be delighted to be able to afford something like this on your own. In fact, I'm surprised that you can, a flat like this in Tooting which everyone knows is so expensive nowadays," Sophie said smoothly. "You must have had a huge deposit," she added.

I placed my hands onto the kitchen counter, ready to confront her, but she had turned away, walking back to the living room with the biscuits.

Guilt at using mine and your joint savings to buy the flat reared its head. Sophie suspected. That was why she had come round, to worry me, not because Jill wanted to see the flat.

But the savings were in both our names, surely that meant that I had done nothing wrong? Surely I couldn't be done for that? You had disappeared. The most that could happen was for me to repay you some of the savings if you came back. If. If you came back and did not want to live with me.

* * *

"I love it!" Jess did a little jig in my living room while Rachel smiled approvingly from the sofa. "What a gorgeous flat and in Tooting too, such a great place!"

"Yes, property has shot up here, you'll make tons of money on this place," Rachel said, ever the sensible accountant.

"How are you feeling, now you live here?" Jess asked as I bent to refill her and Rachel's wine glasses. I paused while I collected my thoughts.

"Better than I did," I said firmly. "I always thought that it would be such a wrench to leave the other flat, with all my memories of John, but actually it's a relief. But mixed emotions. I always wanted to be on the property ladder but with him."

Tears threatened to erupt. They were never far away these days. Before Jess and Rachel could say anything, I jumped up.

"Something I want to show you." Opening the inbuilt cupboard door, I extracted my new house card from the purple file.

"What do you think?" I watched them closely.

"This is nice . . ." Then Jess opened the card and her face fell. "Oh . . . not nice."

Rachel's mouth opened. "Ominous," she said. "Or trying to be."

Jess shook her head, her mouth a tight line.

Amid my whirling emotions I felt the buds of satisfaction spring up. People — they — had tried to deny that this was happening to me, had smoothed it over. I hadn't even told them everything. Rachel had seen my bouquet in Northumberland and so was probably more open to believing me. I eyed her closely again. She certainly seemed shocked. As did Jess.

"Tell the police," Jess burst out. Then: "Do you have any idea who it is?"

"I think it's Sophie," I said instantly, surprising myself. I had not even acknowledged to myself that Sophie had now powered forward to be suspect number one.

The night was dominated by talk about everything that had happened to me since you disappeared and we were no closer to solving the mystery, apart from agreeing it could not be you.

The consensus was that it could well be Sophie. Rachel was drawing up notes about everything that had gone on. I was glad that they had finally become interested in the sinister happenings since you left. But there was a spark of guilt that I was dominating the conversation.

"Jess, your wedding is in a few weeks!" I exclaimed. "Let's talk about something happy and nice, I don't want to dominate with my negative, miserable time."

There was one hurdle to get through before that. The anniversary of your disappearance.

Jess raised her shoulders and put her arm round me. "I don't know what to say," she said. "Yes, it's coming, and I am stressed and anxious and excited, I guess all the things you are when getting married! But I want to talk about you, Eve, and the awful things that are happening.

"And I know it's coming up to a year." She glanced over at Rachel. They had obviously both been talking about it.

"I cannot believe that . . ." The incredulity and sadness in her voice brought a lump to my throat.

"I can't either," I whispered. I took a deep breath.

"I should be trying to have a fresh start, with the new place, despite that thing." I glanced at the card, laid face down on the coffee table. "And I don't think John is coming back, but I want that more than anything."

I felt so heavy, weighed down with it all, I slumped back against the sofa cushions.

"You shouldn't give up," Jess said fiercely. "A year in the scheme of things is nothing — you must keep trying, we will *all* keep trying, giving out leaflets, going to matches, whatever, we can't give up."

Deluded Jess. "I've tried that," I wanted to shout. I've done the notices in newsagents, the leaflets, going to a football match on a lead and getting sod-all from it, pacing round a cold city, visiting hostels, doing press interviews, my magazine column. And nothing.

You had missed an entire year, you had missed our wedding day, you had missed me — *us* — buying our own property. You had missed us trying for a baby. I could have been pregnant now. My life had stood still for a year. I had trodden water. I felt like I was always going to tread water.

But she was right.

"Of course, I will keep trying," I said quietly. *But I will not be Julie, I will not be Julie, I won't.*

I changed the subject, to something that had been niggling at me since the hen do.

"I'm not sure if I'm betraying her confidence, but I'm worried about Vicky," I said hesitantly. "Do you two know what's going on with her?"

"No." Jess sat up, looking alert.

Rachel raised her shoulders. "She mentioned she and Ian had been having a few arguments when we were at the hen do."

"Okay." I took a deep breath. "I'm not sure I should be telling you, but she never said not to tell anyone, so here goes . . ."

I ran through the events of the last night of Jess's hen do. The sleepwalking, Vicky's acknowledging that she wanted to break it off with Ian, that it seemed to be a rebound. I didn't mention the layout of my bed and pillows.

Jess clapped a hand to her mouth. "That's awful," she said. "I had no idea."

"I didn't either," Rachel said slowly. "But I do know that she was seeing someone last year, she really liked him, but he was living with someone, and she was really torn up about it. I mean, she felt terrible about it, and then gave him an ultimatum, but he chose to stay with his girlfriend. She was devastated. I was surprised that she met Ian so quickly and got so serious, given how upset she was."

"Well, I knew none of this." Jess exhaled slowly.

"Me neither, apart from what happened the other night," I said. "I'm surprised she'd get involved with someone who had a partner though, she's always been so moral and, well, quite strait-laced, I guess."

"She only told me about it because she came to stay for the night at mine," said Rachel. "She was ashamed. She really fell for him though. I guess sometimes it's hard to live up to your morals when you're in love."

I nodded in agreement, surprised. It was unusual for Rachel to speak so empathetically about emotions.

* * *

Eve thought she was escaping me. She was so excited about the move. But I popped her bubble. I still knew where she was. She was shocked to get my card welcoming her to her new home. I'll always know where Eve is.

CHAPTER 23

The organ played gently in the background. My hands were clasped so tightly around my handbag that the veins stood out. The last thing to get through and then I would be free. I repeated those words over and over. You should have been sitting beside me, a wedding ring glinting on both our fingers. Instead, Vicky sat stiffly beside me. She didn't look in the best shape either. The engagement ring on her finger had gone. I hadn't had the chance to speak to Vicky, as, in contrast to most people, I had come up that morning on the train. The wedding was in Clewesham, a small town in the Sussex Downs and did not take long to get to from London. I felt guilty that I didn't come up last night, but I couldn't face the cloud of excitement surrounding the bride, the happiness on everyone's faces, Jess's proud parents.

Should have been me, should have been me, should have been me, thumped along with every heartbeat.

Luckily, Jess understood. "That's a shame, a few of us are going for a meal, but don't worry about it," she said. "I understand."

The sunlight dappled through the stained-glass windows of the church. It was an ancient building down a cobbled street. It was the first time that I had stepped into a church since you left. I wanted it to cure me, to soothe my troubled soul. I wasn't religious but putting down the order of service, I clutched the pew and closed my eyes.

"Please God, please God, let me be happy again, let me find peace."

I had just realised that I hadn't asked for you to come back when Vicky's voice was in my ear: "You okay?"

She didn't look okay. Her face was pale with a yellowish tinge, despite the foundation. Her mouth was drawn down. No doubt I looked the same.

"Just saying a little prayer," I whispered.

"Oh right." Vicky looked uncomfortable. She rubbed her foot up and down her leg. "It can't be easy for you." She flung her hand vaguely around the church. "All this."

I opened my mouth. I swayed between wanting to pour out my emotions to clamming up and pushing it all away. This time I wanted to let it out. It seemed like Vicky had the same idea. "It's hard for me too," she muttered.

"I meant to say, Vicky, Jess and Rachel said that you weren't with Ian any more, I'm so sorry."

"Thanks," Vicky mumbled. "I called it off. I doubt you're surprised after what happened at the hen do. I just couldn't go through with it."

I touched Vicky's arm. "You did the right thing."

She continued, "It was rebound, I think I told you that I was with someone before. It was never going to work but I was mad for him, we had such a connection, I have never felt like that . . ."

"Hi, ladies." Clive slipped into the pew beside us. Vicky's face instantly closed. Cursing his bad timing, I exchanged awkward kisses.

"You're cutting it a bit fine," I said, tapping my watch.

Clive shrugged. "Ha, well, the bride isn't here yet, nor, obviously, the bridesmaids — I can't wait to see Rachel all togged up in her bridesmaid gear!" He chortled eagerly, pulling at his tie.

189

Their relationship was going from strength to strength, I noted — but my thoughts came to an abrupt stop as I realised the colour of his tie was lilac, the tie that was meant for our wedding, in fact.

"Why are you wearing that tie?" I pointed at it. The organ broke into "Morning Has Broken". "That was for us, for John and me, at our wedding. Why are you wearing it?"

Clive wiped a clammy forehead. He was always sweaty.

"Sorry if it upsets you, I'm so tactless — is that the right word? — sometimes." He banged his forehead. "But honestly, I didn't mean it like that. I wanted to honour John, I hated the thought of his, your tie, lying in a drawer, forgotten and sad. I thought if I wore it today, it would be a nod to him. He should have been here, I thought I was acknowledging that with the tie." He pulled it again sheepishly.

"It's okay, your best intentions were in place." I sighed, averting my eyes from him. I couldn't bear the flash of that colour.

"So, this is great, isn't it? Rach is so excited," Clive continued. He had no idea when to stop.

I glanced over to the front of the church. Jack was pacing around, looking nervous. His best man, his brother Joshua, looked like he was trying to make him laugh.

I scrutinised Jack. He always reminded me of the little brother I never had. Spiky hair, glasses, slightly geeky-looking. He had asked me out before Jess. I hesitated, ummed and ahhed, as after all he was so nice. Too nice.

"Well, they're a bit late, aren't they?" boomed Clive, glancing at his watch.

"Brides always run late," said Vicky loftily. "It's only five minutes."

The organist broke into another music piece. I picked up the order of service, to be confronted by a happy, loving photo of Jess and Jack at the top, arm in arm and grinning widely. I flung the pamphlet down, hating myself as I did so.

The talking got louder in the church. People were getting a bit restless, most having arrived at least half an hour early.

Just get on with it, I thought with a flash of anger. *Goodness, Jess, do you have to make a big scene, taking ages getting ready?*

I held the pew. I needed to get a grip. I needed to get through the day and then it was another milestone I could put behind me.

The organist paused.

Clive glanced towards the back of the room.

"They're taking a while." He forced a guffaw of laughter. "Her hair must be taking ages."

Jack was moving from foot to foot, hands clenched. His best man whispered in his ear with a forced grin. Jack couldn't raise a smile. I looked at my watch. It was coming up to half an hour.

"Brides are always late!" I uttered a falsetto laugh. "And Jess has gone to town — make-up artist, amazing veil to get into, it'll be that."

I hoped that I didn't sound too bitter. I hoped that she would stop messing around and make an appearance soon. I wanted this whole thing over.

"Do you think everything's okay?" Vicky wondered, glancing at her watch. "I mean they're staying five minutes' walk away."

"It'll be fine." I brushed it off, watching Jack. He was speaking with his parents, his forehead so furrowed I could see it from my seat.

His mum looked calm, stroking his arm. I knew exactly what she would be saying — don't worry, brides are always late — and his face became more relaxed as she spoke.

Clive was scanning his phone. "No text from Rach, so guess all okay."

"Of course it is," I said irritably. *Hurry up, Jess.*

The organist paused again and wiped her face. She spent a while flipping through her music book. The chatter in the church was loud without the organ. The vicar stood in the corner, looking nonplussed. Even Jack's mum looked anxious now. I looked at my watch. Forty-five minutes late.

"I hope they're okay," Clive said, tapping out a text to Rachel.

"Of course they are, it's a five-minute walk," I snapped.

Clive's face twisted in unexpected irritation. "I know that, Eve, no need to jump down my throat."

"Sorry." I was contrite, despite the fact that he thoughtlessly wore the tie that symbolised my wedding, which was now being twisted in his large fingers. "Just stressful, isn't it?" I gave a weak smile.

"Sorry." Clive removed his chubby fingers from the tie that you and I had taken so long to choose, poring over the exact colours. "I am being a bit over the top, it's just that we — I mean, me and Rachel — thought Jess seemed a bit downcast last night, but probably just wedding nerves." He gave a nervous cough.

Jack stood very, very still at the front of the church. I felt a wave of sympathy. The women in front of me, I wasn't sure which side of the family they were from, were straining their necks towards the entrance of the church, which unfortunately held no sign of the bride lingering outside it.

"Fifty minutes," Vicky murmured. She looked anxious; her thoughts seemingly pulled away from her own situation.

The organist laid her hands on the keys. It looked like she had given up for the time being. Then there was a creak — the door to the church opened and in stepped Jess's mum, Jenny, and Rachel, clad in a pale green bridesmaid dress. Jenny had a fetching yellow hat perched on her dark hair. Staring straight ahead, the two marched quickly down the aisle.

"What the . . ." Clive murmured.

A silence. Rachel's heels click-clacked on the stone floor.

I watched, almost mesmerised. Jenny swept Jack and the vicar before her and they, with Rachel, disappeared behind the pulpit.

Talking broke out. Voices rising and falling.

"What the . . ." Clive repeated, a drop of perspiration dripping on to his crisp white shirt. I was glad the tie escaped.

The vicar emerged from behind the pulpit.

He strode to the pulpit, grim-faced, as an expectant silence washed over the room.

"I am very sorry to have to announce that unfortunately the bride has called off the wedding. I am very sorry indeed."

Jack, Jenny and Rachel had crowded out of the internal door. I thought I saw a tear streaking down Jack's face. I felt terrible for my earlier thoughts in the church. Next to me, Vicky looked stricken.

"You may all leave, in your own time." The vicar gestured vaguely with his hands.

In silence, we left the pew. Jess's behaviour about her wedding skidded through my mind and I realised that I wasn't actually surprised. All the "John leaving has made me think . . ." this was where it had led.

I touched Rachel's arm outside the church.

"What happened?"

The sun shone down, making her squint in my direction. A beautiful day for a wedding.

"I don't know," Rachel said helplessly. She shrugged. "She was quiet last night. This morning, she looked awful, barely spoke and then announced, out of nowhere, that she just couldn't do it. She gave no explanation. God, we all tried to persuade her, but she was having none of it. She just kept staring straight ahead, saying she couldn't do it." Rachel looked and sounded shaken.

"Can I see her?" I asked.

"I guess. She's in her room at the hotel."

"Want me to come too? I will, but actually, I feel quite cross." Rachel squared her shoulders. "She had months to cancel. It is not fair on poor Jack."

Typical, straight-talking Rachel. I felt a rush of affection for her. I touched her shoulder.

"I'll go on my own. I know where the hotel is."

"Okay. Room 10. On the first floor."

As I turned to go, I caught sight of Jack standing just outside the church. His mum's arm was interlinked with his, and his dad framed him on the other side. He looked at me, dazed.

It didn't take long to get to the hotel — a few minutes' walk down cobbled streets. A graceful Regency building confronted me, the perfect place to spend your wedding night, I thought, as I entered the light and airy lobby.

I walked up the stairs and heard muffled voices. I paused and then knocked with some trepidation on the door.

"Come in," called Jess's dad, Brian. I hoped I wasn't intruding as I entered softly.

Jess was still in her wedding dress, bridal make-up on, hair pulled back. She looked beautiful. She stood up when she saw me and I noticed again how much weight she had lost, her waist slender in the simple gown, with its delicate lace sleeves.

"Oh, Eve, hello," Brian sighed. He looked smart in his suit. He rubbed a hand over his eyes. "What a pickle, eh, what a pickle."

I thought Jess would have lost it, be crying and falling over herself trying to explain, but she was dry-eyed and silent.

"I had better go to the church, speak to people, see that poor boy." Brian flashed a glance at Jess, but she was unmoved. "See you later."

He shuffled reluctantly out of the room, probably dreading the confrontation that awaited him outside the church. I wanted to hug Jess, tell her it was all okay, but she was cool, calm and composed so it didn't feel right. I sank on to the bed.

"Are you okay? What on earth happened?"

Jess sat down stiffly in the chair by the window.

"I've had doubts for months and months. In fact, I wonder if I ever felt like he was right for me, even at the start, but of course I could be over-analysing things."

"This is why you kept saying to me that what happened to John made you think about your relationship, this is why you were crying at your hen do," I interjected.

Jess nodded.

"But surely John going missing didn't lead to you realising that you didn't want to marry Jack?" I carried on.

I was annoyed — I couldn't put my finger on why at first, but it came as Jess opened her mouth to start speaking. Your disappearance was the most devastating thing that had ever happened to me. *So don't try to claim it as your life event. It's mine,* my mind whispered. I felt ridiculously possessive, somehow, of your act.

"I don't understand why John disappearing would make you leave Jack," I almost snapped.

"I don't know." Jess shook her head. "It just opened a can of worms in my head, you know how a shocking event can make you think."

I shrugged, still feeling angry.

"And it made me realise that life is too short to just carry on the same path when you are not happy . . ."

"Maybe John felt like that too, maybe that's why he left. You make me think you're endorsing what John did, that he didn't love me and was right to leave," I said, my voice hard.

Jess put her hand up. "No, no, I'm not, I honestly don't mean that. And if it were about you, he would just have finished with you, not gone missing." She paused. "Sorry, I'm not explaining it well. It — when he left, I saw how devastated you were and how much you loved him, and I realised I would not have been like that if Jack had disappeared, as distressing as such an act is."

"Okay." I was slightly mollified, trying to ignore the ache that had started again in my chest. "But why do you think you went off him or never loved him enough?" I pressed on.

"I don't know really, I'm just not sure I was ever really attracted enough to him, it was like we were really great mates."

"But at our age it shouldn't just be about lust, friendship counts for a lot," I interrupted. Then I wondered if you hadn't agreed with me. I thought you were the closest person to me, but you can't have felt the same way.

"I'm not talking about lust specifically." Jess sighed. "I know that's childish. But I wanted to feel more, I felt I was settling, and he was starting to irritate me. Trivial things that I used to find endearing annoyed me more and more, like when he screwed up his face when he was thinking and sometimes looked really vacant . . ." She trailed off. "I'm sorry, I sound awful. I tried to bury it, and I did succeed, like I did get excited at the hen and when I was choosing my dress, but then I realised that it was more about the wedding and then I moved from looking forward to dreading this day.

"This morning, I felt such a weight on my chest, but I thought, I can't do that to Jack, and my parents have spent all this money, I will get through it, perhaps it will all be okay. But I felt worse and worse and when I got into my dress, I realised I couldn't go through with it, I physically couldn't. I just blurted it out to Rachel as we were getting ready. Luckily, Jack's sister was in another room."

"What did Rachel say? Was she shocked?"

"Yes, she kept trying to say it was wedding nerves, but I was adamant. I simply couldn't, can't do it."

For the first time Jess's composure slipped slightly. "Then I told Mum and Dad."

"Bet that went down well."

Jess smiled ruefully. "They were horrified. And Dad kept banging on about the cost."

"So how do you feel now?" I asked. "You seem so composed; do you feel bad about Jack? Sorry, that's not a criticism," I added quickly. "And sorry I feel like I'm in journalism mode interviewing you! I don't mean it like that."

"No, I don't mind, it helps me straighten out my thoughts," Jess said pensively. "I feel awful about Jack, but I'm actually relieved at the same time. I know my life as I know it has changed, but my relief outweighs guilt and sadness."

"I guess you've been suppressing these feelings for so long, you will feel like that," I offered, wondering if you had felt like that. *Stop it, stop it. This is about Jess now, you don't belong in this moment.*

Jess nodded and jumped up. "Help me out of my dress?"

I patiently untied the ribbons that laced up the back.

Jess stepped out of her dress and flung it on the floor. I stopped myself gathering it up and smoothing out the crumples.

"You've lost weight," I marvelled, watching as she pulled on jeans and a T-shirt.

"Yes, and not just through dieting for the wedding," Jess said. "All the stress over Jack . . . at least I get something out of it, not the fat girl any more, hey." Her voice was hard.

"You were never the fat girl, I hope you don't mean something by that, that I thought you were," I exclaimed. Jess was acting out of character, I almost felt I didn't know her. The normal Jess would have been crying and hugging and warm with make-up smeared on her face.

"Oh, come on, everyone thought I was chunky." Her upper lip was raised, like a snarl but then it was gone as soon as I blinked. She grabbed an opened champagne bottle and slopped it into two used glasses.

"Was meant to be for celebrating the wedding, but who cares."

I held my glass uncomfortably. Jess raised her glass.

"To new beginnings." Her voice was flat.

* * *

"I can't believe it." A bead of sweat dripped down the side of Clive's face. He was always hot and sweaty, I thought with some irritation. How could Rachel be attracted to him? I watched as Rachel clutched his knee and he draped his arm round her. We were sitting in the local pub. Vicky was with us too. We'd debated whether to go back to London but Rachel, ever the pragmatist, had said that as we had paid for the hotel rooms, we might as well stay the night. But it was more than that — we wanted to be all together, chewing it over, not in our individual places back at home.

I wasn't sure where Jack and his family were, probably they had got the hell out of the town. We had asked Jess if she wanted to join us. She was tempted, and I could see her eyes light up briefly. But she reluctantly said that she needed to be with her mum and dad. They were really not happy.

"I mean, they seemed so happy," Clive blundered on, taking a large swig of his pint.

"No, I don't think so," I said straightaway. "She has actually shown her doubts a lot the last few months — Rachel, did you notice? She seemed subdued and down about the wedding and repeated a few times that John leaving made her think." I swallowed down the irritation that rose as I spoke.

"Well," Rachel frowned, "she never said that to me, but I did think she seemed downcast at certain times, like shopping for the bridesmaid dresses." She took a sip of wine. "I think she's made a mistake regardless," she said. "They were good together."

"But not if she felt she had fallen out of love with him," Vicky burst out. She took a large gulp of her gin and tonic. "I felt it wasn't right with Ian and I called it off. Jess has done the same thing."

"Er, bit different. You didn't get to the altar," Rachel said dryly.

Vicky flushed. "It was a hard decision," she said. "Just because we didn't get to the aisle didn't mean it wasn't really traumatic."

"More so for him," Rachel said bluntly — then realising her error, she added, "Sorry, sorry, of course it must have been terrible for you too, I didn't mean it like that."

We rushed on; nobody wanted to talk about Vicky's broken engagement with the blow of Jess calling off the wedding.

"She implied to me that a major reason was because of John disappearing, said it made her analyse her relationship and she realised she wasn't happy," I said cautiously, testing the water. I tried to swallow the lump of resentment that appeared in my throat.

"Makes sense." Clive drained the remnants of his pint. "Made me think about things too, like life's too short to be messing around . . ." He gave Rachel a sloppy grin.

"Well, it looks like it had the opposite effect on you to Jess," I said grimly.

Rachel said, "Maybe that was the trigger but there must have been more to it than that."

Suddenly Vicky gripped my arm. "Look," she mouthed.

Weaving their way through the pub were Jack, his parents and his sister, who held his arm tightly. Jack was staring at the floor, but he looked up briefly and saw us. He hesitated, then letting go of his sister's arm, he moved slowly towards us.

Clive was on his feet, gripping Jack's arm and pumping his hand. "Mate, we are so sorry, I mean what a shock, never ever expected that in a million years." Then he floundered. He was like a great fat fish coming up for air. I cringed and glanced at Rachel; did she not find him irritating?

"Thanks," Jack interjected in a small voice. He had always been small and slim, but he seemed even slighter than usual; diminished. His hair, so smooth and tidy this morning, was sticking up wildly. His glasses were smeared.

"We're so sorry, so sorry," Rachel, Vicky and I all chorused. Rachel, normally so composed, must have felt flustered as she jumped awkwardly to her feet.

"I must admit I never thought I would get jilted at the altar," Jack attempted to joke.

"Oh mate, look, anything we can do, anything at all . . ." Clive started.

Shut up, my mind screamed.

Jack smiled politely. He turned to face me. "Could I have a quick word?"

A pause.

"Yes," I mumbled. What was this about?

I followed him outside. Jack headed to the low stone wall that surrounded the pub and sank down onto it. He fumbled in his pocket and brought out a packet of cigarettes and a lighter.

"I'd given up, but I think today counts as special circumstances," he said.

"Jack, I am so sorry," I started, unsure of what to say. "Can I help in any way?"

"Jess hasn't been acting right with me for weeks." Jack cut straight to the chase. He inhaled deeply. "You might not tell me, and I know your loyalties are to her, but did she say anything to you, before what happened today?"

"No." I shook my head. It was kind of the truth. "She never said anything directly, no."

"See, the interesting thing is, her behaviour started changing about six months before John went missing. Then when he went, it became dramatically more noticeable. I should have called off the wedding myself, but I loved her, I hoped it was wedding nerves, I don't know, I feel a fool now."

"How did she change?" I asked carefully.

Jack blew a smoke ring. "Distant, off, much less physically affectionate, seemed like her mind was elsewhere."

"She told me that John disappearing made her re-evaluate everything," I admitted. "And I did wonder if she was getting cold feet about getting married, at times."

Jack pursed his lips and shook his head. "Yes, she said that to me. Really angers me actually. Isn't it enough that selfish bloke wrecked your life, without destroying other people's."

He threw his cigarette lighter hard on the pavement.

"He won't wreck my life," I muttered.

"What?" Jack's voice was steely. "I don't think it helped that you went on to her all the time about it. That put thoughts in her head. Jesus, did you have to do that?"

I gasped, taken aback that soft and gentle Jack could sound so angry and cold.

"She was my best friend," I snapped back, my own annoyance rising rapidly. "Of course I spoke to her. If things had been right with you, it wouldn't make her re-evaluate her life."

Jack raised his cigarette butt menacingly above his head, staring at me. I shrank back, my hand protectively against my face. Surely, he wasn't going to throw it at me?

He made a *ppffft* noise and let his hand slump.

"Goodbye, Eve."

There was a note of finality in his voice. I watched as, hunched over, he sloped back into the pub. Shaken, I waited until he disappeared though the pub door before getting to my own feet.

"He's just taking his anger and hurt out on you," Vicky advised when I went back to sit down with the others.

"It's so unlike him," I said, glad when Clive plonked a fresh glass of wine for me on the table. I glanced about but couldn't see Jack and his family. They must be sitting at the back of the pub. "I found him threatening."

"The guy has just had the worst day of his life. He won't be himself," Rachel counselled.

What was worse, being jilted on your wedding day or your fiancé going missing, probably dead? I weighed it up in my mind. I knew which I would prefer.

CHAPTER 24

D-day. The day I had been dreading. An entire year since you went missing. I couldn't believe it. A whole year. I poured hot water into my little cafetière, and it was in front of my eyes again — the people, all those people surging from the doors of the underground train and not one of them you. It had been there from the minute I woke up that morning. The last glimpse of your dark hair standing up slightly on end, your slim shoulders encased in your beloved Adidas top. My breathing came fast as the panic of that day washed over me. It followed me as I showered, dressed, and made my coffee.

An entire year and just one supposed sighting of you at Crystal Palace. I didn't believe it was you. I tried to push the other possible clues about you from my mind — the cards, the flowers, the missing things, I didn't believe that was you either.

I took my coffee into the living room. The Missing Association had suggested that I raise more media awareness about the anniversary, but I refused. I was being selfish, but it hadn't worked the first time and it didn't work on our wedding day. Besides, I had my column to write. I would rather write my feelings myself, then relay them to someone else to write.

Instead, Sophie carried out the media interviews. She loftily implied that I was selfish and cowardly. I didn't care — I knew she was delighted to take the limelight. Her rightful place, as she saw it. *Let her get on with it.*

The letterbox slammed. The post was early. I stood up, foreboding washing over me. I wondered what surprise was waiting for me this time. I inched slowly down the corridor. Lying on the mat was a postcard. I picked it up. It was a cheesy card, with Seville plastered on it. I turned it over.

Seville. You loved Spain. You loved Seville. We had a wonderful holiday there shortly after we first met, wandering the narrow, cobbled streets, drinking wine in the piazzas. You were learning Spanish. Why did it never occur to me that you would go there? *Because your passport hasn't been taken.* Sharply turning over the postcard, I ripped off the redirection sticker to see if underneath I could see your precious handwriting, some hint that this was definitely you. My name and old address were printed, not written.

The rest of the back of the card was blank.

Tears streaked down my cheeks as I tried to make sense of it. Could this be you? A message to me that you were alive? The gentleness of the innocent postcard jarred sharply with the cruel messages and gifts I had been receiving since you went missing.

Despite the sadness I was relieved — this could be a positive sign that you were still here and that you weren't behind the sinister gifts and appearances. That you still cared and thought about me. That you wanted to give me a message. That you were alive.

I took the card back into the living room and stepped out onto the balcony.

The sun came out and I took a deep breath. I refused to believe that this was a message to me that you would return. But something shifted inside me, a turning point. That it was your decision. There was nothing that I could do about it. Just a few months previously, I would have been frantically packing a case, booking a flight, hell-bent on getting myself out there to try and find you, bring you home, despite the passport puzzle. Now I wasn't moving. You had made your choice. Now I needed to make the decision to get on with my life.

* * *

My phone rang at work. A withheld number. I hesitated but then quickly answered, as I always did when I didn't know the number, in case it was news about you.

"Hello."

"Ethan Thorpe from *London Daily Eye*."

"Oh, hi," I said slightly coldly, heart sinking. I hoped he did not want me to do any more coverage.

"Listen, I've been told that you're not keen to do any more coverage. But I wondered if I might be able to persuade you . . ."

"It's too late surely, the anniversary has been and gone," I said more abruptly than I meant to. *Leave me alone.*

"Well obviously that would have been ideal, but it was clear that you didn't want to be approached, and I thought I would wait a little, so that it wasn't so raw . . ."

"It's only a week later," I said grimly.

"Well, yes . . ."

Ethan's poise had slipped, and he sounded uncomfortable. "I wondered if I might be able to persuade you to speak to me again . . ."

I lost concentration as BlackRose80 came into my mind, the letters strong, black and menacing.

"No," I said sharply, interrupting him. Then feeling bad — after all, he had been nice — I added, "I'm sorry, that sounded rude, but actually, I don't think I need to. You're probably not aware, but I've started writing my own column about John's disappearance, and . . ."

"That's what I'm calling you about! We are very aware of your column, and we want to syndicate it, so we can run it in our newspaper. Would you be up for it?"

"Oh." I shook my head slightly, and a smile spread slowly across my face. "Really? Well, certainly from my side, but you would need to check with our publisher. I'm sure he would be pleased as it raises our magazine profile, but you would need to go through him."

"That's fine. Can you give me his details?"

I gave Paul's details, my heart light. I loved my job, my career, and now it was coming through for me — a reason to go on, to have a life without you.

I said goodbye and jumped up, pacing over to Paul's office to peek in and see if he was there.

"He's in France on a business trip for a few days," his PA informed me.

"Ah." I scuttled back to my desk. Oh well. I was practically sure he would say yes, but it would be nice to speak to him about it.

I pulled out my Dictaphone, intending to transcribe my interview with Ruby, whose dog had swallowed fifty stones but had survived (we were a bit thin on stories that week), but instead, I pulled up a new Microsoft Word document. I would write my column instead. It was all swimming in my head and I wanted to release it. I was at the point of New Year. New Year without you. *I was determined to go out, be with people and socialise* . . . I started tapping away.

My hands flew over the keyboard. Stopping for breath, I decided to click on my Instagram account for inspiration. My latest magazine column had been posted on Instagram and I checked it constantly, to see how many likes, views and comments I had. I gasped — almost one million views and eighty thousand likes.

"Thank you — a story that needs to be told, for all missing people out there." Tillylovescoffee

"My brother went missing five years ago. It brings me such comfort to read your columns. I am not alone." MaritimeSophie

I was helping people and raising the profile of this issue. I felt so grateful for the position my job had put me in, for the opportunities it gave me. I saw that I had a direct message. I opened it. And froze.

"You haven't mentioned me in your column yet. I'm waiting."
BlackRose80.

Their profile picture, unsurprising, a bouquet of black roses wrapped in red paper. Like the bouquet sent to me. I could barely breathe. My hands sank onto the keyboard. The desire to write my column was gone. There were no posts or followers, and I was the only one she was following. She was closing in on me, destroying my pleasure in my columns, in my affirmation that I had a life after you.

Her. She. I assumed the person was a woman. But it could be a man. It could be anybody in my life.

I scrolled through my phone to find the police number and walked quickly outside. As soon as my call was answered the words poured out of my mouth about the Instagram comment, the online message on my *London Daily Eye* article, and the "new home" card.

As with the black roses, the incidents were logged. I was told to call straightaway if anything else happened. I felt relieved that the police's concern had ramped up compared to my previous call.

I got back to my desk when Gemma stalked past me, giving me a frozen, throwaway look.

I tried and failed to continue writing my column, BlackRose80's message going round and round in my mind, when my phone rang.

"Hello?"

"Ethan here. I've heard back from your publisher already and he thinks it's a great idea! He's asked me to meet you to sort the details out."

"Ahhh." I sighed, torn between delight and unsettlement at what had happened earlier.

"Shall we do one night, over a drink, might be more relaxed?" Ethan spoke quickly.

"Umm. Oh okay."

I tried to conjure up Ethan in my mind, but he was vague. I remembered a cheery face, smiling hazel eyes and a mousy hair colour. Not like your beautiful indigo eyes and sculpted features, with hair so dark that it was almost black. So striking that your face was imprinted in my mind from the moment I met you. In contrast, I could barely remember Ethan.

Sadness and despair battled surprise and flattery. As they charged at each other I found myself saying coolly, "Thanks, yes, that would be nice. When do you want to meet?"

Two minutes later I laid my phone down on my desk in a daze. We were meeting on Friday, at seven in a pub near me in Tooting. What was I doing? The comparisons started again with you, not striking, not the charisma, not the characterful face . . . Then I remembered the postcard. The possible message from you to say that you cared for me, thought of me, but weren't coming back. That you left without a glance. That you thought about moving to Hong Kong without me.

My heart hardened and I relished the feeling. I was strong and powerful when I was angry. I deserved better, I deserved happiness. Ethan might not have your striking looks and charisma, but he wanted to meet me for a drink. He seemed kind.

Then I gave myself a shake, I was assuming he was interested in me. He might not be! This was for work and maybe he just fancied doing boring old transactional business over a drink.

I tried to place Ethan and BlackRose80 in a corner of my mind and focus on my plans that night. I was seeing Jess, Rachel and Vicky. It was our first meet-up since the wedding and I knew that Jess was struggling, despite being the one to call it off.

When I walked into our local in Tooting that evening, she was sitting at a table nursing a glass of red wine. The others had not arrived yet.

I hugged her firmly. "You okay?"

"Yes," Jess sighed. "I just feel so guilty. Jack's taking it really badly. I shouldn't have let it get to the stage I did. I should have finished it months before."

"It's hard," I offered weakly. "It must be so difficult confronting those feelings and then getting swept up in the wedding plans."

Jess nodded. "That's it. But I feel so bad, and my parents are so disappointed and have lost a lot of money and I just feel so sad in the flat. Even though I know that I don't want to marry him, all the memories in the flat make me depressed and it's difficult to move forward."

"Exactly how I felt." I paused as the despair and feelings of being haunted in my and your shared flat swept through me. Then I gave myself a mental shake. This was about Jess now; she had heard about my misery for months.

"What are you going to do about the flat, it must be tricky as you both own it?"

"I'm trying to buy him out, but he's being awkward, I don't blame him but if we reach an impasse, we might just have to put it on the market."

Vicky and Rachel turned up at the same time.

After a flurry of orders, Rachel slammed her hand on the table. "Vicky and I have been chatting on the way here and we think a girls' weekend away is in order, maybe Devon or somewhere on the coast, but anyway, somewhere lovely to chill and cheer Jess up."

Jess smiled. "Sounds lovely," she said. "Thanks for the suggestion, ladies."

"We were thinking in about two months' time?" Vicky said eagerly.

Their suggestions of location swept over me. What happened to me was much worse, Jess chose to leave Jack, you did not just leave our relationship, it was more . . . They never suggested a weekend away for me. I hated myself for my petty churlishness. It wasn't a competition.

"You okay?" Vicky asked. "You seem quiet."

I hesitated, then reached into my bag. I laid the post-card, slightly dog-eared from all my handling, on to the table. "I got this on the anniversary of John's disappearance."

Jess picked it up. "Spain," she said softly. "He loved it there, didn't he?" She turned it over and after seeing no clues there, turned it back.

"Looks like it is him," Rachel said.

I was surprised. "I thought you would say it was a hoax," I said.

"Why? I can't think who else it could be. Unless it is whoever was sending those sick things to you," she said. "But this is different. I don't think that the person who did that sent this."

I was so relieved that they believed it was you too that tears welled up.

"How does it make you feel?" Jess asked gently.

"Sad, relieved." I tried to weigh up which feeling was dominant.

"So, there's no more horrible happenings?" Rachel asked delicately.

"Well . . ." The Instagram message from BlackRose80 reared its head. I couldn't face telling them that night. It was too raw and I didn't want to feel more anxious and scared than I already was. I didn't want their pitying, surprised looks, raised eyebrows. I'd tell them another time.

"Not for a while." I touched the wooden table. "I was convinced that I would get something on the anniversary. But just this. I can't believe that something that should really have brought me to my knees has been a welcome surprise."

"Well, it's a contrast to those other awful things," Rachel said. "And it has hopefully given you a clue that he is still out there."

"The not knowing was the worst," I agreed.

"Hang on." Vicky leaned forward earnestly. "Are we sure that it is him? How can we know for sure? The person sending you this stuff sounds sick. Could they not have decided on a change of tack?"

Rachel's mouth widened and Jess bit her lip. They glanced at each other. It was surprising that she should say that; it was unlike cautious, careful Vicky. But then again, she had been through a break-up herself. And we weren't planning a girls' weekend to help her get over her relationship ending either.

Vicky continued, "And what about the fact that he never took his passport?"

"Why did you say that?" Rachel was exasperated. "What have you achieved by mentioning that?"

Vicky's cheeks flamed. "I'm sorry, I didn't think. That was tactless. But I think it's important to look at the other options. I don't think that Eve should assume this is John and not that sicko. I think that could be dangerous."

I felt everything shifting again, and a sinking feeling in the pit of my stomach. I had been going to tell them about Ethan. I hadn't the heart to now.

* * *

It was a bad day for both of us. The anniversary. But while Eve could take comfort in that fabulous column of hers, which is going to catapult her into an even better career, no doubt, I don't have anything like that. It makes me angry. It makes my plans even better and more disturbing, I hope.

CHAPTER 25

I can't do it. I can't do it. The beat of the words matched the rhythm of my walk as I headed to the underground after work.

It was my meeting with Ethan. I felt presumptive, embarrassed and guilty all at once, laced with dread. Vicky had sent the tiny positive foundations that I had started building after the postcard crashing down. She was right — how could I know that the card was from you? More likely BlackRose80.

I felt self-conscious using that name, but after all, what else did I have. I felt like they were still there. Waiting. Walking past a coffee shop, I saw a man sitting outside taking a drag on a cigarette. He stared out and his eyes met mine. My heart jumped as I quickened my pace. I knew I was being paranoid, that he was just gazing out ruminatively, but I was being watched. My new flat felt oppressive, I was uneasy despite the double lock on my front door, the locks on all the windows. All my lights were on every night. But it felt like there were eyes in the walls. Someone was still watching me.

I tapped my Oyster on the scanner as I walked through the underground gates. I chanted all the names of all the people who knew me and you. Our circle of friends. Sophie. Grace. Gemma. It could be anyone. Ethan? The train lurched as I gave myself a mental telling-off. *Come on.* The chances that he was involved were a million to one.

But it was more than that. The postcard made me feel that you did care; that you were alive and gave me a tiny close of the gate on it all. Now it was like a gaping wound again. You still could be dead. What was I doing, meeting a man after what had happened? It wasn't even a date but meeting Ethan in the evening made me ashamed. I would sort out the syndication details. Be perfectly pleasant. Then be on my way.

I approached the bar, feet dragging slowly. The streets were crammed with people out for drinks and a bite to eat, pleased it was a Friday night and wanting to let off steam. I entered the bar, which was small and quirky, and importantly, less than a year old, so I had no memories of you and me here.

It was crammed and my heart sank. I hoped I wasn't going to have to stand as well as make polite conversation with a man I wasn't sure that I wanted to meet. Then I saw someone motioning and there was Ethan sitting in a corner at a table. *At least he has got us a table*, was my first thought, followed by: *He has a wide smile and his eyes crinkle at the corners.*

"Hi." I plonked my bag clumsily on the table, my voice high-pitched.

"Hey." Ethan lurched forward slightly, and I thought he was going to peck me on the cheek, but he seemed to think better of it as he abruptly stopped.

"Good to see you. Thanks for coming."

"You're welcome," I squeaked.

"Can I get you a drink?"

"A white wine, please." I was tempted to ask for a large one, but it didn't sound very demure. Ethan disappeared into the crowd at the bar, and I sank down on a seat. I liked his smile and twinkling eyes. He was nicer looking than I remembered. I still wished it were you. *It's not even a date*, I reminded myself sternly.

Ethan weaved his way back past bodies five minutes later. "Sorry, the bar was really busy," he said.

"It's okay." Again, my tone was a couple of notches higher than usual. Where had this voice come from? I cleared my throat, determined to sound normal next time.

Ethan asked about my journey, whereabouts in Tooting I lived. I answered politely, waiting. Finally, he got to the point.

He drew out his Apple Mac. "Right, the syndication," he said briskly, and my cheeks flamed for thinking this meeting could be about anything else.

We went through dates, both to get the column over and when it would be published, plus a contract. He asked me to sign it digitally. I hesitated, wondering if Paul should be signing this — but he did tell Ethan that I would sort this. Jutting my chin out, I signed it proudly. My column would now not only be in a prominent women's magazine but a major London newspaper. I could help people, raise awareness. *And further my career*, a little voice whispered. I remembered BlackRose80's comments at the end of the online article. I hoped I wouldn't get any more when my column was printed and up on the paper's website.

"Another drink?" I asked Ethan politely, shuffling around with my bag, expecting him to say no.

"Yes, please. Same again." Ethan smiled, closing his laptop down and slipping it into his bag.

"Ah, okay!" I grabbed at my wallet in my bag.

I realised then how much I wanted this to be more than a work meeting. I smiled as I ordered the drinks and meandered back to our table. I didn't know anything about Ethan. But I wanted to know more. I was hungry for details about his life. Where did he come from, what was his first job, did he support a football team, who were his friends, what university did he go to?

As the questions poured out, I realised that I really liked his relaxed manner.

I laughed self-consciously. "Sorry, I feel like I'm interviewing you, my friends say that I always do this, that I might as well have a notebook and pen with me, I guess just part of being a journalist."

"I'm the same," Ethan chipped in. "Good thing we're both journalists."

You were, too. A painful reminder.

"I am going to act like a reporter now, but I honestly don't mean to be nosy." Ethan leaned forward. He looked like he was going to clasp my hands, but instead placed them palm-down on the table. "Are you okay, after John? What happened was awful and I can't stop thinking about it and how you are getting on."

He sounded so kind. I didn't normally like opening up to strangers. But I found myself speaking.

"You know some strange things are going on, I told you in the interview," I said. "It's making things much harder. I'm scared."

"Yes, I remember. I mean you only briefly mentioned it, but things were going missing . . . sorry I didn't ask you more." He looked guilty. "I probably should have asked you more."

"No, no it's okay." I hesitated. "I actually got a horrible message after the article was printed. BlackRose80." The name sounded cheesy and almost laughable as it rolled off my tongue. Maybe I was overplaying it.

"What?" Ethan looked confused.

I explained about looking on the comments page online and seeing BlackRose80's comments. "They said they knew me, and they said, 'I am still here'."

I explained about receiving the black roses on what would have been our wedding day. "They symbolise death." The wine tasted bitter in my mouth. Maybe I shouldn't be telling Ethan all of this.

"Sometimes I think I dreamt it," I continued. "When I looked again for BlackRose80's comments, they were gone."

"Yes, the web moderators get rid of anything inappropriate," Ethan said.

"I was upset, I wanted to see it again, analyse it, it almost made me feel like I dreamt it," I continued as if he had not spoken. "And actually. I got a message from them on Instagram the other day after posting my column . . ." I relayed what happened. "Can we stop them posting comments on your website, under my column?"

"Of course. I'll let the moderators know and they'll be blocked, and in case they post under another name, I'll get them to really keep an eye out."

Ethan drummed his fingers on the table. "They say they know you and John. Do you have any suspects?"

It was good to speak to him. My friends sometimes clammed up when I spoke to them about it, or there were certain things I couldn't say. Perhaps it was better to speak to an outsider, who didn't know you and who barely knew me.

I considered his question.

"Everyone."

* * *

We stumbled out of the pub. The bar opposite us was lively, spilling into the street. The wine had gone to my head. I wondered if I had talked too much about you, about the things happening to me. It felt so refreshing to tell him everything though. He was interested, asking searching questions, giving me ideas, regarding whoever was doing these things to me. I felt I could confide in him more than my friends and parents, even though Rachel, Jess and Vicky were much more supportive now.

"Another drink or do you want to go home?" The corners of Ethan's eyes creased as he smiled. I wanted to trace them with my finger.

I stared at the pub opposite, with the laughter and happy people. I wanted to be part of it. And I wanted to keep talking to Ethan.

"Another drink," I said firmly.

CHAPTER 26

The sun streamed through my Juliette balcony window. I squirmed as flashbacks from last night ran through me — telling Ethan everything, stumbling slightly to the pub over the road, his lips on mine. A smile played at the corners of my mouth as I recalled that. His warm arms around me, I wanted to sink into him. He could take it all away from me. I had been worried that he would want to take the kiss further, but he hadn't. A gentleman. Maybe I wasn't such a horror, such a terrible person that someone would actually put into place an elaborate plan to disappear from me. Maybe I was attractive, interesting and funny.

I wandered into the shower.

Ethan had asked if we could go out next week. Just half an hour after I had left him at the Tube, he had texted saying what a nice time he'd had and was I free Wednesday or Thursday. I messaged back and we were seeing each other Wednesday.

The water felt deliciously hot and satisfying as it poured on me in the shower. I delighted in the cleanliness of my skin when I dressed. Since you had gone, I was embarrassed to admit it, but I had taken to washing just three or four times a week. It was too much effort.

I put the kettle on and scooped coffee into the cafetière. The fresh smell permeated my nostrils and I smiled. I took pleasure in the moment. You were still missing but I was alive again. Silly really, after one kiss and a nice chat, to feel so content in the present but even if this ended, I saw a future again, a road to happiness. After you, I thought my life was over, but this offered me a pleasant glimpse of what could be.

My phone beeped. It was Vicky. *R we still on today. 11.30 at Mommas?* We had arranged to meet for brunch, Vicky had kindly offered to come to Tooting.

Yes! I responded.

I took a sip of my coffee, and it assaulted my taste buds and I grinned again. A fresh cup of coffee, standing in the streaming sunshine, with a second date with a nice man. Yes, perhaps my life wasn't over.

* * *

I sipped my cappuccino at Mommas, the talk from other tables particularly loud, but I delighted in it, I felt alive, part of something.

"You seem in a good mood," Vicky said teasingly, after we placed our orders.

"Yes." I hesitated, then plunged in. "I actually had a date last night and you know what, I feel good!"

Vicky slammed her cappuccino down, looking surprised. "Wow, that's soon," she said.

My good feelings took a wobble. "John went a year ago," I snapped, I had to defend myself. "When I say it was a date, it actually started out work-related. It was with Ethan, the one who interviewed me for *London Daily Eye*. The newspaper wants to syndicate my column and we were meeting to sort that out. But then it seemed to turn into a date!" I paused. "John was the one that left, not me."

Vicky held her hands up in fake protest. "Sorry, I didn't mean to upset you, you were just so devastated . . . it surprised me, that's all. I hope you find happiness."

She took a prim sip of her coffee.

"It is just a date," I repeated weakly. "It feels nice to be desirable again. Someone who hasn't yet walked out of their life to get away from me."

Vicky frowned. "Come on, you know it wasn't that simple."

"I know, of course, but that is how I feel, and I am in this situation not you. Sorry, I wish I hadn't mentioned it, I wanted a bit of escapism chat." I shrugged. "I thought that you'd be pleased for me."

Vicky leaned over and touched my arm. "Sorry," she said flatly. "I just feel a bit down about Ian and I took it out on you."

"I'm sorry." I wanted to say that she had decided to split up with him, he hadn't left her, his life, everything, never to return, no explanation. But I pressed my lips together.

"You'll meet someone else," I said. "If I can, you will. Ian wasn't right, Vicky, after everything you say." I leaned forward and touched her arm. "But it's not him you're really upset about is it, it's the guy before?"

Vicky's mouth tightened and she blinked rapidly. "Yep, you're right."

She fiddled with her coffee cup, tracing the handle. "It's not like me, you know what I'm like, careful, not wearing my heart on my sleeve. But I fell for him, from the moment I met him. He joined my school last year. The new English teacher. As soon as I saw him, I noticed his beautiful blue eyes. But it became more than that. We got on so well. The same tastes in music. We both loved walking. We could talk for hours about books. American poetry — remember, my special subject at uni? It was his too! We loved to talk about Walt Whitman and . . . well, I totally fell for him. But there was a major obstacle. He lived with someone."

She clutched the napkin.

"It's not like me at all. You know I would never ever normally get involved with someone taken — but I did. That's why I never told you or the others about it. I didn't tell anyone. I was so ashamed. And I thought that you and Jess would judge me, being engaged and settled and all."

Even though I already knew that she'd been seeing someone who was already in a relationship, I bounced between sympathy and surprise. Vicky was usually so moralistic and upstanding. She once told Jess off for kissing someone who had a casual girlfriend in our first year at university. She must have been in love. My heart went out to her. I tried to ignore the spark of resentment I felt against her for the partner of her boyfriend. Gemma's beetle brows and thickset jaw hovered in my mind.

Vicky continued, "We started seeing each other. Oh gosh, I was obsessed, consumed with him. In the end, he said he couldn't bring himself to leave her. He felt too bad. I think that despite the way I thought we clicked he obviously didn't like me enough to leave her. I mean, they weren't married, not that that makes my behaviour right, but it would have been easier for him to walk away from her."

"So how did you meet Ian?" I prompted.

Vicky sighed and finished off her cappuccino. "It was a couple of months after it all finished. I was still heartbroken, but my friend, Pippa, I think you met her years ago, persuaded me to come out. Ian was her friend and, on the night out too. He was cute and complimentary to me, and interesting with a good job, and I was desperate to stop feeling so awful. I was attracted to him and flung myself into it. But I didn't really know him. And little things started to annoy me. He used to clear his throat and cough all the time, set my teeth on edge. And he wasn't into literature and . . . oh, I don't know, I jumped in headfirst and it was a mistake. I knew I had to break it off."

Vicky had never spoken about her feelings for this long and this in-depth, for as long as I had known her.

The food arrived at that point so there was a polite silence while the waitress placed two plates of avocado and feta on toast on our table.

I leaned forward to sympathise with her. To tell her I understood her heartache.

But she withdrew her hand from my fingertips.

"Well, if you can, I guess I can!" Her voice was brittle.

I leaned back, surprised.

"What do you mean?"

"Move on."

"Look, it probably won't go anywhere," I exclaimed. "It just felt so nice to be with someone again, who liked my company. Who doesn't seem to want to escape his life to get rid of me." My throat dried as I eyed my loaded plate.

"I'm sorry," Vicky said. But her voice was still hard. "I guess I'm mulling something over. You said that you had a horrible message posted on the newspaper website after an article Ethan wrote? Rose something. Then he pursues you. It worries me a bit. Is he something to do with that message?"

My mouth dropped open. Vicky looked defensive. "I mean, probably not. But you can see why I'm concerned. After everything . . ." Her voice trailed off and she took a bite of her toast, avocado spilling out of the corners of her mouth.

"He doesn't know me, what would be the motivation?" I splayed my hands helplessly.

Vicky shrugged. I pushed my plate away. I wanted to get away. I'd wait ten minutes and I would ask for the bill.

* * *

It didn't take her long, did it? She was apparently devastated over John's disappearance, but just a year later, she's met someone else. I hadn't. She had also started writing her own column — award-winning, no doubt. I hadn't. It was his anniversary and she had help and concern and people wrapping their arms around her. I know I couldn't have expected that but it still grated. I was angrier than I had ever been. I had an idea. Maybe it would finally make it into that column of Eve's.

CHAPTER 27

My date night. I wanted to get home and get myself ready, so I even took the Tube, to be quicker. Hot commuters pressed themselves against me, and I tried not to see the sea of bodies from a year ago. A man with foppish dark hair in an Adidas jacket leaned against a pillar, glued to his phone. I tried to ignore the emptiness in my stomach.

I marched up the escalators once at Tooting Broadway underground station, ignoring my pounding heart. I needed to get to the gym more. I used to go, but since you went, I lost my motivation for it. We were going for an Italian meal in Tooting. I liked the fact that Ethan lived close by in Mitcham.

A parcel lay on the floor when I opened the door. Wrapped in innocuous brown wrapping paper, my name and address were printed on it. My heart sank. I knew it wasn't good. I took it into the living room and placed it on the coffee table while I sat on the sofa, staring at it. I picked it up. It was light. It felt like I was staring down on myself from the ceiling as I slowly tore the paper open, like an out-of-body experience. Inside was a card and a plastic bag.

Something was both solid and soft in the plastic bag. I plunged my hand into squelchy wet gunge. I pulled it out and there lay solid pink offal. I thought it was liver but looking closer I saw tubes. A strong smell emanated. It was a heart. I emitted a sound between a retch and a scream.

Whose heart was it? Was it human? I ripped open the envelope. A card with a broken heart pictured on it, and inside:

Do you like your present?

The heart lay on my table, large and livid, its smell enveloping me. Retching again, I called the police.

They answered promptly and fortuitously I was transferred to Kate Matthews, the original police officer who managed the case. I found her a bit gruff and short, but she knew my history and she acted like she cared. We hadn't spoken for months but she knew instantly who I was.

It was hard to get the words out. "A heart . . . been going on for ages." I agitatedly listed the other events, even though I had already reported some of them. My voice was confused, rising and dropping. All the time a pink flame in the background, growing until I imagined taking over my sight, my eyes. This was my tipping point.

"We'll have someone over to have a look." Curt but an underlying kindness.

One more task that I had to fulfil.

Ethan, I'm sorry, but I can't meet tonight. There's been another incident. Will explain more when I see you, but the police are coming over.

I hesitated, hunched over the phone. Then decided to go for it. Typing in a flurry, I wrote: *I am so sorry, I was really looking forward to it. I very much hope that we can rearrange very soon xx.* I stared at it, and removed one x.

After pressing send, I wondered if I should call one of my friends. Vicky and her insinuations from when we met for coffee came to mind: *Ethan wrote the article and then BlackRose80's message appeared on the website.* I could almost hear her saying, "You meet him for one date and then get a heart posted to you."

I dismissed that thought almost instantly. The phone fell into my lap, as I stared at the pink and red mass on my coffee table. Blood had started to seep across the mahogany wood.

A brisk knock on the door had me off the phone and practically running away; I couldn't be with it on my own anymore. Kate Matthews and a colleague I didn't recognise stood there. "Hi, Eve, this is my colleague, Joe Davies." I shook his hand distractedly and showed them into the living room.

"There." I pointed. As if they could miss it. "Is it human? Is it John's?" My voice reverberated around the room.

Instantly Joe was at the heart, professionally rolling out some kind of cloth out of the rucksack that he was carrying.

Kate looked me directly in the eye. "I would say not. I believe it's an animal heart, designed to scare you. But until we do tests, there's no way of knowing for definite."

She sat down on the sofa. "You need to tell me what's been happening. And then we need to go to the police station, and you need to give a statement."

I was filled with relief. I wasn't on my own any more. My phone beeped.

Eve, I'm so sorry. I wanted to ring but understand that may not be appropriate. Let me know if there is anything I can do. Thinking of you. Ethan x.

Joe pulled on plastic gloves and picked up the pink mass in his hands. *Please, please let it not be your heart.*

* * *

I was exhausted. It was eleven in the evening and I was only just back from the police station. It had taken ages to make a statement. I felt purged though, like a weight had been taken off my mind. It was the right thing to do. The police had taken it seriously, had said that I should have recorded every incident with them, right from when I heard someone trying to get into my flat. I was redeemed. I had not been imagining it, had not been exaggerating. They had given me a panic button and I was to call the instant something else happened. The heart was being tested. I would hear tomorrow.

I poured myself a hefty dose of whisky and paced about my living room. I needed to find out who was doing this to me. It almost consumed more of my thoughts than you did. I thought of the postcard from Spain and the familiar sad, empty feeling crept up my body. But I dismissed it. Concentrate. I needed to find out who it was, and I felt sure it was someone I knew. Sophie. My mind screamed. I refused to contemplate Ethan. My one piece of sunshine, and this had been happening a long time before I met him. I would not entertain the thought.

Sophie was going to be paid a visit. I wasn't sure how, but I needed to somehow work out if it was her. I gulped the rest of the brandy and fell into an uneasy sleep.

Something pink and fleshy and seeping blood was being pressed into my face. My hair and pillow were wet with tears when I woke from my dream.

* * *

My phone rang. Anonymous number. Which, in my mind, was usually bad news.

"Hello?" I couldn't keep the panic from my voice.

"Hello, Eve, Kate Matthews here," she said evenly and with no emotion. "We've done tests on the heart, and it is a sheep's heart."

My legs weakened, and I clutched the wall. I was in the kitchen at work. "Thank God," I breathed.

"Yes, I understand. It's a relief it isn't human. But to be sent a heart . . ." Kate paused. "We have to get to the bottom of it. Anything, anything at all, you must let us know."

"Yes," I muttered, my unease rising. "You — you don't think I'm at risk, do you?"

"We will make sure you aren't." Not the most reassuring answer.

But the heart wasn't yours. Relief flooded through me. I needed to get back to proof my pages in the magazine. It was going to press tomorrow. But one thing first. Sticking the kettle on and scooping coffee into my cafetière, I scrolled to Ethan's text.

Are you ok? Can I help? XX

Two kisses. I was a teenager again. Someone had my back. I barely knew him but I wanted to snuggle into his arms. *Take it away, look after me.* It was pathetic, but I wanted someone to protect me.

Bit better, I tapped out. *I can't really explain it over text, are you free Friday? XX* I pushed send quickly before I could agonise over the number of kisses.

Straight away. He pinged back: *Absolutely xx.*

Some warmth felt like it was trickling over the iciness in my chest. I poured water into my cafetière and was rummaging in the fridge for the milk when Gemma walked in. As usual, she gave me a sweeping glare before turning away and going to the coffee machine. Usually, I felt guilty but this time a flash of anger swept over me. What I did was very, very wrong, but it was a year ago, I was going through hell. I opened my mouth to speak, then closed it again. She would only go and tell management and then I might be out of a job.

I was about to turn away myself when something caught my eye. Delicate black bows on her white top. A neat black collar. Tucked into her black skirt. The hole I had made when I grabbed the top had obviously been patched up. It was a good job because I couldn't see any stitches. My breath caught in my throat. Why wear that top, the top that made me almost lose my mind? I reminded myself sternly that she was entitled to wear any top that she wanted and that it had been me that had been in the wrong in the first place.

But it must mean something to her. I clamped my lips together hard. *Don't speak to her, don't speak to her.*

She turned around and, clasping her coffee cup, glanced down at her top, back at me and smiled. Her horn-rimmed glasses and unmade-up face were in sharp contrast to her glamorous blouse. I watched her sashay out of the kitchen and leaned back against the counter weakly. That was just plain nasty, whatever I did surely didn't warrant that. I found it hard to believe that she wore that top without thinking, a pretty top that went well with her skirt. It felt deliberate. It was such a contrast to her behaviour when I first met her.

Me attacking her had made her despise and hate me. Unless . . . I paused and made myself face it. It was more than that. Perhaps something *had* been going on with her and you. My more positive mood came crashing down. Why did I let myself feel happy about Ethan, one date with a guy I didn't even know. I loved you and you were gone forever. I had been delivered a sheep's heart yesterday. Someone hated me that much. I headed slowly back to my desk.

Sarah gave her usual awkward grimace when she saw me. She had never been comfortable since you went and had acted even more awkwardly since the incident with Gemma. I reached into my bag and pulled out the crumpled piece of paper with my list of who was behind the events happening to me. I grabbed my pen and under Gemma's name added: *She wore that top again.*

* * *

She was leaning over me. Thick brows, hair scraped back. A black rose hung out of her mouth. The white top with pretty bows had a gaping hole, out of which her writhing heart hung, pounding and pumping.

I woke up, my own heart hammering, fumbling for the lamp switch. Four o'clock, my alarm clock said. I closed my eyes and tried to cleanse my mind of thoughts. I would not be turning the light off though.

CHAPTER 28

"Are you okay?" Ethan looked so concerned for my welfare, warmth blazing out of his hazel eyes, that tears filled my own eyes. He gave me a huge hug and pecked me shyly on the lips as the hustle and the bustle of Tooting Broadway Tube at rush hour continued around us. I couldn't remember your eyes ever looking so caring. They must have, of course, but your disappearance had created a gap so yawning I found it hard to see past that dark chasm.

I squeezed my hands together and pinged on what I hoped was a bright smile. "Let's go for a drink and I'll tell you about it."

Ethan took me gently by the arm and we walked to a big old cavernous pub with dimly lit corners and old sofas. It was busy, but we managed to find a sofa right at the back.

"Sit." He smiled. "A white wine?" He weaved his way to the bar, and I sank back into the sofa, relaxed for the first time since I was sent the heart. The worn old sofa was enfolding me in its arms. The chatter of people excited that it was a Friday and the Stone Roses song in the background soothed my spirit. I closed my eyes, and it was a pleasure just to think of nothing in particular. It was a while before Ethan came back clutching a glass of white wine and a pint for him.

"Sorry, it was really busy," he explained, plonking them down and sinking onto the sofa next to me. His knee touched mine and it felt nice. He was solid and sturdy. He liked me. I couldn't imagine him taking off and never ever returning. But then I never imagined you doing that either.

"Do you want to talk about what happened or would you rather talk about other things?" Ethan asked.

I was bursting to talk about it. Fleetingly I wondered if it was a clever idea. It was hardly the light, giggly, flirty stuff of a second date. But I took a breath and did it anyway. The heart in my hands, my shock and worry that it was yours. The fact that it was a sheep's heart. The card with a broken heart on it, and its note: *Do you like your present?*

"I can't help feeling that it's retaliation for my date with you, someone knew I went out with you." With a shock I realised I had not put that into words to anyone.

Ethan shook his head. "That is disgusting." Shocked, angry and protective all in one. Someone cared about me.

Ethan took a long sip of his drink. I could see his mind working, almost relishing the problem. He was definitely a journalist.

I pressed on: "It's got to be someone who knows me, maybe someone who knows that I've been on a date. Probably a friend or a work colleague maybe."

I filled him in on Gemma, even shamefacedly telling him about the way I attacked her.

Ethan frowned. "I think you have a point. To wear that top, that does seem more than thoughtless."

"Do you think that something went on between them?" I asked him.

"No, but I think she wanted it," Ethan said diplomatically. He paused. "You say she seemed mature and kind and empathetic at the start, then changed so dramatically — that's odd. I know she's only behaved like that since you grabbed her but you have to wonder if something was going on."

I told him about Sophie and my suspicions. He nodded instantly. "Yes, I agree that she might be involved — God, it's so sick though, how could John's sister do something like that, how could anyone?" He took another sip of his drink. "But I think it's someone who knows you both, who has a grudge against you."

"I'm going to visit Sophie and — I don't know how — try and find something out," I said. "Vicky is also on my hit list." I had filled him in on Vicky's strange behaviour. But Ethan was unconvinced.

"But she didn't seem to have especially close links with John," he said slowly. "I know she's upset about her own relationship ending, but it seems a bit extreme to go from that to, well, a heart."

We had finished our drinks. I realised with a start that all we had talked about was my situation and you.

"Oh God, all I've done is rabbit on," I said guiltily. "I am so sorry I promise that we won't talk . . ."

Ethan leaned forward and kissed me. I felt tingles down my spine.

"I'll talk about it until the cows come home. I want to help," he said, and placed his mouth on mine again.

CHAPTER 29

Hi Sophie, any chance I could come round to see you soon? I'd like to see your new place and I need to speak to you about stuff that's been happening.

I sent the text, opened *The Times*, and took a sip of my flat white. The hustle and bustle in Mommas made me happy. It was Saturday morning after my night with Ethan. My mouth turned up slightly at the corners. Then I felt an instant flash of guilt, was it too soon to like another man, did that make me shallow . . .

Then I thought about you, if you were alive, starting a new life, perhaps in Spain, perhaps elsewhere, leaving me without a backwards glance and I hardened. The livid heart tugged at my sleeve; I deserved some happiness.

We had gone to the cosy Italian two doors down from the pub last night. Over pizza and a bottle of red we discussed my situation in more detail but then turned to other things — music (we both loved Britpop, the Cure and Arcade Fire), cinema (both enjoyed horrors as a secret guilty pleasure and thought that *The Graduate* was the best film ever), our friends, our social lives, our work, what we thought of Brexit. I couldn't remember the last time that I spoke to someone like that — no, actually I could. I tried to block out thoughts of other cosy evenings at other Italians in the neighbourhood, with someone whose favourite film was also *The Graduate*, who I could talk to about anything. But you obviously did not feel like that with me.

After the meal we headed out onto the street a little unsteady and I loved the bright lights, the chatter, the cars blaring past, I felt part of something, not cocooned in my sad little world, my face pressed up against a glass wall as I watched everyone else move forward with their lives, while I just kept pedalling backwards, to before you went.

Ethan held my face and kissed me, and I was excited like a teenager again. We walked back to mine and kept stopping to kiss and hug. His arms around me protected me from the heart, from the other thing in my life, I could have stayed in his arms forever. I was so tempted to invite him in to my flat, but I hesitated. I wasn't quite ready.

"We've got all the time in the world." Ethan smiled.

I took a sip of coffee, grinning widely as I remembered that and caught the waitress's eye.

"You look happy," she trilled.

"I am," I said without thinking. Then quickly: "Great coffee!" Which it was.

Ethan and I were seeing each other mid-week. I got the feeling he wanted to see me earlier than that, but did not want to overwhelm me, and I was grateful to take it slowly, although secretly I would have loved to see him tonight. To keep the wolves from my door, to push that heart away.

My phone beeped. Sophie's name popped up. Surprised at how quickly she responded. *Sure. Tomorrow?*

No kiss at the end but the most cordial text from Sophie that I'd had for months. I texted back quickly.

Yes, great. What's your address?

Sophie had moved back in with Jill shortly after you went missing, but recently had moved out again and as far as I knew, was renting a flat in Sydenham, south east London.

I placed my phone down carefully. "Another flat white, please," I said to the server.

I had to think, to plan, this was my one chance to find out if Sophie was behind these events. The heart and black flowers overpowered all of the others. I had to somehow search her flat. My heart sank as I realised how unlikely it was that I would manage this, and anyway, what would I find . . . my phone beeped again. Expecting an answer from Sophie, I grabbed my phone. But it was Rachel.

Hi lovely. We've decided on our long weekend! I saw Jess and we think Devon, cottage on a cliff. You still okay for those dates? X

The sea, sand, quaint cottages and cream tea, a chance to escape my problems. I smiled. The idea was starting to be appealing. Another message came through. Sophie. With her address, then: *seven ok?*

* * *

I got off the train at Sydenham and trudged down the high street. *I hate you. I don't want to see you. But I have to get answers.* How I would get those answers I did not know. Either cajole her or search her flat. Either had huge barriers.

I turned into a street of smart Victorian houses, converted into maisonettes and flats. I knocked at 3C. Thudding down the stairs and then the door opened. Sophie's face peered out. Not as pinched and pale as usual. I noted that like the last time I saw her, at my flat, that she had some colour in her cheeks, had put on a few pounds.

"Come in." Her tone was friendly. I walked up the narrow stairway and into a high-ceilinged, front room with period features.

"This is nice," I remarked, sitting down rigidly on the sofa. I always found conversation with Sophie taxing.

Sophie leapt up. "I'll give you a tour." I was surprised at her energy. She proudly showed me her spacious kitchen, which could fit a table and chairs, and the small balcony that led off it. Her bedroom was a good size and she had an attractive bathroom with a roll-top bath. But I wasn't really concerned about the size of the rooms or the period features.

I tried to clock her layout, where her bedroom was, where the storage was, where I could conceivably find a clue.

Sophie led me back to the living room. "Glass of wine?"

She was the most welcoming that I had ever known her. "Yes, sure," I said, eying her suspiciously.

She proffered me a glass and sank into an armchair. "I'm cooking lasagne. I hope that's okay."

"Lovely," I said distractedly. "How are you, Sophie, about John?" Cut straight to the chase.

Sophie looked surprised. Then her mouth turned down. "It's hard, obviously." She was obviously resentful of me bringing it up. "But you know, I have to move on now, it's been over a year, I can't make it all about him, I have to think of myself and live my life."

I waited for her to ask about me and how I was coping. Nothing. Okay.

"This is a change," I said carefully, biting my lip to stop the hateful spew emanating: *You made me feel that your feelings were the only ones that mattered, that they were more important than mine, that you would never recover.*

"Has anything happened to make you feel better?" An idea suddenly popped into my head, and I wasn't surprised at the biting of her lip, the flush of her cheeks, the shifty look at the ceiling.

"Well, after going through hell," she said dramatically, "I never knew it was possible to feel like that. I actually met a guy two months ago and things are going really well, and I am happy for the first time in ages."

So did I, I wanted to say and a flush of warmth spread up my chest to be replaced by sadness for you. Had your sister and I abandoned you?

I still said nothing. The pause became pressing. When it became clear that she was not going to ask about me, I opened my mouth.

"I'm pleased for you." I tried to make my tone friendly and non-confrontational, fighting down my anger. "Tell me about it."

Sophie's eyes brightened.

"I met him online." Her voice took a challenging note. "It's difficult to meet people in real life . . ."

I threw my hands up. "Hey, I agree. All my friends meet people online."

Nothing wrong with online dating, but I could see it affected Sophie's pride. I swallowed a smile.

Sophie visibly relaxed. "Yeah, that seems to be one of the only ways at the moment, glad it's not just me. Anyway, he's called Sam, thirty-five, an accountant and it's going well." She smiled. Her teeth showed. I had never seen her grin revealing her teeth. "He makes me happy."

Despite my dislike of her, my emotions touched hers. I never thought I would be happy again and now, even if it didn't last with Ethan, I knew I could achieve it. It clashed with my sadness about you. I hoped that you actually were in Spain and happy.

"You deserve it." I did my best to sound sincere. "John would have wanted that."

Sophie beamed. "Thanks. I needed that."

I waited for a question about how I was coping, if I was okay, if I thought about meeting someone. Nothing again. I had an idea.

"It must be a big thing for you, telling friends and relatives," I began, ignoring the fact that I was neither, but desperate to get rid of her so that I could search her flat. "Please feel free to ring him and chat if you want, I understand."

"Thank you, I appreciate that. It took a lot to tell you. But I don't need to ring him. I spoke to him before you came over, and anyway, I'm seeing him tomorrow."

I sought for another excuse to search about her flat. A bathroom trip seemed in order. A dodgy tummy to buy me time . . .

But then Sophie stood up. "I need to finish off the lasagne. Won't be too long. Stay here if you want or you can come with me and chat while I do it."

She didn't seem thrilled with the latter option. "Ah, I'll just stay here and chill if that's okay, I've a couple of messages to send. Take as long as you want."

I waited and heard her traipse out on to the balcony off the kitchen (Sophie was a secret smoker). My window of opportunity, but where to start, bedroom or living room? I hesitated, torn. But it seemed like a bedroom might be a more obvious place to find something personal.

I walked quickly and quietly to her bedroom and made for her bedside drawers, blindly piling through each one, hands raking through old bills, stained notebooks, old lipsticks and condom packets. I wasn't sure what I was looking for, but it wasn't any of these. *Where else?* I saw her wardrobes and flung open a door. I raked through her shoes half-heartedly.

My heart raced as I tried to think where else I could find signs, signs of what I didn't know. All the time, like the beat of a drum, a voice in my head repeating: *This is crazy, give it up.*

I was about to leave the bedroom and go rummaging through Sophie's living room, despite thinking it unlikely I would find anything there, when I saw a Clarks shoebox peeking out from under the bed. Sparking inspiration, I knelt down and rummaged around. Socks, old newspapers, an empty can of coke. Nothing. I pushed the shoebox back under the bed, intent on searching elsewhere, when I felt something slip and slide about inside. It didn't sound like a shoe. I pulled it out again and opened it. Probably something random. Why was I even checking when time was running out . . . A white mug lay there. I picked it up and a footballer's face grinned up at me, arms outstretched. *Hand of God.* Your Maradona mug. And inside some familiar-looking keys. The keys to our flat.

The mug clattered from my outstretched fingers back into the cardboard box.

That was the first thing that went missing. I knew I had been right, despite the scorn from everyone about noticing something so minor. The keys glinted at me. I thought back to footsteps in the hall, the sound of small heels click-clacking, coming back from being away and seeing pillows moved and ruffled, sensing that someone had been there . . . your watch gone. I glanced from side to side, but I didn't think I had more time to search.

Then I heard footsteps coming down the hall, my heart leapt but I sat there paralysed, staring at the keys and mug.

"Eve, where are you?" Sophie pushed the door open and stared at me, looking surprised. Then she took in the fact that I was kneeling by the bed, the open box and its contents. Her face flushed, and her brows drew together. A small sharp knife was gripped in her hand.

I edged away to the window. "What the hell?"

"I could say the same thing." Sophie's voice, despite the colour in her cheeks, was measured. "What are you doing going through my things?"

I gestured at her hand. "Why are you holding a knife? Put it down, please."

Sophie didn't move. Was it her? The one who sent me a heart and came into my flat, creeping around as I lay in bed, who sent me black roses, who sent me the "congratulations on your new home" card? I was caught against the bed.

Sophie took a step forward and I cowered. "If you must know, I got the knife out to chop an onion for our lasagne. I went to check you were okay, still holding the knife, and couldn't find you in the living room."

I calmed down. "Nasty things have been happening to me, Sophie, since John went," I began. "Things going missing. Someone entering my flat while I'm in bed. Horrendous things sent to me." I glared at her. "An animal heart ring any bells?"

"What are you talking about?" Sophie was calm. She still held the knife.

"Well, what's this?" I gestured at the mug. "That's the first thing that went missing. You did it. You denied it at the time. You have the keys. No one else does. So, you had access to the flat, to enter and scare me and take stuff, like John's watch."

"I took the mug because it meant something to me. My mum gave it to my brother when she was seriously ill with breast cancer. I knew how much he cherished it, I wanted to feel close to him. Can't you understand?" Sophie's eyes looked suspiciously bright. "I denied it to you because I thought you might think I was weird, but more to the point I thought you would hassle me and try and take it back."

She took a step forward.

"The keys? John gave me a spare set. Don't you remember when I needed to stay at yours when you were away on a work trip, as I was between flats? John said to hang on to them." She shrugged. "So, you thought I was capable of all that kind of crazy stuff?"

I stared at her.

"Yes, frankly, because look at the evidence here. And I know you don't like me; you didn't like me being with John. You didn't want anyone to be with him. You wanted him to yourself."

"Yeah, you're right, I didn't like John being with you because I don't like you." Sophie enunciated each word crystal clearly. "You nagged, oh God how you nagged him to marry you, all the time, he was young and you put such pressure on him. You took him away from me and Mum, his family, I hated that."

I opened my mouth, fists clenched, but she continued.

"You were jealous of my relationship with him; you tried to destroy a sister–brother relationship and, you know what, there did start to be more of a distance between us, like he was worried about seeing me and opening up. How sad is that? We had no dad, our mum had cancer."

"Whatever I did, what you did was unacceptable. I could go to the police," I retorted. "You know I was sent black roses on what should have been our wedding day? But of course you do. And I can't believe you let yourself into the flat when I was sleeping. I knew I heard heels!"

I glanced down at her feet. Even at home Sophie was wearing pumps with small heels.

Sophie stared into the distance. "Black roses are the symbol of death, aren't they?" she said.

I started walking, out of that room, into the living room to grab my bag and coat and then out of that flat, out of Sophie's life. I knew I would never see her again.

Sophie came to the door of the bedroom to watch me go, still holding the knife.

I turned to her, as I opened the front door jerkily. "It's such a shame that this happened. Don't you think that John would be devastated about this relationship breakdown between two women that he adored?" I didn't know why I was saying this; she had stalked me and I was frightened of her and of what she might do. But still I felt so sad about you.

Sophie slowly lowered the knife, and I wondered if I had got through to her.

"Mum and I were the women he adored," she said slowly. "And I don't believe he's alive."

I allowed the first part to pass me by. But the second — she had always been so sure he was out there, somewhere. I felt like she was giving up on him.

"I'm sad you've changed your mind."

I don't know why I didn't leg it out of the front door, but I was rooted to the spot. It helped to think that you were alive, that you were living a life elsewhere. I could justify moving on, buying a flat, meeting Ethan. Now all that faded and in my rising guilt I wondered how I could meet him again.

Sophie stared at me. "I think he's dead," she said. And then she closed the door quietly in my face.

* * *

Eve got it wrong. So wrong. It made me smile and shake my head. I'd got away with it, so far. And hopefully would continue to get away with it. Sophie would come under fire for any new . . . 'events'. I didn't care, I'd never liked Sophie either. One thing I agreed with Eve about. Let her be the scapegoat.

CHAPTER 30

"Unbelievable." Rachel slammed her coffee cup down. "What a . . . I was going to say cow, but it's worse than that. I can't believe she crept into your flat and did all those sick things. I'm sorry that I didn't always believe you."

A train thundering in almost drowned out her words. We were off on our girls' weekend to Devon and were waiting at Euston to catch the train.

"Well, I'm just so relieved I know who it was. It's haunted me, those awful things, especially the black roses. I'm so glad that I now know that it wasn't John doing it.

"You know, she told me happily that black roses were the symbol of death."

"She's sick," Rachel repeated. Then: "Will you report this to the police?"

I hadn't thought about that. "I guess I should as they are now involved. But I'm not sure what they'll think about the evidence, I'll have to think. They weren't interested when I told them about the mug."

"But things have changed since then. She could go to court and be prosecuted," Rachel boomed.

I wasn't sure I liked that idea; despite everything Sophie had done.

I glanced at my watch. Jess and Vicky should be joining us soon. I was actually looking forward to our weekend. I had an answer now to what had been happening and I wanted to bury Sophie and assign her to a back page in my life. Since I found out about her terrorising me, I felt an overwhelming relief. Besides, I had had three more dates with Ethan, and it was going well. My phone beeped and it was him.

Have a brilliant time. You deserve it. The familiar tussle of happiness versus guilt and loss over you.

Jess and Vicky appeared at the café, tugging bags.

"Sorry we're late," Jess panted, plonking her bag in the middle of the coffee shop. She grabbed my arm. "I'm looking forward to this."

I smiled and enjoyed the feeling of my mouth automatically turning upwards without me physically stretching it.

"Me too," Vicky said.

Her face looked less taut and more relaxed than it had in a while. Tears pricked my eyes. I never expected to feel a sense of calm again, of happiness, after you left. You were still bubbling under the surface, but I had my friends, a nice flat, and could actually take some satisfaction at times in the day without my feelings robbing me of my breath. And I was seeing someone so nice, who helped restore my confidence in myself.

And I had found out who had been stalking me. Sophie. Now I knew my fear had almost evaporated. I was almost sure that my confrontation with her had marked the end, but if not, at least I knew the source. And these things stuck a thick plaster over the wound of you leaving.

We bustled to catch the train. Even Vicky looked less pinched. She asked me cordially over Ethan and expressed pleasure that it was going well.

"Champagne!" shouted Rachel excitedly as soon as we got on the train. "Or at least fizzy wine!"

We sank into our first-class seats. Yes, we had treated ourselves.

We tucked into our fizz as soon as we could. I compared it to the train we took for Jess's hen do and again gave myself a pat on the back for how much better I felt compared to then.

"Cheers to us all and especially you, Jess and Eve!" Rachel said.

A cloud passed over Vicky's face.

"And Vicky too!" said Rachel hurriedly.

We clinked glasses. Rachel was acting out of character, I thought. She was normally reserved and understated. She took a big gulp of her drink and placed her glass down erratically on the table.

"So Clive and I are moving in together," she said, her voice rising in a slight squeak.

"Oh my gosh, congratulations!" I yelled, determined to sound pleased for her.

Then I examined my feelings and rather than my usual despair that everyone else was happy and moving on with their lives while I had pressed pause, I realised I was genuinely happy for her. Although I shuddered slightly at getting intimate with Clive — I tried to put my night with him in a box and throw away the key — he was a nice man. And if they stayed together, I could always have a connection to you. Otherwise, I might have lost touch with him. I realised I was pleased to always have a link.

Jess and Vicky quickly cried out congratulations in my wake and we clinked glasses again. I appraised their faces, but both looked relaxed and happy for Rachel.

Rachel moved the subject on swiftly. "Are you okay, Jess?"

Jess took a firm sip of her champagne. "I am, actually," she said evenly. "I feel much better. I feel guilt still and I do miss Jack, I miss chatting to someone, asking about my day. But I know it's right. I feel relief, such relief."

Rachel grabbed her hand. "I am so pleased," she said warmly.

"And, Eve, thank goodness you know the truth. I still can't believe it."

Jess and Vicky nodded. I had told them already about Sophie.

"You can rest easy now," Vicky said. "No one is going to torment you like that again."

I nodded. "I feel like I can stop looking over my shoulder." To my surprise my voice shook. "It was consuming me, and you know, it sounds dramatic, but I felt in danger, that this person could actually hurt me."

Jess touched my shoulder. "I always thought Sophie was strange and just not right," she said. "Especially the day John went missing. Remember what she was like? Dominating everything. Making that drama in the police station. It was all about her. About her and her feelings. Sod anyone else. At least you are free of her." Her face was tense, her mouth a straight line.

I smiled. "Yes, I'm free." I was light, like a dandelion clock floating, despite the fact you were still gone. I was going to use this weekend as a new beginning, to throw off the cloak Sophie had wrapped around me, the suffocating feeling that I had lived with for over a year and the pain your disappearance had inflicted on me. I would start again. No shadows in the corner. Just my flat, my job, my column and, yes, Ethan. A warmth spread up my throat. I smiled over at Vicky, Rachel and Jess. Jess stared out of the window. Vicky was looking at the floor. Rachel met my eye and winked.

CHAPTER 31

"Well, this is rather nice!" Rachel ran out of the wide-open patio doors and into the garden of our holiday cottage. Stuffed with lavender and roses and herbs of all types, it was extremely attractive. But the jewel in the crown was the little gate at the bottom of the garden, which led out onto the narrow path on the edge of the cliff front, dropping down to the glorious blue sea stretching as far as the eye could see.

I ran down the garden and out of the gate, smiling at the sun blazing down, the warmth on my bare arms and the smell of the roses — the weather was being kind to us. I gazed at the sea. I could do anything, anything with my life, it wasn't over, I realised as I sniffed the salt on the air.

Rachel joined me.

"I'm really pleased about you and Clive," I said, and I meant it.

"Thanks," Rachel said. "You know, I'm actually surprised he's my type. I am well aware he's a bit bumbling."

I opened my mouth to refute this, but she shook her head smilingly.

"No, he is! But that's okay. He has a heart of gold and I love him."

"Ah Rach." I slung my arm through hers. I was happy for her. It was good to feel happy for someone else without feeling the familiar tug of envy and wistfulness.

"By the way, I do know about you and Clive," she added quickly.

I dropped my arm, my face flaming. I had assumed that Clive would never tell her, *I* was certainly never going to mention it.

"Oh." I was floored, and a blaze of anger and embarrassment leapt up inside me.

"Sorry, I know it's embarrassing; I don't mean to make you feel bad and I honestly don't mind," Rachel said quickly. "I mean I guess I was a bit shocked, but I know it was a one off. Silly old Clive — can't keep his mouth shut! He had a few too many pints as usual and blurted it out!"

I shook my head. "Well, I'm relieved you're okay about it, I didn't want you to know but maybe it's best it's out in the open. And you don't need me to say that it didn't mean anything."

Rachel smiled.

* * *

"I've forgotten my PJs!" I shouted, swaying slightly as I reached the door of my room. While a cottage, it was generous enough to have four bedrooms, so we all had one each. It had been a great night. Champagne at the cottage, and then dinner in a restaurant on the harbour front. We had reminisced rather than talked about big, serious topics like Jack, you and Ian. For that I was thankful. It was not even eleven but we were all exhausted and had polished off a fair bit of wine in a short space of time. I felt giddy but in a nice way. I was looking forward to sinking into my bed and replying to Ethan's WhatsApp.

"Anyone got some I could borrow?"

"I've got a T-shirt!" Jess called from the bathroom, the sound of water running as she washed her teeth. "It's in my top drawer."

I smiled to myself. Typical that she would have unpacked everything for just three nights. All my clothes still lay higgledy-piggledy in my suitcase.

I wandered into her room and headed for the chest of drawers. A pink T-shirt lay crisply on top of an assortment of underwear and socks. I laid my hand on it and was about to pick it up when I felt something hard. I lifted the T-shirt and saw a glint of silver.

I instinctively knew what it was before I even saw it. The silver watch, slightly worn on the inside, the chunky square face: 11.05.

Your watch, still working perfectly.

I froze. Then reached out to pick it up.

Clutching the watch, I sank onto the bed trying to organise my thoughts. How did Jess have your watch? My relief at pointing at Sophie as the perpetrator started to disintegrate. My breath caught in my throat. Surely, she wasn't capable of this. Her kind eyes, her arms round me every step of the way after you went missing. My best friend.

The door opened and she wandered in, white, freshly washed teeth gleaming at me as she smiled, already dressed in pyjamas.

I stood up on unsteady legs and dangled the watch from my hand.

"Why do you have John's watch?" To my surprise my voice was calm.

Jess's eyes widened then dulled.

She took a step towards me. "I can explain."

I moved back. "Did you do those things, was it you, not Sophie?"

Her mouth tightened and an altogether more unfriendly look, something that I had never seen before, appeared.

"You need to listen to me. I want to explain, and we might wake the others. Come outside with me."

Without a word, I followed her out through the patio doors into the garden, down the path to the gate and out to the cliff. The watch felt like it weighed five stone in my hand.

A slight breeze ruffled my hair and I stared into the darkness as the waves broke on the rocks down below.

"What's your explanation?" My voice was faint, as I struggled to process what had happened. "Surely there's an explanation?" My voice was pleading.

Surely there was a sensible reason, as otherwise everything I knew, my foundations, were ripped apart.

"Let me tell you . . ." she said, in a voice I didn't recognise. Her face suddenly looked alien. Where was the amiable dimple, the smile in her hazel eyes? Where was my best friend?

The breeze whipped through her hair.

"Why have you got John's watch?"

It lay slack in my hands.

"John and I had an affair for six months," Jess said.

I clung to your watch, my stomach plunging as if I was on a rollercoaster.

"We'd always got on well, and one night I popped over unexpectedly to see you. I can't remember why, but you were out. John let me in and offered me a drink. We chatted and I found myself confiding in him about my doubts about Jack. God, I had them so long I don't know why I went as far as I did with him.

"I'm sorry, this will be hard to hear, but he opened up a little about your relationship. That he felt under a lot of pressure to commit and get engaged, but that he just wasn't sure . . . the sadness and worry he felt about his mum's cancer, his sister being so dependent on him and no dad and so forth.

"I was surprised, to be honest. So surprised. I thought you both had the perfect relationship. I know you got paranoid about him and how committed he was, but I thought that was rubbish. He always seemed so attentive."

I could hear the waves lapping down below, glued to the spot as I waited for Jess to continue.

"The next week, John was in Balham meeting Clive and said he'd got a book that you wanted to lend me, and he'd drop it off. Jack was out that night. I was pleased, but I refused to explore that feeling.

"He turned up at ten, I offered him a drink and then, well, we opened up to each other again. One thing led to another, and we kissed. And yes, went to bed."

Her voice softened. "I'm sorry, I know you won't want to hear this, but I fell hook, line and sinker, I couldn't help it. Years of not much passion with Jack and then to feel so attracted to John, oh wow, I couldn't believe it."

Jess's mouth on yours, her dark wavy hair falling over your shoulders, you caressing her face . . . the kaleidoscope of images played on in my mind . . .

"Go on." My voice was almost swept away by the wind.

"We saw each other when we could. Snatched evenings and lunches when we could. I adored him. I honestly — I lived to see him. I prayed he would leave you for me."

She didn't even apologise.

"But I soon started to see how troubled he was. Much as it pains me, he didn't feel as I did, I mean he liked me, but being brutally truthful, I think what he did with me was a symptom for his doubts about you and of his troubles — his angst about his mum, his sister, his dad, his life."

The wind pulled my hair off my shoulders. I took a step away from the cliff side and waited.

"I confided in him about my true feelings. I was in love; I would leave Jack. It was the wrong thing to do, he pulled back from me. Said he felt so guilty, that he was wrecking two lives. He didn't end it as such, but I felt desperate when he left that night. I couldn't bear for him to leave me; I would do anything.

"He came round the Friday before he disappeared. He came round to finish it. Said he felt beside himself with guilt. He couldn't lead me on, he couldn't do this to you, he didn't know what to do, felt he shouldn't be with anyone. I felt so desperate, I told him that I was pregnant, that I had just found out. That my pill must have failed. That it was his. That I hadn't slept with Jack for months. That I was going to keep it.

"All a lie. I don't know what came over me, I was just desperate to keep him, and it tripped off my tongue. He was horrified. Hardly said a word and then left abruptly. I realised I had made a big mistake."

You had told me you were working late that Friday. You making us breakfast in bed the next day, us choosing our rings, drinking champagne — and all the while you were hiding your affair with Jess, the fact that she'd told you she was pregnant. Then I remembered your quietness as I chattered on about our wedding plans.

Do you think they are happy?

The pieces of the puzzle were falling into place.

Jess continued in her new, hard voice, a world away from her usual soft, easy-going tone. "Then you called to say that he had disappeared on the Tube. I didn't know what to think at first. I assumed it must be because of what I said . . . I actually thought there was a chance at first that he would come to mine, that it would all be okay, even though I had lied, even though I knew the chance was slim. It didn't sink in for a few days that this could be permanent that he had gone missing, walked out of his life.

"I could have said something, but I didn't want to disrupt my life for nothing, and I clung to Jack despite my feelings, he gave me comfort, I still had someone. I had to put a face on it with you. But God, it was difficult. And I did — I do — feel guilt, but I think what I did tipped him over the edge, it was only the final thing that made him walk. However, I should never have lied."

Jess. My best friend in the world. Her kind eyes and empathetic face when she came round the day you left. Her advice to ring round your friends, her arms round me, taking me to the police station. My crutch.

"But why?"

Jess stared at the watch hanging limply in my hand. "I told you."

I squeezed your watch.

"No, no, I mean why did you really do it? I know you fell for John, but I still don't understand how you could do it, betray me like that, what made you take that step, when we were such friends. Best friends."

My cheeks were wet. I didn't realise that I had been crying.

"Okay, you want to know why?" Jess took a step towards me. "I might have been your best friend, but you weren't mine. I hid it well, didn't I, but underneath I have often hated you."

Her words were like stones hitting me. This wasn't the Jess I knew. Her kindness and humour, where were they? Her warm voice replaced with an ice-cold enunciation.

"I really liked you but then that changed. You had something I wanted so much, so, so much. Remember how I wanted to be a women's magazine journalist too? Remember how we both had that ambition? I wanted that since I was seven years old, when I tried to put together a little magazine with my friend. I devoured every magazine I could since I was young, from my mum's *Chat* and *That's Life* magazines, and other weeklies, to *Glamour*, *Grazia*, you name it. Remember how we both worked on the university magazine, of course you got the features editor role, but I worked damn hard at articles."

"Of course I remember. But you could have been a women's magazine journalist, you decided to get into business-to-business trade publications," I said, still not understanding.

Jess's voice rose. "And why would I go to a business magazine, eh? Because I couldn't get a job on a women's magazine! I tried so hard, remember my work experience on that beauty magazine, and that one aimed at retired women? They never offered me jobs. I applied to so many magazines, websites, I started even branching out from women's magazines to anything that was vaguely a consumer publication. But nothing, just nothing. And I had to watch it all come so easily to you, Eve. Winning the features editor role at the university newspaper, and I was just as good as you. *Just as good.* Remember you were mates with Kate the editor? Then you got that work experience on that *Only 16* magazine — and they offered you a job practically straight away. Then you moved seamlessly to *Real Lives*, working your way up the ladder."

Anger started to mix with my despair and shock. "I did not get that job on the uni paper through Kate! I barely knew her; I don't know where you got that from. And I worked so hard at *Only 16*. Door-knocking until midnight one night and staying outside another house all day to get the people to sign a contract and talk to us . . ."

"So did I!" Jess said. "I worked bloody hard at my work experience too, but I never got offered anything. Do you know how many applications I made to women's and consumer magazines and websites, not even just for advertised jobs but applying on spec. Three hundred! Three hundred rejections or even worse, just no reply. And I had to watch you move magazines in that time and get promoted and promoted."

Her shoulders were shaking. "And you know the worst thing?" Her voice was suddenly low and I moved forward to hear it.

"You never once offered to use your contacts to help me. Not once. Some best friend."

"But I thought you were happy in trade press. You never said you wanted to still try and get into women's magazines!" I was indignant. "You should have asked. Of course I would have helped you . . ."

"Oh, come on — you must have known that I would rather be in women's magazines than that truck magazine I started on!" Jess snorted. "Why should I have to spell it out? I was proud. I wasn't going to have you pity me even more than you probably did when comparing your shiny career to mine. But you knew how much I wanted that career while at university and you knew I applied for tons and tons of stuff, and nothing."

"I'm sorry. Maybe I was a bit consumed with my own career and life. You should have just said, and I would have helped. To my mind, you gave no clue."

Another side that Jess had hidden from me. So well too.

"Actually, I'm not sure that is the worst thing." Jess went quiet. "At my hen do, you brought up my magazine being on the TV as a funny story. How could you show such a lack of empathy and awareness? Summed it up, didn't it — lording it over me on my hen do. Mocking me. It took everything I had to laugh and pretend it was hilarious, when all I wanted to do was throw my glass into your face. And I thought, you know what, you deserve it all."

The last pieces of the puzzle fell into place.

"I take it you were the person who did all those things to me — not Sophie?"

Jess's face was now in darkness, but I could sense a smile. "You told me about the Maradona mug going missing. I thought it was your mind playing tricks to be honest. Obviously I was wrong. But it got me thinking. I missed John so much, I ached for him, and I knew you had a framed photo of us all the New Year's Eve before he went missing. I felt it would bring me comfort, a proper physical photo, not just some WhatsApp pic and would remind me that we really did have something between us.

"I had a key John gave me. One time, you were away with work, and he gave me the key as it was his newspaper deadline day and he'd be late. It meant that I could go over to your flat as soon as I finished work and wait for him. He never asked for it back and I wanted to hold on to it. Anyway, I used it to go in and get the photo, when you said you'd be out. I did feel bad and didn't mean it to be sinister."

Jess stopped. "But then it developed. I couldn't stop thinking and thinking. About how you'd won when it came to our careers. You achieved everything you wanted and then some. Despite me having just as much talent and putting everything into it, I failed. I just felt all this rage from all those years boil over.

"I sneaked into your flat when I was drunk one night. It was pitch dark. I was wearing heels and they made a sound, I assumed they woke you. You shouted, 'John!' I got a massive shock, didn't expect you to wake up, and I fled.

"Well, I got away with it, didn't I. And I got off on that. You had another one-up on me — you could openly grieve John and I couldn't, and I don't care that it was only six months. My own heart was broken. I was trying to fling myself into my wedding plans, but it made me sick if I'm honest. I knew me and Jack should end but I felt like I couldn't be completely on my own after John."

Fumbling with her fingers, Jess started again.

"I felt a thrill, I wanted to go in again and so I skived off work one day, pretending I had a stomach bug. I knew you were at work, but I felt nervous. I had a hunt around the flat. I'm not sure what I was looking for. But in my hunt I flung some cushions on the floor and rumpled up the duvet. I wanted you to know someone had been in there. I looked in your drawers and in the top drawer, among his underwear, I found his watch. I remember you getting it for his birthday and he always wore it proudly. I remember when we first kissed, it was on his wrist, and it rubbed against my arm. I took it, because it reminded me of him, again not to be nasty actually. I took it on our weekend away, just for reassurance, you know, just so I could pick it up when I wanted, it was near me."

I pictured your watch on your wrist as we kissed, its cool feel against my skin when you held my hand. The way it glinted in the sun on your tanned arm on holiday. The images entwined with Jess's description of her and you.

"But after those events, I got worse. I really feared he had killed himself and wasn't coming back and of course I felt guilty. But I wanted to cause you pain for making me feel like crap for years . . . for getting that great big dose of luck when I didn't."

I shook my head involuntarily. Jess raised her hand, her fingers stretched taut. "You got lucky and I didn't," she said calmly.

I opened my mouth to reply, to say that yes while I did get some luck, I worked so hard too. I also wanted to work on a women's magazine more than anything. I too had harboured the same dream since I had been little.

But Jess carried on: "I knew your wedding theme was lilac, John told me. So, I sent a tie of that colour to you. And do you know what, it felt like a release."

I shook my head. All the rich food that I had eaten that night set in my stomach, heavy as a rock. My Jess, where was my friend? I did not recognise this person.

"You could win an Oscar. You came over as nothing but a kind, concerned friend," I whispered.

"As you did, but you didn't help me with the thing I wanted the most, did you."

Anger tightened my jaw. "And that justifies you having an affair with my fiancé, playing malicious tricks on me, making me feel I was going mad, and terrifying me and illegally entering my flat?"

Silence. Then Jess continued her narrative. "So, the next thing that happened was that time you saw my eye through the peephole. I wore a bright coloured green lens for that . . ."

"And the black roses on my wedding day, BlackRose80?"

Jess took a deep breath. "I loved him so much and he left, and I hated you for it, and I hated that you could openly grieve, and I couldn't and I hated that you won in your career, you had the one thing I wanted the most — I told you all this." She gestured sharply with her hand. "I wanted to make you suffer and black roses, yeah, well, it was a tragedy, wasn't it, it was like he died for both of us."

The tricks ran through my mind, the witches' card, the new home card and . . .

"The postcard from Spain?" I asked.

Jess's voice softened. "Actually, that wasn't me."

A pause, as we both considered the meaning of that. Then my mind turned to the last 'gift'.

"How could you send me that heart, how? It was disgusting, horrible . . ." Tears ran down my face.

Your disappearance devastated me, but this was worse. The affair was bad enough, but I couldn't get over the tricks, the lying, the hiding of what Jess really felt about me. For a second time, everything I knew had turned upside down and was turning away from me.

"It was meant to be. Something tipped me over the edge. The final straw was your column on John going missing. Oh, the irony that I contributed to make your career and profile even more of a runaway success."

Jess's voice shook. She took another step towards me. "You'll be winning awards for that column, won't you? You'll probably get another even better job. You'll probably get on the telly with it. It makes me want to explode!"

She took one more stride towards me, her hand stretched out.

CHAPTER 32

Jess

I take a while to get ready. I play Absolute 80s on the radio loudly; I firmly apply my Red Velvet lipstick. Then I scrub it off and just dab some lip balm on. I don't want to look too made-up and like I thought this was a date.

I pull out my phone to re-read Ethan's messages.

I'd really appreciate speaking to you, thanks for replying . . .

Next text: *I just need to make sense of it. Could you meet one day this week?*

. . . OK great, Tooting tomorrow at 7?

I'm not stupid enough to believe that Ethan wants to meet me for anything more than to seek answers about Eve. But I'm enjoying it, nonetheless. I'm meeting a nice man. If Eve liked him, I'm sure I will. I need some escapism.

The pub is warm and cosy. There are people jostling at the bar, calling out merrily to each other. I exhale heavily, not realising how stressed I've been. So nice to be around alive, vibrant people. I see him instantly. I recognise him from the photo he sent me on WhatsApp. Blond-haired and hazel-eyed. Different to John's dark, brooding handsomeness. But nice-looking, even better-looking in the flesh.

Jealousy tightens my throat. Eve always got gorgeous men. I got Jack, every girl's mate. I swallow and try to dissolve the stiffness in my throat. His eyes are hollow-looking, he is definitely here to talk about Eve, to seek answers. I get up closer and his skin is pale and there are shadows under his eyes. They were hardly together, but it has hit him hard.

I plaster a gentle half smile on my face and widen my eyes. Walking over slowly to him, I place a hand on his shoulder.

"Ethan?" I modulate my voice to a low tone, just enough to be heard above the crowd in the pub. He looks up at me quickly and slowly rises to his feet.

"Hi, thanks for meeting me. What can I get you to drink?"

He's chosen a window seat, tucked away. Nice. I take my jacket off and settle in.

"Glass of wine, Sauvignon Blanc if you don't mind, thank you."

Ethan says, "That's Eve's favourite wine too!"

I give what I hope is a reflective smile. "Well, best friends have a lot in common!"

Ethan strides to the bar to get my drink.

He appears again in my view clutching a beer and my wine. He does not look like he is taking any ounce of enjoyment in the night. Ah well, give him a break, go slow. I can't believe I am thinking about him like this, as a possible romantic lead. But if Eve likes him, I will. Of that, I am sure.

Ethan takes a ruminative sip. I wait, trying to look calm and patient. I clench my lips. Wait for him to speak. I arrange my face to a look that I hope is gentle and serene.

"Thanks a lot for meeting me," he says at last. "I just feel like I need to talk to one of her best friends. Who was there. To help me try and process it. It doesn't feel real, and maybe talking to you, well, I feel like I need some closure."

I open my mouth but having started he wants to get more off his chest. So, I take a sip, make that a gulp, of my wine instead.

"I know we were hardly together. I mean just a few weeks really. It was so fleeting, but it left such a mark on me.

256

I really saw a future; despite everything she went through with John. We had a connection."

His words sting. I give myself a mental shake. Why should what a stranger says about Eve upset me? Because she always has one up on me, with the amazing career and the fabulous man, while I was stuck on a fusty old trade publication with Jack, every girl's best friend. I swallow another sip of wine.

"She said I made her smile for the first time in ages." His eyes light up briefly.

"It must be so hard." I touch his hand briefly, as a show of solidarity and sympathy and his eyes widen slightly. *Okay idiot, just trying to be nice*, my mind screams. I won't rise to it.

"Eve went through a terrible time, as you know," I say slowly. "And I know that when she met you, she was still in the depths of despair about John. That weekend, she seemed in good spirits." I pause. "Initially.

"But when we got the cottage, we had a bit of a heart to heart and . . . oh, I'm not sure I should say this." I keep my eyes downcast. My mind scrambles ahead to fill in my story.

Ethan takes a breath. "No, you must tell me, I'm looking for answers," he says urgently.

"Okay, well I will tell you everything." I stare directly at him. He fixes his eyes steadily on me.

"She said she was pleased that she had met you, that it was a distraction . . ." Ethan flinches briefly. "But she still loved John with all her heart, and that you were just helping take her mind off it."

Ethan is very still. Impulsively I grab his hand.

"She said she wanted to like you like that, she really did, but that she just wasn't over John, and that she couldn't see it lasting. She really wanted to, you know, head over heart but her heart said no, and she still felt distraught over John."

I bow my head slowly, to conceal the little half grin that was turning the corners of my mouth up slightly. He is falling for this hook, line and sinker.

Ethan opens and closes his mouth a few times. He's not so good-looking when he does that. Never mind, I won't dwell on that and press on.

"I'm not sure if the others realised. She was good at putting a face on it. Then obviously she vanished that night and we had no idea where she was. At first, when we woke up in the morning, we presumed she went for a walk or whatever and then we found her phone in her bedroom which concerned us, I mean it's unusual to leave your phone. And then I must admit, because of what she confided to me, I was starting to really worry. And then, well, you know the rest . . . she was found by someone walking their dog on the beach."

Ethan lets out a heavy breath again. "So, what do you think happened to her, why did she end up on the rocks?" His voice shakes.

I pause. "I believe she committed suicide, but that is just my opinion. Rachel believes that she fell from the cliff by accident. I think she killed herself because of John. I am sorry," I end faintly. My ears ring with a scream, and I am back at the cliff face.

* * *

The thought of Eve's column catapulting her to even greater career success, even to possible fame, give my limbs a life of their own. My legs propel me forward and my arms shoot out and I push her. Her face looms in front of me — her eyes wide, staring at me. A flash of fear, of shock. And sorrow, which I try not to think about. My ears fill with her scream. It is just a single shriek, but it echoes off the cliff face. And then she is gone. I look over the side of the precipice and nothing, just blackness. The waves crash against the rocks, but that's it. I continue to stand, staring into the darkness, the wind whipping my hair. My hands shake. Did I murder her? My mind is scrabbling to put the pieces together. What have I done? How could I?

I shout, my voice wild, into the unforgiving darkness: "Oh, Eve. Eve! No! I am so sorry." I want to rewind time, just thirty seconds, a minute, so she's back with me, back on this cliff.

"No! Eve! Please stop. Just please, somebody make it stop." Everything is despair and horror and blackness. Is that just the wind, or can I hear a police siren? I take a step towards the cliff edge. To

*jump after her? I deserve everything that's coming to me, I say to myself.
I am a selfish, evil, lying bitch. And I have just killed the woman who
is supposed to be my best friend.*

*I scream, a wail of helplessness and hopelessness and fear that
empties my lungs and seems to go on forever. Then I collapse on to the
grass, a pathetic, sobbing mess.*

*I don't know how long I stayed there in that awful, apparently
endless night. But then light returns to the sky and the fog starts to clear
from my mind. It can't have been a siren or if it was, of course the car
couldn't have been looking for me. Not at this stage. And then . . . well,
how would anybody know that I was ever here?*

*The old bitterness creeps back into my soul. You deserve it, Eve.
All those things you had that I wanted and you never tried to hide from
me. Smug, weren't you? So fucking smug. You could have helped me,
couldn't you, Eve, but oh no. You had to have all the glory, never any
room for anyone else in the endless success story of your life. And to top
it all, you had John. No sneaking around trying to hide an affair for
you. My resolve hardens. You deserve it, Eve. I walk away.*

* * *

I blink, and I'm no longer at the cliff face, staring into blackness, but back in the busy bar. Its noise jars on my nerves.
Ethan's shoulders rise up and down and he stares into his
pint.

"I feel like I'm navel-gazing and being selfish, but I'm —
ah — so upset that she didn't feel for me like she made out.
I mean I shouldn't feel deceived, but I guess I wonder why
she lied. I suppose maybe she wanted to like me and believed
she did at that exact moment in time.

"I actually thought we had a future. It was such a brief
moment really, in the scheme of things but I felt such a
connection, and I loved her personality, so open and gentle
and . . ."

He drones on and I stiffen, the usual flames of jealousy
licking my mind as I consider Eve's career, John then Ethan,
versus my job, Jack then no one. I am being drawn into a

dark tunnel of my own musings when Ethan says, "Sorry I'm going on."

"No, no," I say quickly. "Don't be silly. You've had an awful shock. As we all have." I manage to perfect a little wobble in my voice. Ethan's eyes crinkle in sympathy.

"Look, my honest opinion is she wanted to like you and no doubt she did, but it was just too soon after John. She was still very unsettled and affected by those horrible, well, I don't know what you would call them, but tricks, I guess, played by John's sister. All this meant she wasn't ready."

"Oh yes, she was so upset, she talked a lot to me about that. Evil, twisted, messed up." Ethan shakes his head at a total loss. "I can't get over the sheep's heart, I really can't."

I feel a small moment of pride. I wanted to think of something particularly shocking and sinister and it seems like I achieved it. Took me some effort as well, seeking it out. I had to order it from a small butcher in Clapham. I didn't enjoy holding and squeezing that sloppy, spongy thing into the envelope.

Ethan's thoughts turn back to what I told him Eve said about him. "Anyway, I have to say I'm a bit stunned I was just a distraction, but I'll get over it. Funny, she seemed so into me, considering what had happened. I mean she was very open about John, but I thought we had a good chance of making a go of it. Oh well, all incidental anyway. After what's happened. Just such a tragic waste."

Wow, he believes me. If only he knew that he had given Eve hope back and a reason to get back to living. I feel a warm feeling rise in me. This has been so easy.

Tears fill his eyes. I didn't want to see them drip down his face, to hear ugly sobbing and a running nose. I stood up. "Would you care for another drink?" I say softly.

Ethan blinks furiously. "Yeah, why not." I slip away to the bar, hoping that by the time I am back, he will have composed himself.

I smile at Ethan as I plant the glasses down. To my surprise he says, "Sorry. I feel like I've dominated the conversation, going on about me and my feelings. You're her best friend; it must be awful. She talked a lot about you, telling me about you and that you go back years. Her very best friend, she told me," he repeats.

Is that a stab of remorse? It's not enough to make me back out, to regret what happened. I want to move the conversation on.

Luckily, he says, "Tell me about how you met, I think university, right?"

"Yep, correct. First person I met when I arrived, she had the room opposite . . ." I keep my voice light and breezy as I dutifully recount our experiences at university, being careful to be very flattering about Eve, crossing my fingers under the table.

Actually, at one point the present slips away as I relive a day with Eve, just after we graduated. I talk about it as I see her falling.

I feel another pang, but then remember how she trumped me. She had the two things that I wanted the most desperately in my life. I smoothly keep to my story.

Ethan even smiles a bit at times. "Tell me about yourself," he says suddenly.

I don't know what to say. I hated my best friend. I had an affair with her fiancé. I played sinister tricks on her.

"Well, I'm a journalist too," I start brightly, "but not in the same league as you and Eve," I add with my practised self-deprecating laugh. I have it polished to perfection after all those times friends, acquaintances, even strangers were wide-eyed at Eve's glamorous job versus either a bored smile, or even a laugh at mine.

"Oh, Eve's writing is so impressive," Ethan says. "I mean I knew she had to be good to be in her position, but her columns were both beautifully written and raw, they got right at the heart of the matter. The newspaper was so excited to syndicate them."

I clench my knuckles tightly under the table.

"Sorry, that was rude, I didn't mean to interrupt. What type of journalist are you?"

"I'm online editor of a pensions publication."

I wait for the corners of his mouth to turn up, or his eyebrows to furrow but all he does is take a sip of his beer. "That's very interesting."

I look at him sharply to detect a hint of sarcasm.

"There are so many issues affecting pensions at the moment, cost of living crisis, interest rates increase and — well, you don't need me to tell you!"

He does seem genuinely interested.

"People tend to laugh or look a bit bemused when I tell them, I mean it's dry stuff. Not exactly flashy," I find myself confiding in him. "Not like Eve's job," I add, careful to keep my voice light.

"I think it's so interesting. It touches upon so many topical issues, political, economic, social." Ethan looks engaged as he puts his pint down. "People can be funny about trade publications. I'm not sure why. I started on one. I eventually went on to *London Daily Eye* as a news correspondent, but I wouldn't mind going back to business. I'd love to write on the business side for a newspaper."

He's lovely. I unclench my hands and find myself opening up to him, only about certain things of course, but I find myself telling him about Jack, about jilting him at the altar. About my doubt and my guilt.

Ethan is engaged and interested. Leaning forward. A little pocket out of the Eve topic. I do my best to appreciate it.

"I felt like that about my ex," he begins. "I mean I told Eve about it too."

I try to stop my shoulders tensing.

"We lived together for a couple of years, and it just didn't feel right. I almost got in your situation, I almost proposed because it was the right thing to do, but I realised at the last moment I couldn't."

He takes a gulp of drink. I lose myself in our conversation.

My phone beeps and Rachel's name flashes up. *You about for a quick chat? Because Eve's cause of death is not natural, there will need to be an inquest, to record a verdict. They need witness statements . . .*

I push it away impatiently. I don't want to read and think about that now. I'm fed up of Rachel too, bleating on repeatedly that she doesn't think that Eve killed herself because she had turned a corner and had new, good things in her life, like her flat and Ethan.

I slip the phone into my bag.

Our talk widens. Holidays, travel, films, music. Growing up. Ethan went to a private school.

"Oh, so did I!" I say, eyes widening. I went to a comprehensive, but who cares.

"I love Arcade Fire, the Cure, the Smiths," Ethan declares.

"So do I!" I know enough about the Cure and the Smiths to chat, but I don't like them. He doesn't need to know that. Eve loved them though. She used to bang on about "The Walk" song by the Cure. "I love 'The Walk'," I announce. "It's one of my favourites. Reminds me of so many things." My voice trails off. *Thank you, Eve. Just don't ask me why I like it.*

"I was fourteen and for a period I felt out of place, like I didn't fit in at school. So I used to go home and lie on my bed afterwards and listen to that song and I don't know why, but I liked its darkness. I felt less alone, somehow, like there was more to life than school," Ethan volunteers.

I try to concoct a similar story, but it's beyond me. I can't even remember how the song goes. Luckily, he moves on to another subject.

I take in his long lashes, almond-shaped eyes and his floppy blond hair. I like him. I want to plant my lips on his and kiss for hours. Typical Eve to get yet another great, gorgeous guy. What she can do, I am going to try and do.

I can't believe it when the bell in the pub rings for final drinks. Ethan looks startled too. He drains the dregs of his beer and stands up. The noise has upped a notch as drunk and merry people laugh and jostle and pile out of the pub. We quietly head out.

Please give me hope, give me a reason to feel something, I beg silently, staring at his back as I follow him out.

We stand outside the pub. Ethan moves closer to me, slightly invading my personal space. I don't mind. "Thank you. You gave me some answers. Obviously, some were not what I wanted to hear, but I needed them." He bows his head, and a shot of disappointment reverberates through me.

Then he says, "But despite the sadness of all this, I did enjoy meeting you. It feels good to have a bond with Eve still, despite the fact what I've heard is not what I'd hoped for."

I ignore the part about Eve and a jolt of pleasure judders through me. I hold my breath.

He says, "But I can't see you again, Jess. You remind me too much of Eve. I had such deep feelings for her, despite our short time together. And I still do, even though I now know she didn't feel the same. I need to move on somehow, to put this behind me, and if I'm to do that, I can't have any reminders of her in my life."

I am floored. I genuinely thought he was going to ask me to see him again. I had been planning my response in my head — demure and regretful, but quietly pleased.

Now I feel empty. Empty and furious. I'd been planning to break that bond he had with Eve. Now I won't have the chance.

"Okay, fine — if that's how you feel," I say shortly. I try to add, "I understand." But the words won't come.

A slight look of surprise passes over Ethan's face. "I'm sorry," he says. "But I'm really grateful that you agreed to meet me. You've answered some of my questions and I appreciate that a lot. It's helped me massively."

That makes me even more angry. I'm struggling to keep my emotions in check. He touches my shoulder sympathetically. I want to slap his hand away. Instead, I arrange my face into a bland mask.

"I'm glad." I try not to spit the words out. "All the best, Ethan. I hope it works out for you."

He turns and heads off down the street, his hands in his pockets. The emptiness in my stomach spreads through my whole body as I watch him go.

Even now Eve still manages to get one up on me.

I wait until Ethan has disappeared from view before I start to walk in the opposite direction. But I don't know where I am going. Everything I've done is starting to sink in, and I feel sick.

Much as I don't want to admit it, Eve has left a gap in my life.

CHAPTER 33

She comes towards me, hair scraped back, glasses perched on the end of her nose, a baggy grey coat primly buttoned up to her chin.

"Thanks for agreeing to meet me," Gemma says.

Eve was right. She definitely doesn't make the best of herself.

We both stare out at Tooting Common. Young families dash past on scooters and bikes. Shouts of laughter come from the playground.

Gemma. The one that John had grown close to. Eve had talked about her often. Was I sharing him not just with Eve but with her too?

"Why do you want to meet?" I fight to keep the hostility out of my voice.

Gemma sighs and twists her hands in her lap.

"I'm sure Eve told you about my history with both her and John. I was shocked to hear what happened to her. I feel so bad. We've not had the best relationship. I wasn't very nice to her after she grabbed my blouse. I know that."

"Did John buy you that blouse?" I interject. I already know the answer. But I need to look detached from it all. Innocent.

"No!" Gemma raises her voice. "I admit, we had a friendship that was intimate emotionally in some respects, but he never, ever bought me that top."

I know. Because the blouse that had been on John's bank statement is hanging up in my wardrobe.

Gemma shakes her head. "Look, I feel very bad about what happened to Eve and to John, and it's selfish but I wanted to meet someone close to them. I feel worried about what role I might have played, if she did — well, you know . . ."

Her voice tails off. "She must have been so upset when I said there was some kind of bond between us and then I wasn't pleasant to her. I could have been kinder. But she shocked me when she grabbed me like that."

"Did anything happen between you and John?" I ask, trying to keep my voice level.

"No! Nothing physical. I was honest. There was an emotional bond, you know, we were going through similar things. We'd always got on well. I admired him at work."

Work. My heart hardens. While both trade publications, there is a world of difference between my sleepy monthly pensions magazine and John and Gemma's shipping newspaper, which was well-known even outside the maritime sector.

Gemma is like Eve: a hugely successful journalist, albeit in the business-to-business sector. She has won awards. I know because I googled her. No wonder John had a soft spot for her. He would have admired her. Not me, on my little-known fusty monthly.

I look at Gemma and I hate her. I put her in the same career category as Eve. Rungs and rungs above me. Eve and Gemma have so much up on me. John was never going to go for me in the end. Why would he with those two on the scene?

A small child screeches past on a bike, screaming with joy, head held back, hair flying. It reminds me of another time, not so long ago, when a little boy shouted happily as he passed by on his scooter on the common. Eve had sat with me as we bit into ham sandwiches and shared a laugh. Eve and I often used to wander and sit in Tooting Common, grabbing an hour at the weekend or after work.

Gemma wants reassurance about her behaviour. I give it like a robot. And then before I know it, I say, "I'd like to keep in touch. Shall we arrange to meet up again? We're both suffering. We can help each other."

I cringe at my cheesiness but Gemma's face lights up. "I'd like that."

I see Eve sitting on the exact same bench as we are on now. Her hair blows over her eyes and lips, displaying only the tip of her nose. She is talking earnestly. I've forgotten what about. I wish I could remember. I blink and feel almost surprised to see Gemma there instead and not Eve.

Fancy a drink next week? We can talk more, I text Gemma as I walk briskly home.

I feel flat. Any satisfaction I've gained from meeting her is draining as if down a plug hole. She's not Eve, and I've lost out on Ethan. But most of all I miss John. I fell for him, everything about him, from the tips of his long eyelashes to his sarcastic sense of humour.

And then . . . I see someone. The man wears a red track-suit top, just like the one John was wearing when I last saw him. His dark hair is longer than I remember but it's the same foppish style. Faded grey, slightly scuffed trainers adorn his feet. Even the walk and the posture are the same — a quick, purposeful gait, hand in pockets, head down. Then when he turns his head, I know it's him, I recognise his profile, the slightly beaky nose, cleft in the chin and patchy stubble. All those times when I thought it was him and it wasn't; this time is different. My breath catches in my throat as I sprint forward. "John!" The man stops and turns to face me, an eyebrow raised quizzically.

It isn't him.

* * *

Dear Eve,

It's been a long time since I've written a letter. I've tried many times to write to you and have ended up scrapping it. This time, I'm just going to put all my thoughts down on paper and see what happens.

You might not want to read what I have to say, and I totally understand. I'm so truly sorry for what I've put you through.

The day I went, I didn't plan to go. You got on the Tube and I suddenly felt I couldn't get on with you. I couldn't go back to our flat and my life. My feet were glued to that platform and then as the carriage doors closed, I had to get out, away from the crowds surrounding me, away from everything. I ran up the escalators and I kept on running when I got out of that station.

I just couldn't go on with my life as it was. I had wanted to marry you, but it felt like another thing crushing me, another thing expected of me. I've always been scared of such a big commitment. It's a cliché isn't it — my dad walked out of my life forever when he left Mum, and I've been fearful ever since of marriage and all that comes with it.

Mum's illness consumed me. I felt like I couldn't lose her as well as my dad. And Sophie — you two have never got on. I know you're not keen on her, Eve, and to be honest I don't blame you. But in the end, she's my sister, and she depended on me. I guess I've always felt like more of a father to her than a brother. She wanted me to look after her, to always be there for her, and I felt pulled both ways between you. I couldn't be all that you or Sophie wanted, and I let you both down.

All this was weighing on me so heavily, and redundancies at work didn't help. My job was such a major part of my life, it validated me. I know you understood how I felt about that, Eve, because I know how much your career means to you.

I had to do something to get back some control of the situation, so I went to the doctor and was prescribed *antidepressants. You probably wonder why I didn't tell you. I felt so empty, I didn't know where to start. I hoped that this medication would get me back to the person you knew.*

This next bit is going to be very hard to write and, again, I'm so sorry. But I need to be absolutely honest with you. However, I guess you might even know this by now. I had an affair with Jess. It went on for six months. She popped round to our flat when you were out, and I was feeling particularly down. That's obviously not an excuse for my behaviour, but I don't want to leave anything out.

She provided me with an escape. I could forget all my commitments and responsibilities. I didn't think about where it would all lead, I just went with it. But then, it was obvious she wanted more. She told me that she loved me.

I felt so suffocated all over again. All my own fault, but I didn't know how to get myself out of this mess. I started thinking about going off on my own abroad to work and start again, to extricate myself from everything. I kept thinking about Hong Kong. But it was more like a fantasy to be honest. A way to comfort myself if things got too bad. I did ask Mark, who as you know lives out there, about jobs, but I didn't seriously pursue it.

Anyway, I knew I had to finish it with Jess. I hated myself. Jess didn't deserve me to lead her on and I didn't want to betray you anymore. The night before I disappeared, I went over to hers to call it off. She told me she was pregnant. I felt terrified, Eve. Everything else and now this. I couldn't breathe and I couldn't see a way out.

I tried to hide it from you, I wanted to give you a good day looking for our wedding rings, even though it was a farce because I had betrayed you so deeply.

So that's the place I was in when you got on that Tube. I saw the train coming towards the platform and I couldn't take it anymore.

I walked for miles. I had cash on me and paid for a night in a hotel on the outskirts of London. I wanted out of my life. So, I made it to Seville. As you might have guessed after I sent you a postcard. I always loved it there, as you know.

You might wonder how I made it there, without a passport. I applied for a second one through work, because as you know I used to travel a bit with the job. The reason was ostensibly so that I could apply for a visa for one country and still travel while I waited. But deep down I viewed it as a potential means of escape. I'm sorry, Eve — another secret I kept from you.

I've got a job as a waiter and as part of it I have board in the restaurant's hotel. It's very basic and I live hand to mouth but that's how I've liked it until recently.

I stuck to my routine; I didn't think outside those boundaries. All I thought about was my shift, and then small things, like a wander round the city, a coffee on the square. A walk by the river. I blanked everything out of my mind. You, Sophie, Mum, Jess.

But then, I just started thinking about you again, Eve. Like waking up with you and going into work together. That coffee shop near the office where we used to go to dissect our latest stories. Eating lasagne in our flat. My favourite times.

And I wanted Mum again, to hug her and know she was still on the mend. I wanted to check Sophie was ok.

But the baby Jess was expecting grew bigger and bigger in my mind and I just couldn't face what I had done. Pathetic, isn't it? I need to man up and be a dad. But I felt paralysed. It was safer to stay put, to keep on hiding from my responsibilities.

But that was before I read your column about me going missing. I was scrolling through social media and saw it. I was sickened at what I had done to you and Mum and Sophie. I knew I wanted to put it right, to return to the people I love.

I'm coming back, Eve. Even though I don't know what I'm facing.

The things I have done are unforgivable, and I totally expect that you won't want anything to do with me. But I

271

would so much love to see you, to speak to you, to explain more.

I still love you.

John

THE END

THE JOFFE BOOKS STORY

We began in 2014 when Jasper agreed to publish his mum's much-rejected romance novel and it became a bestseller.

Since then we've grown into the largest independent publisher in the UK. We're extremely proud to publish some of the very best writers in the world, including Joy Ellis, Faith Martin, Caro Ramsay, Helen Forrester, Simon Brett and Robert Goddard. Everyone at Joffe Books loves reading and we never forget that it all begins with the magic of an author telling a story.

We are proud to publish talented first-time authors, as well as established writers whose books we love introducing to a new generation of readers.

We won Trade Publisher of the Year at the Independent Publishing Awards in 2023. We have been shortlisted for Independent Publisher of the Year at the British Book Awards for the last four years, and were shortlisted for the Diversity and Inclusivity Award at the 2022 Independent Publishing Awards. In 2023 we were shortlisted for Publisher of the Year at the RNA Industry Awards.

We built this company with your help, and we love to hear from you, so please email us about absolutely anything bookish at feedback@joffebooks.com

If you want to receive free books every Friday and hear about all our new releases, join our mailing list: www.joffebooks.com/contact

And when you tell your friends about us, just remember: it's pronounced Joffe as in coffee or toffee!